# UNDER THE RADAR

# Books by Fern Michaels

Up Close and Personal
Fool Me Once
Picture Perfect
About Face
The Future Scrolls
Kentucky Sunrise
Kentucky Heat
Kentucky Rich
Plain Jane
Charming Lily
What You Wish For
The Guest List
Listen to Your Heart
Celebration
Yesterday
Finders Keepers
Annie's Rainbow
Sara's Song
Vegas Sunrise
Vegas Heat
Vegas Rich
Whitefire
Wish List
Dear Emily

The Sisterhood Novels

Under the Radar
Final Justice
Collateral Damage
Fast Track
Hokus Pokus
Hide and Seek
Free Fall
Lethal Justice
Sweet Revenge
The Jury
Vendetta
Payback
Weekend Warriors

Anthologies

Silver Bells
Comfort and Joy
Sugar and Spice
Let It Snow
A Gift of Joy
Five Golden Rings
Deck the Halls
Jingle All the Way

# UNDER THE RADAR

## FERN MICHAELS

**Doubleday Large Print
Home Library Edition**

ZEBRA BOOKS
KENSINGTON PUBLISHING CORP.

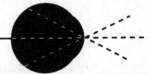

**This Large Print Book carries the
Seal of Approval of N.A.V.H.**

# Chapter 1

Charles Martin slipped quietly out of bed, careful not to wake Myra. He looked around the dim room, trying to figure out what, if anything, had wakened him from his deep sleep. All was quiet in the huge room. There was no air-conditioning making humming noises on Big Pine Mountain because it simply wasn't needed. He looked toward the open windows, where the sheer curtains moved with quiet gracefulness. Turning his head, he tried to decide if one of the dogs might have barked or if the birds were rustling in the big pines outside the window. Except for

Myra's soft intake and exhalation of breath, the silence was deafening.

Charles knew sleep was out of the question because he was wide-awake. He got up and made his way to the bathroom, where he showered, shaved, and got dressed. The red numbers on the digital clock sitting on the mantel said it was three in the morning, an ungodly hour to be waking up to start the day. Not that rising at that hour was entirely outside of his experience. When he was planning a mission for the girls, sleep was something he usually did without.

In the kitchen, he made coffee. Just as he was pressing the button to start the automatic drip, he realized something was *wrong*. He looked down at his trembling hands. His hands *never* trembled. Never. He jammed them into his pockets as his mind raced. Myra was sound asleep, which meant all was well with his dearly beloved. One of the dogs, Murphy or Grady, would have alerted him if something was amiss with the Sisters. The phone wasn't ringing. So what could possibly be wrong? He listened to the silence around him as he tried to figure out if it was him or something else. Something was spooking him, and he didn't like the feeling. He'd never had such an ominous feeling before. Even when he'd been a covert agent for Her Majesty, he'd had nerves of steel. He'd always been cool and collected, no matter what the situation, his mind never going off on tangents.

Charles almost jumped out of his skin when he heard the last cheerful plop coming from the coffeemaker. He poured a cup and carried it to the War Room, where he checked his incoming e-mail and faxes. There was nothing to be seen, both machines glaring at him like two angry dark eyes. *What the hell is wrong?* He turned and walked back out to the main part of the house and opened the front door. The velvety night was dark and quiet. He walked over to the bench under a tall pine and sat down. The pungent scent of pine was so strong, he felt light-headed. Sipping his coffee, he lit up one of the cigarettes he thought no one knew about. He puffed furiously, hoping the cigarette would calm his twanging nerve endings.

Lowering his head as he tried to grapple

with what he was experiencing, Charles let his gaze drop to the watch on his wrist. He could read the numerals clearly in the eerie blue light of the halogen lamp in the center of the compound: 3:45. He raised his head to look around. He'd never felt as lonely as he felt just then, that very second, in the whole of his life. He wondered suddenly if he was going to die. He shivered. For some reason, he'd never given his own death a thought until then. He immediately discarded the image. He squeezed his eyes shut as he tried to grapple with his feelings and his morbid thoughts.

Desperate, Charles fired up a second cigarette. After the first two puffs on his previous cigarette, he'd let it turn to ash. He inhaled deeply and coughed. Terrible, ugly, nasty habit, but he could understand why people smoked. Suddenly, he felt calm. The hand holding the cigarette was rock steady. His head felt clear, his senses sharp. *This is it,* he told himself. *Either I'm going to die, or something is going to happen,* right now.

The special encrypted phone he was never without vibrated. In that single instant Charles knew he wasn't going to die. He was sharply aware of the night around him, the rustling of the pines, the cough of a frog somewhere deep in the forest. For one second he thought he could actually *hear* the clouds move overhead. His uncanny sixth sense told him there was a possum or a raccoon within spitting distance. The sudden glow of two yellow eyes confirmed his feeling. A maple tree to the left of him rustled impatiently in the early-morning breeze. Off to the right, he could hear the creak of the cable car in its nest in the housing unit as the morning breeze kicked over into a light wind. Except for those rare times when he slept so deeply a building could have fallen on him and he wouldn't have woken, he had always been a poor sleeper, waking just the way he'd woken a little while ago. It had taken him a long time to get used to the mysterious moans and groans of the stationary cable car as well as to all the other mountain noises.

Dreading what he was going to hear on the special phone but needing desperately to know who was on the other end, he flipped it open and brought it to his ear. He rather thought he said hello, but later on he simply couldn't remember. What he did remember was the brisk voice that said, "Sir Malcolm," by way of greeting.

It was already midmorning across the pond. For his special friend to call him at that hour had to mean something very serious was wrong somewhere, and somehow it affected either him or the Sisters. Somehow Charles managed to find his voice.

"Tell me straight off, Bess." He took a second to wonder why he was calling his friend "Bess." Normally he called her "Liz." Bess was reserved for times of crisis. "Don't blather on, I can take it, whatever it is." Charles's long years of friendship allowed him to speak with such familiarity to the most powerful person in all of England.

"Very well. But, please, sit down, Sir Malcolm."

"Bloody hell, Bess, would you still tell me to sit down if I was in bed? Even the squirrels and birds aren't awake yet. I woke about an hour ago, knowing something was wrong." Then Charles's voice changed, it grew softer, almost pleading when he said, "Just tell me, and I'll deal with it."

Charles listened, the color draining from his face. *Now,* he thought, *I really am going to die. I really am.* The voice nudged him for a response twice before he could make his tongue work. "I heard it all. Thank you for calling me. Yes. Yes, I will be ready." The special phone went back into his pocket.

In a daze, Charles walked back to the main house on leaden feet to his bedroom, where he packed a bag in the dark. He looked down at Myra, who was still sleeping soundly. He wanted to touch her, wake her, to tell her . . . so many things. Things he didn't understand. Instead, he left the room as quietly as he'd entered it.

Across the compound, Annie, on one of her nocturnal trips around the house she lived in, saw the lights go on in the main house. It wasn't all that unusual to see the main house lit up in the wee hours of the morning. Charles was a notorious non-sleeper, often working through the night, especially if they were on a mission. He was a master at those ten-minute power naps the media touted. But something prickled at the back of her neck, right between her shoulder blades. She always referred to the feeling as her own personal warning system. She didn't stop to think as she put on a robe and slippers and quietly left the house. She walked across the compound and up the steps to the main house.

Quietly opening the door, Annie walked out to the kitchen, where Charles was sitting on a kitchen stool, staring into space. To her mind's eye, he looked terrible. She poured coffee and sat down on the opposite stool. That was when she saw the bulging duffel bag.

Annie's stomach muscles crunched into a knot. She didn't bother beating around the bush. "Where are you going, Charles? It's not even light out yet. Were you going to leave us a note or just . . . disappear? Does Myra know you're leaving? Of course she doesn't, or she'd be here in the kitchen with us. You need to say something, Charles, and you need to say it now."

"I . . . I have to go away, Annie. I'm not sure when I'll be back or even if I will be back. I had some . . . Well, let's just say I had some disturbing news that I have to act upon immediately, and there was no time . . . What I mean is . . ."

"You're sitting here right now. I am sitting here right now. That means to me that you had time to wake Myra, wake all of us, to tell us whatever the hell is going on with you. What does that mean, you don't know if you will come back? Exactly and precisely, what does that mean? What are you waiting for? Ah, a helicopter, right? Are you going to tell me or not?"

Charles looked down at his watch. He had eleven minutes until the British helicopter set down on the mountain. "Fetch the others, Annie, but be quick. I just have eleven minutes."

Annie ran. She rang the bell on the front porch of the cabin she lived in with the girls. She shouted to them to meet her in the kitchen of the big house, then ran, stumbling to Myra's room, where she literally pulled her from the bed.

"Get up and dress, quick, Myra. Charles is packed and ready to leave. A helicopter is coming, and he said he might never come back. Get with it, Myra, stop staring

at me like a lunatic. Dress! That's a goddamn order. Don't forget your pearls," she
added as an afterthought as she raced out
of the room. That was a stupid thing to say;
Myra was never dressed until the pearls
were around her neck.

Annie arrived back at the kitchen just
as the others stumbled across the dining
room in various modes of dress. Myra was
the last one in, sloppily dressed in a sweat
suit. She was trying to smooth down her
hair as she looked around in a daze. Then
both hands flew to the pearls around her
neck.

"Eight minutes and counting," Annie
said breathlessly. "Go for it, Charles. The
highlights, since time is short. We can fill
in the blanks ourselves."

"What's going on?" Myra demanded,
an edge to her voice as she eyed the
bulging duffel bag at Charles's feet. Her
hands feathered the pearls at her neck, a
sure sign that she was agitated.

"I had a disturbing phone call from . . .
from a friend across the pond a little while
ago. It seems my son was in a plane crash
and is in extreme danger."

"Son! What son?" Myra screeched at the top of her lungs.

The others chimed in, wanting to know why he'd never mentioned a son.

Charles stiffened. "You weren't told because I didn't know I had a son until two hours ago. A long time ago, when I was just a lad, there was a young lady . . . It's a long story. I was a commoner, she wasn't. I left to go on to other things, and I assumed she went back to her family in South Africa. Not only do I have a son and a daughter-in-law, I have three grand-children. None of whom I knew about. It seems my son wanted it that way on orders from his mother, who is deceased.

"I have to go. I want you all to under-stand I have no other choice."

Overhead, the solid *whump-whump* of the helicopter could be heard.

"And you expect me to believe that?" Myra shouted, tears rolling down her cheeks.

Charles's tormented voice hung in the room like a death knell. "Yes, Myra, I do expect you to believe that. Because it's true, and I've never lied to you. I have to say good-bye now. I'll be in touch when I can."

Speechless, the women just stared at Charles as he bent to pick up his duffel bag.

"Don't bother getting in touch and don't bother coming back," Myra said coldly, the tears drying on her cheeks as she turned away to stare out the kitchen window at the darkness outside.

"Myra . . . please . . . try to understand . . ." When he realized Myra was not going to back down, Charles let his shoulders slump. He started toward the door. A second later he was gone, the door closing softly behind him. There was a sense of finality to the sound.

The women rushed to Myra, all of them babbling and jabbering, but it was Annie who grabbed hold of Myra's shoulders and shook her like a rag doll. "Don't be a fool, Myra. Are you out of your mind? That man needs you right now, the way you needed him when Barbara died. Hurry, you can fight with him on the flight. If you don't go you'll regret it for the rest of your life. Go!"

The others pushed Myra toward the door. "But I'm not dressed . . . he lied to me . . . Well, maybe he didn't lie but he should have woken me to tell me . . . I can't just . . . go. I need my *things*."

"You don't need your things. You have your pearls, you don't need anything else," Annie shouted to be heard over the landing aircraft. "Run, Myra!"

The women raced from the room, out onto the porch, down the steps, across the compound as they half-dragged and half-pulled Myra to the helicopter pad. Somehow they managed to catch up to Charles, who was so stunned that he stopped in his tracks, his arms extended to clasp Myra to his chest.

The other Sisters stood in a huddle, the wind from the helicopter blades almost blowing the hair off their heads. They waved furiously, shouting words that couldn't be heard.

When the bird in the sky was just a speck, they trudged back to the main cabin, Annie in the lead.

Back in the kitchen, they fell to their assigned tasks and within minutes they had breakfast on the table.

"Eat! You know Charles's rule: first we eat, then we talk," Annie ordered.

The Sisters made a valiant effort to eat the pancakes and eggs, but for the most part all they did was stir the food around on their plates. Murphy and Grady waited patiently, knowing the food would find its way into their food bowls.

The minute the table was cleared and the dishwasher was humming, Isabelle poured fresh coffee. "Let's talk," she said as she plopped down in her chair.

"Charles has a family he didn't know about. How is that possible? Charles knows everything. How could he be igno-rant of an entire family? If it was a secret, how did Her Majesty know about it?"

Something funny was going on, they finally agreed when all the questions they asked one another had no answers.

The Sisters' concern turned to them-selves.

"We're rudderless. There's no one at the helm. What are we supposed to do?" Kathryn demanded.

"It's not exactly like we're busy," Nikki said. "We're *missionless,* if there is such a word, at the moment."

"Yes, but what if something comes up?

What do we do then?"Alexis asked. "And I hesitate to mention this, but we haven't heard a word from our president-elect and the pardon she promised us. Maybe this is a good time to, you know, sort of look into it."

"Why don't we have a party?" Yoko suggested. "We can invite Lizzie, Maggie, Jack, and Harry, and anyone else we think it is safe to invite."

"That's definitely out of the question. That's one of Charles's rules. We can't go against it, as much as I would love to have some fun and see Jack," Nikki said.

"So . . . we just sit here on this damn mountain and wait to see if Charles comes back. He said straight out he might not return. We need to make some plans," Kathryn said.

"Girls! We are not rudderless. I am, as of this moment, appointing myself as our new PM and will take the helm," Annie said.

Her Sisters laughed. "Annie, they only have prime ministers in England. You can't be a PM," Alexis said.

"No, no, no. I didn't mean prime minister.

I meant point man. Or, in this case, PW, which means point woman. I considered saying point person, but PP doesn't seem quite right."

A couple of the girls snickered.

"That's another way of saying I'm taking charge! If there are any dissenters, now is the time to . . . uh . . . dissent."

A rousing chorus of *yahs* echoed in the kitchen just as Annie's cell phone rang. The Sisters looked at one another, their eyes full of questions. Annie put the specially encrypted phone to her ear, murmured a greeting, and then listened to the excited voice on the other end of the line.

Annie's expression went from disbelief to utter disbelief when she said, "Pearl, I have my own crisis right here on the mountain, and I can't get excited about what's going on in Utah. Besides, it isn't even light out, so it has to be around three o'clock in Utah, which raises the question: What the hell are you doing out there on some back road in the middle of nowhere at this hour of the night? I'll get back to you when I have time."

"What? What?" the other Sisters demanded.

Annie shrugged. "Like I know. I could barely understand her. Somebody's bus broke down. Not Pearl's."

Annie's phone rang again, then Nikki's pealed. Yoko pulled her phone out of the pocket of her robe just as it rang.

"Will someone answer the damn phones already?" Kathryn blasted.

Everyone started talking at once, on the phones and among themselves.

Five minutes later the Sisters were pacing.

"I'd say Pearl does have a crisis. But, I don't see how we can help," Nikki said.

Annie's phone rang again. She barked a greeting, then said, "We're discussing it now, Pearl. What do you mean, what should you do? Sing songs. Play games. That's what we used to do when our parents took us for buggy rides a hundred years ago. I'll get back to you."

The Sisters argued back and forth for a good ten minutes before Annie stood up and stomped her feet. "Listen up! Are you all saying we are not capable of helping out a fellow Sister? All right, all right, she's *almost* a Sister."

Before anyone could respond, there

was another wave of phone calls. Judge Easter, Lizzie, then Maggie calling in.

All Annie would say is, "We're taking it under advisement."

"Maybe we should have told them about Charles and Myra," Isabelle said fretfully.

"And maybe we shouldn't," Annie said spiritedly. "They don't live on this mountain, so that makes them the auxiliary or the second string. That means they do not, I repeat, they do not need to know *everything.* I don't think Charles or Myra would want their private business being talked about, even with friends. We're family, so to speak, so it stays right here and goes no further. But, we need to have a show of hands to show total agreement."

Annie's Sisters knew she was spot on as five hands shot in the air.

"All right, then. My first decision as PW is that we are all in agreement, and we act accordingly. I don't know what that means exactly, so we'll more or less wing it for now. Now, let's sit down and figure out what if anything we can do to help Pearl without Charles and Myra and still keep their business private."

# Chapter 2

Within seconds, the high-tech world that none of the Sisters truly understood kicked into high gear when their special phones warbled a symphony that left the women breathless.

Annie's beringed fingers wiggled in the air, the signal for each of them to say who was calling according to their caller ID displays. Confusion reigned as one call clicked off and another one came in at the speed of light.

Pearl.

Maggie.

Lizzie.

Nellie.

Jack.

Harry.

Bert.

Annie wagged her finger. "Okay, we know why all the phones are ringing. We have to make a decision to shelve Myra and Charles, then we have to decide what if anything we can do for Pearl. That's not to say we aren't going to help Myra and Charles at some point, but for the moment, Pearl's problem seems to be the most pressing."

Isabelle leaned forward. "I don't know if I'm comfortable with that, Annie. We're just going to . . . what, ignore whatever it is that's going on with Charles? Shouldn't we be thinking about a way to get to England to help? I understand all about Pearl but she's not really one of us. I don't mean to sound ugly, but that's the way it is. She helped us, we helped her. It was supposed to be a one-shot deal. End of story."

"Charles doesn't want our help," Nikki said. "If he did, he would have left instructions for us. Look, this is as personal as it gets for Charles, and he doesn't want us mucking around in his private life. We have to accept that and the fact that he may very well not be coming back. I understand where you're coming from, but I think Annie is right. We have to shelve Charles and Myra."

"Utah is not around the corner. I should know, I had that run for years when I was driving my rig," Kathryn said, "especially at Christmastime when I used to haul Christmas trees. Let's face it, who can we call to help us? Charles never shared his roster of contacts with any of us." She looked pointedly at Nikki, and said, "Unless you know how to access all that secret spy stuff."

"I can try, but Charles never . . . I just helped him, he didn't share secrets. There is some guy he depended on named Avery Snowden, but that's all I know for sure. Let me make sure I understand what you just said, Kathryn, and what I think you're all worried about. What you're thinking is, we can't take on a mission without Charles. Well, if that is what you're thinking, you're wrong. We can make it work. We all know people, our second string know people. If we pool our strengths and our knowledge, I wager we can pull this off."

"Does that mean we're going to help Pearl?" Alexis asked.

"Damn straight that's what it means," Annie said.

Yoko hopped off her chair and danced around the room. "That's all well and good, but what does Pearl do in the meantime? We should call her, get her to some safe haven, then kick it up a few notches. Until we formulate a plan, we let the second string kick some ass. Charles always dotted every *i* and crossed every *t*."

"I do like the way that sounds, dear. I'm going to call Pearl right now and get the particulars. The rest of you start calling the others. Someone make some more coffee, this is going to be a very long morning. Wait! Wait! One more thing," Annie said, drawing herself up to her full height. "This is *WAR!*"

"Well, damn," Kathryn said as she punched in Bert's private cell phone number, a number no one in the Hoover Building knew existed. Her legs felt rubbery when there was no response. She didn't bother to leave a message.

Two thousand miles away in Las Vegas, Lizzie Fox's encrypted cell phone rang. She reached a long arm over Cosmo Cricket's barrel chest to snag the phone off the night table. Her sleeping partner groaned loudly enough to shiver timber. He did his best to roll over, but his bed, while huge, didn't quite accommodate someone his size plus a partner. Lizzie stifled a laugh as she giggled a greeting. And then she listened. Before she snapped the phone shut, she said, "I'm on it and on my way."

Cosmo Cricket, legal guru to the Nevada Gaming Commission, groaned again. "You just got here, Elizabeth! Tell me I didn't hear what you just said." He rolled over and the bed felt like it was tilted on two legs.

Oh, how she loved the sound of her name on Cosmo's lips. Lizzie leaned over and kissed the big man so soundly she felt his ears radiate heat. "I know, but I have to go. The good news is, I'll be back.

I promise. We talked about this, Cricket, and you said you understood and would never stand in my way . . . in regard . . . to . . . certain things."

The big man propped himself up on one elbow and stared at the woman who had somehow, magically, made him fall in love with her. "I did say that, didn't I? Go on, do what you have to do. If you need me, call."

Lizzie planted a second liplock on the big man that made his whiskers sizzle. "Count on it," she said breathlessly.

"Where are you going, can you tell me?"

"Utah."

"What the hell's in Utah?"

"A bus full of stranded pregnant teenagers."

"Oh," was all Cosmo could think of to say.

*Oh, indeed,* Lizzie thought as she stepped into the steaming shower, her mind already on the problem at hand.

While Lizzie was showering and plotting, retired judge Nellie Easter Cummings flipped open her special phone, the phone that drove her almost-brand-new husband, the recently retired FBI director, out of his mind because each time it rang it represented a crisis of some sort. She wasn't completely sure but she thought Elias looked forward to the ringing phone.

He sipped his coffee, his impatience showing by the way he tapped his bare foot under the table. One of Nellie's nine cats, the one called Miss Patty, pretended to nibble at his toe so that he would pick her up. He obliged, and she purred her thanks by settling herself in his lap. He stroked the soft yellow fur, hoping he would calm down the way the cat had.

Elias forgot about the delectable breakfast sitting in front of him as he watched Nellie close the phone and shove it in the pocket of her smock, something she'd started wearing of late.

"That was Lizzie Fox. She's in Las Vegas doing . . . well what she's doing . . . is . . ."

Elias laughed. "You can say it, Nellie. I know what the two of them were/are doing. Cricket's a great guy. I hope that marriage comes off. From what I can see, the two of them are great together. Almost as good as you and I." He laughed.

Nellie's face flamed because down deep she was a prude, something she always denied vehemently.

"It seems Pearl has gotten herself into a bucket of trouble out there in Utah someplace. Through no fault of her own," she added hastily. "Pearl always travels during the middle of the night doing her . . . her underground railroad thing. And she always tries to use back roads with the people who help her. She came across a bus that had broken down with a load of pregnant teenagers. She needs the Sisterhood. But . . . according to Annie something else is going on—something with Myra and Charles; they've left—and she really wouldn't talk about it. What all that means, Elias, is, the girls don't know what to do. I imagine they are trying to figure out how to make everything work without Charles at the helm. I'm thinking we might want to take a trip to the mountain. To help. The more heads the better. What's your feeling about that?" Nellie's tone and words were jittery-sounding, the way they always were when her special phone rang.

Elias let his hands flap in the air to show he was okay with a trip to the mountain. Miss Patty arched her back, hissed, and leaped to the ground to show her total disdain for anything other than her own feline pleasure.

"I'm also thinking we should make a stop at the *Post* and have a little talk with Maggie. Will that work for you, Elias? Because you'd be doing the driving, and I know how you hate to drive in the District."

"That will work," Elias said as he heaved up from the table. "I guess you want me to shower, dress, and pack for us while you . . . uh . . . make some more phone calls." He wouldn't admit it for the world, but he always got perked up when Nellie's special phone rang. Retirement was beyond boring.

Nellie nodded as she cleared the table and stacked the dishwasher. Then she waited until she heard her husband's footsteps on the wide plank stairs that led to the second floor of the farmhouse. She picked up her phone and hit the speed dial, and within seconds heard Maggie Spitzer's voice coming through loud and clear.

"I'm on it, Nellie," Maggie said before the judge could utter a word. "Annie okayed the use of her Gulfstream, and it's being readied as we speak. I'm sending Ted. The plane will set down in Vegas to pick up Lizzie. I'll work the desk. Get up to the mountain as soon as you can." She listened for a moment. "No, no, don't waste time coming here, just hit the interstate. I'll call Nikki now and tell her you're on the way. Just off the top of your head, do you know how far it is from Utah to Montana?"

"I don't have a clue. Google it, dear," Nellie said before she hung up. She looked around the kitchen to make sure she was leaving it neat and tidy. She filled the cats' water bowls and food bowls. She'd changed all their litter boxes when she first got up that morning. Her cats would survive for four days without her. If her stay on the mountain was longer, she'd simply call Pritzy Alouette, her cleaning lady, who would come to check on things and take care of the cats.

As she climbed the stairs to the second floor, Nellie mumbled and muttered to herself about retired Supreme Court justices who didn't know how to stay out of trouble. "I'm getting way too old for these shenanigans," she mumbled. But, like

Elias's heart, hers always kicked up a couple of beats when word came through on the encrypted phone that her help was needed.

If she could just figure out what was awry with Charles and Myra to make them leave the mountain. In a British helicopter, no less.

Less than forty miles away, Jack Emery waited his turn to be called up to the front of Harry Wong's *dojo* to receive his coveted black belt. He thought of all the years of training, all the bruises, the sore muscles—not to mention a few fractures—he'd endured since enrolling in Harry's martial arts classes. He'd religiously followed every instruction and even managed to pick up a smattering of Harry's language. The words always sounded ominous and deadly, so he thought he should memorize them. On occasion he'd utter one or the other of them, and Harry would laugh like hell, which probably meant Jack had said "manure" in six different ways.

Bert Navarro nudged Jack's arm. "Bet you thought old Harry was never going to give you that belt, huh?"

Jack nodded. "He passed me over twice because I wasn't ready. Even I knew I wasn't ready, so it was okay. This time I just told him I'd beat the living shit out of him if he didn't come through."

Bert grinned. "What'd he say?"

Jack laughed out loud. "He told me to 'sit on a pointy stick and spin.' Then I told him I was going to tell Nikki to tell Yoko to tell him she'd beat the living shit out of him and, voilà, here comes my black belt. As we all know, our fearless leader, also known as Harry Wong, the second-best martial arts expert in the land, is only afraid of one thing: Yoko." Jack laughed at his own wit, then sobered when Harry fixed his steely, slant-eyed gaze on him.

"This is a ceremony, gentlemen, even though it is only a ceremony of three. Rituals and rules apply. That means no laughter, no jokes, and no cell phones ringing. Since you think you can ignore my rules, Mr. Emery, drop and give me two hundred push-ups. Like *now*. Director Navarro, since I saw you instigate that little scene that just transpired, drop and do the same. *Now!*"

"Eat shit, Harry. I did a hundred when I got here," Jack said. "Give me a break."

"Yeah, eat shit, Harry," Bert said.

Harry offered up what he called his Number 6 Evil Grin and dangled a brown belt that was to go to Bert, along with Jack's black belt, back and forth. He reached behind him to pull out a pair of pink scissors that Yoko had given him for his ribbon-cutting ceremonies. He opened the scissors and prepared to slice at the two belts in his hand. "Last chance."

Jack and Bert almost killed each other as they raced to the middle of the sweat-soaked mat in the center of the floor.

"Now, repeat after me, gentlemen. Harry Wong is the Master of his *dojo*. The Master of his *dojo* is to be respected and obeyed. Unconditionally. Say it in between each push-up."

"Fuck you, Harry," Jack huffed as he struggled to do the Master's bidding.

"Yeah, Harry, fuck you," Bert groaned.

"Count! Shout out loud so I can hear you. Do it in synch," Harry said, the Number 6 Evil Grin still in place.

The black and brown belts hung just

an inch from both men's noses as they did their best to comply with Harry's dire instructions.

Both men were on their eighty-seventh push-up when the door of the *dojo* burst open and Maggie Spitzer stormed into the room. She matched Harry's evil grin with one of her own. "Get up!" she commanded. "Harry, sit down and listen to me. Stop with this . . . macho bullshit and listen up. And turn your cell phones on." She turned to face Harry, who was sitting docilely. "If you *ever* make them turn off their cell phones again, I will cut off your advertising allowance and sic Yoko on you. Are we clear?"

"Crystal," the trio said solemnly as they primly folded their hands in their laps.

"Good. We are now involved in a major problem. This is what I know as of the moment . . ."

While the members of the second string were scrambling and scurrying, the Sisters were gathering around the circular table in the War Room on Big Pine Mountain to plot their strategy.

# Chapter 3

Pearl Barnes looked like anything but what she was: a retired Supreme Court justice. She was dressed in baggy cargo pants, a sweat-stained oversized T-shirt, and combat boots laced up to her ankles. Her iron-gray hair was cut short and slicked back. These days her skin was bronzed, dry, and wrinkled. And she could smell her own body odor. A far cry from the way she looked when she was in court: immaculate, coiffed, and perfumed in her judicial robes.

She'd been driving for hours in a special bus with a special engine that promised never to give out on her. It looked like her, old and decrepit, but that was what she wanted, part of her MO so that she didn't draw attention to her illegal activities.

The people she worked with—"volunteered" was a better word, and more to her liking—didn't call her judge because they didn't know about that other life. They called her many names, like Savior, Angel, and Mama. The name that stuck more than any other was Missy. Not Missy something or other, just Missy. But for the most part she answered to just about anything including, Hey Lady!

Pearl looked at the passengers in her bus and winced. She had thirteen pregnant young girls, and if she was any judge, none was older than fourteen. An unlucky number no matter how you looked at it. Then she looked at her two novice volunteers, who looked scared out of their wits, the same way the three other women and their seven children looked scared out of theirs.

They were all looking at her expectantly, wondering what magic she was going to unleash. Her destination was a small rural town called Sienna, where she planned to drop off the women and children, where they would wait in a very special barn until the next relay team surfaced. Now she had fourteen girls and one dead bus driver. The driver she had to forget about for now because when you were dead you were dead, and there was nothing one could do about that. Sooner or later, the Highway Patrol would come along and take the man to the county morgue.

Before Pearl climbed into the driver's seat of the bus, she took one last look at the dead driver and blessed herself. She hated leaving a body alone and unattended, but she had no other choice. She took another few minutes to think back over what she'd done when she'd rescued the young girls. What had she touched? Had she wiped everything clean? She thought she had. Well, she couldn't worry about that. She had to get all her passengers safely to the welcoming barn, a mere twenty-two miles due east.

Pearl turned on the ignition and listened to the engine purr to life. She loved the big old bus. Really and truly loved it. It had carried hundreds of women and children to safety.

As the bus lumbered down the road, Pearl's thoughts were all over the map. She knew very little about the polygamous sect that these children belonged to. She should have known. She was a judge, for God's sake. She defended her lack of knowledge by trying to convince herself she'd never had to deal with polygamy. Men with a dozen wives were too obscene even to think about under normal conditions.

What she'd found really strange was how quiet the young girls were. Even though they were scared out of their wits, they didn't part with any information. With the exception of the one named Emily, a truly chatty youngster, who had told Pearl about the polygamous sect and indicated that she'd miscarried in her fourth month. Mentally, Pearl agreed with her earlier assessment, she had fourteen young girls but only thirteen pregnant ones. It had taken only three minutes for her to come to the conclusion that the youngster named Emily was the talkative one of the group. And even she had not really given up much other than that they were all being moved from a compound in Nevada to

Utah. If Emily knew or understood why, she hadn't divulged that information.

Pearl risked a glance in the rearview mirror. Everyone was either dozing or sound asleep. She wanted to cry for all of them.

Such a dark night, she thought, out there virtually in the middle of nowhere with a crisis on her special bus. And no one knew anything about this situation except for the Sisters on the mountain, Lizzie Fox, and Nellie. All she had to do was be patient and wait.

The cell phone Pearl had removed from the girls' bus, when they weren't looking, vibrated in the pocket of her shirt. She'd also helped herself to the driver's wallet just to make it marginally more difficult for the authorities to identify him. She was tempted to answer the vibrating phone but thought better of the idea. Wherever the bus carrying the girls was headed, surely someone must have alerted someone else that it hadn't arrived. The girl named Emily said they had been sitting in the ditch for almost three hours. Five now since Pearl had gotten back on the road. Yes, it was time for the people at the girls' final destination to get worried. Nellie and the others would have to deal with that end of things.

God in heaven, what was she going to do with the girls? Sooner or later, without a doubt, someone would try to charge her with kidnapping. Well, that wasn't going to happen, she thought grimly.

"C'mon, c'mon, someone call me. Like now would be a good time," Pearl muttered over and over under her breath. When nothing happened, she continued driving. With any luck she'd hit the barn just as the sun came up. At best she had fifteen minutes to go.

A rickety pickup passed her going the other way. The driver tootled his horn, something the people in Utah did out of habit. Pearl tootled back, a cheerful sound in the very early morning. She wondered if the driver of the pickup would be the one to call the Highway Patrol about the bus in the ditch. Then, of course, he would mention seeing the other bus, and the hunt would be on.

It probably wouldn't be a problem since she had magnetic signs and extra license plates to switch out, all compliments of

Charles and his network. Also, thanks to Charles, she had several sets of new identities. This driver's license she was carrying said she was Harriet Woonsocket and lived in Burlington, Vermont. She even owned a small Cape Cod house there, where she paid taxes yearly and got junk mail delivered. The other identities were available in case of need.

In the back of the bus under the last row of seats she had boxes and boxes of books, including Bibles, and other reading material that she passed out to churches and youth groups.

Pearl Barnes, aka Justice Pearl Barnes (Ret), also known as Harriet Woonsocket, alias Missy something or other, was a woman of many names and talents.

She saw the huge yellow sign proclaiming that Snuffy's was the best bar and grill in the state of Utah. She turned off onto a gravel road, drove two miles, and there was the barn straight ahead. She was grateful George was waiting and had lowered the spikes across the road that otherwise would have shredded the tires of her bus into a hundred pieces.

The doors were opening as she slowed and drove right into the cavernous space. The doors closed almost immediately.

"You cut it pretty close, Missy," the big, baldheaded man said cheerfully. "Got some hot breakfast ready for everyone, and the hot water is running full blast for anyone who wants to take a shower. Full load this time, I see. Gonna have to have Irma fix some more eggs. She'll love that. That woman just loves to cook for a crowd."

Two volunteers stepped into the crowd and shuffled half the women and children to the kitchen in back of the barn and the other half to the showers on the other side.

"Something happen along the way, Missy?" George Ellis asked, concern furrowing his brow when he saw the pregnant young girls.

Pearl swiped at the sweat forming on her brow. "You could say that. Listen, we're going to have to stay a little longer than I planned or like." She quickly related the night's events. George soaked it all in like a sponge. "Driver was dead, you say?"

"Very dead. I tried for a pulse. I took his

cell phone and wallet so they aren't going to know who he is, at least right away they won't. I did pass that pickup like I told you. I'm sure the Highway Patrol is there as we speak."

"These girls, what are they saying?"

"Nothing. The one who isn't pregnant is the only one really talking and, beyond telling me who they are, she isn't saying all that much. She did volunteer, quite cheerfully, that she miscarried in her fourth month. There must be some kind of law about this, George. You live here, what do the authorities do about something like this? Those girls are babies themselves, and they're going to give birth to babies. Where are the damn parents?"

"Polygamy is a whole other world, Missy. The authorities pretty much look the other way. Those people out there in that big compound have some pretty powerful lawyers, and they go at it. Just easier to do nothing. I'm not saying that's right, I'm just saying that's the way it is."

"Not for long," Pearl said. "Things are going to change pretty quick, I'm thinking. In the meantime, we have to keep them here until . . . until I can get some help."

"I hear you, Missy. Now, how about some of Irma's pancakes? By now she's probably run out of eggs, so she's switching to pancakes. Our own fresh sausage is always a big hit. You game?"

"George, I am starved, and I admit it. You don't think anyone will come around here asking questions, do you?"

"Doubt it. This acreage is set two miles back. Course, they know I'm here, but they'd call first to ask if I've seen anything. No one wants to take a chance on those spikes in my road, that kind of thing. Most people around here go on trust, and that goes for the Highway Patrol. 'Sides, me and Irma are honorary members. You look dead on your feet, Missy."

"I am, George. Do you mind if I pass on breakfast and try to get a few hours' sleep? Wake me if . . . well, just wake me if you need to, okay?"

"I will, Missy. Your room is all ready, just head on back to it. Irma laid out some clean clothes and towels for you."

Pearl hugged the old man, looked into his eyes, then hugged him again.

George and Irma Ellis had a daughter who had tried to get away from her abusive husband too many times to count. By the time the couple contacted Pearl, who acted on the information immediately, it was too late for the Ellises' daughter. She was found dead in her garage an hour before Pearl could rescue her and her twin babies.

From that day on George and Irma Ellis were Pearl's staunchest supporters and did everything and anything they could to aid her underground railroad, making sure no one else met the same fate as their daughter and their grandbabies.

George looked around the barn and felt his eyes fill up. He and Irma had used all their savings plus their daughter's insurance money to convert the barn into living quarters that no one in Sienna knew about. They'd installed two huge bathrooms with four showers each and two dormitory bedrooms that could sleep twenty-two comfortably. In the back of the barn, George himself had built a kitchen with a huge brick oven you could roast an ox in. All of this had been done on the sneak by Irma and George without building inspectors prying into what they considered their private business. They'd driven miles and miles out of their way to buy fixtures and wiring just so the local shop owners wouldn't know what they were up to.

It had been Irma's idea, once they got under way, to lay down the spiked hump at the entrance to their property. It worked like a charm, and no one came to visit after news got around about the first six or seven accidents. The message was loud and clear: the Ellis family didn't want company. They were probably a bit *tetched* in the head because of the loss of their daughter and grandchildren.

George trundled his big body back to the kitchen area, where Irma was doing her best to chat up the pregnant young teenagers. She shrugged to show him she was not getting any useful information. He mouthed the word "polygamy" for his wife's benefit. She nodded but gave no other indication she knew what was going on.

George walked around the old milk barn, which was big enough to hold all the people currently in it plus five or six more busloads. He went outside and walked the two miles down the lane to his mailbox. Sienna's one and only police cruiser sailed past, slowed, stopped, and backed up to

where George was standing, a pile of cata-
logs and the newspaper in his hands.

"Morning, Deputy Clyde. Where you
going in such a hurry?" George asked.

"Down the road a piece. Bus went off
the road, the driver's dead. No identifica-
tion on him a'tall. No passengers. The
bus is a rental, we think. You see anyone
around here, maybe walking, looking for
help, George? You still got them spikes in
the road that tear up a person's tires?"

"I do for a fact, Deputy Clyde, and, no, I
haven't seen a soul. Heck, it's a two-mile
road to the house. If there were people in
the bus, I'd think they'd head right into
Sienna. Maybe the guy was deadheading
somewhere. You know, dropped off his
passengers and was returning to wherever he was headed. Sorry I can't help
you. I'll watch the local news at noon to
see how it's all going. If you need me for
anything like a search party, just give me
a call."

The deputy nodded and got back into
the cruiser. George watched until the black
and white cruiser was just a speck on the
road before he turned and started on the
two-mile walk back to the barn. Walking to

the mailbox was George's only exercise, and he was proud of the fact that he did it, day in and day out, rain, snow, or sunshine. Just like the United States mail carriers.

A knot settled itself between his shoulder blades. Clyde might act like a hick, but he was sharp as a tack. And Clyde did not take kindly to any kind of wrongdoing on his watch, which was twenty-four/seven. He'd be back sooner or later. Probably sooner than George would like. He had to make preparations for his guests before that happened.

The knot turned into an itch as he walked along in the bright sunshine. How long before the people at the compound—assuming that's where his guests were headed—would call the authorities? Or would this be something they handled with their own people? He had to admit he didn't know. Nor did he want to find out.

George picked up his pace and broke into a trot. Time, he felt, was his, Irma's, and Missy's enemy. Yet time was all they had.

# Chapter 4

If she had been wearing jodhpurs and knee-high polished boots, Annie de Silva could have passed for General George Patton, ready to announce that it was time to go into battle as she waved Charles's pointer at the huge seventy-six-inch television monitor on which Lady Justice stood, balancing the scales of justice.

It was always a moving moment for the Sisters as they contemplated their past, the present, and whatever the future was going to hold for them. Breaking the law, serving up justice Sisterhood style, had its upside and its downside. This was always

the moment when each of them knew
they could bow out or forge ahead. The
question was never a verbal one, but it
was hanging there like an invisible thread,
and they all knew it. One by one they
would nod to show they were on board for
whatever was to come.

The huge clocks on the wall showed
various times around the world. It was ten
minutes to twelve, Eastern Standard
Time. Almost seven hours since their
world had turned topsy-turvy, with Charles
and Myra's departure on the British helicopter and Pearl Barnes's latest crisis.

Annie stepped down and stood behind
her chair at the round table. "Listen up,
ladies. We are on a short leash, timewise.
Pearl needs us, and she needs us now.
We've spent the last hour watching video
of those strange people out there in Utah.
I personally take offense at any man who
claims he has the right to take as many
wives as he wants. Like this man," she
said, pressing a button to show a middle-
aged man, dressed to the nines, on the
screen. "He has one legal marriage and
says he has thirty-seven spiritual—or
celestial, if you like that word better—

wives. Which doesn't say much for those dumb women. That makes thirty-eight wives. The legal wife and the thirty-seven spiritual/celestial wives have given him seventy-eight children. All under the age of seventeen. The man's name is Harold Evanrod, and he is called 'the Prophet' of the HOE sect. It's a splinter group of the Fundamentalist Church of Jesus Christ of Latter Day Saints—the FLDS. The HOE stands for 'Heaven on Earth.'"

"That's an Ermenegildo Zegna suit he's wearing," Alexis said. "I know fashion, and that suit cost him bookoo bucks. Where does the money come from? And the guy drives a Bentley! I don't get it."

"Good question, and you're right, it is a Bentley," Nikki said. "A lot of the families are receiving welfare payments from our government. That means everyone out there is footing the bill for the Bentley and the suit. It's called taxes. Thirty-seven celestial wives collecting welfare checks every week. That's a lot of money no matter how you look at it. And this is going to make your jaw drop: the Pentagon is helping out with huge contracts to those people. I don't know how that works because I just plucked it off the Internet a while ago," she added as she looked down at her notes.

Isabelle waved a sheaf of papers in the air. "This is not only unbelievable, it is disgusting. I can't wait to get there so we can"—she smiled—"take care of things. You are not going to believe what those creepy people do to their own, to the children. And no one does anything."

Yoko started to cry. "In a way it is what my evil father did to my mother and all those other young women he brought here to . . . satisfy those horrible pedophile friends of his. Just tell me what to do, and I will gladly do it."

Kathryn stomped her feet and stood up. "This little mission calls for everything we can throw at those people. I, for one, can't wait to get out there, which raises the question, how are we going to do it?"

"We need Charles's password to get into his . . . his secret files. There is no way we can even think we can crack it on our own, which means one of us has to call him to demand it." Nikki looked down at her watch. "He should be setting down right about now on British soil. Will he cooperate? I don't know."

She had her special phone in her hand and was punching in a number. The others watched her, their expressions tense.

They all flinched when they saw her square her shoulders. The grim set of her jaw told them some unpleasant words were going to pass through her clenched lips, and they were right.

Nikki didn't bother with a greeting. "I need your pass code, Charles, and I need it *now*." She listened a second or two, then the ugly words flew. "I really don't give a good rat's ass about your secrecy and our secrecy. I need it *now*. We have a crisis here that you left us to deal with, and since you aren't here, we have to act independently. Are you going to give it to me or not? Really, Charles. I feel for you, but this is a life-and-death matter for hundreds of people, and the son you didn't even know existed does not enter into what's facing us. You are dealing with your crisis, and we need to deal with ours. I can't help you with your guilt. We all are praying for your son and for you, too. So, your answer is *no*?"

The other Sisters immediately started to jabber, their voices high-pitched, angry, and indignant. Nikki held up her hand for silence. Her voice turned warm in greeting. "Myra, Charles is not cooperating. I need the pass code. If you know it, give it to me, please. Hundreds of lives depend on it. HRM? Her Royal Majesty? I didn't know there was such a title. Oh, Charles made it up. Okay. Are you sure, Myra? Thanks. Call us," she said, and then hung up.

"Okay, every operative Charles ever used, all his sources will be at our disposal as soon as I enter his pass code," Nikki said.

"But if he wouldn't give it to you, why did Myra offer it up?" Yoko asked.

Nikki sighed. "It wasn't that he *wouldn't* give it up. *He* couldn't give it up. There is a difference according to Myra. It's that covert, British espionage stuff. You know, like a cop never gives up his gun, that kind of thing. Right now it really doesn't matter, and Myra wouldn't lie to us. It's splitting hairs, but what the heck; we have it now, and that's all that matters. I'm going on the computer, the rest of you delve into all that polygamy stuff. Be sure you understand what we're getting ourselves into and how we're going to extricate ourselves. Someone needs to call Pearl and tell her we need at least thirty-six hours before we can be there. That's providing everything works to our advantage, and I can get us the help we need."

Annie was already dialing Pearl's number. The retired justice picked it up on the first ring. "Listen carefully, Pearl. We're on board, but we need at least thirty-six hours until we can get there, possibly sooner, but we don't work by the seat of our pants. Now, here is my suggestion: Move your people just the way you would, but this time use that fellow who owns the barn. Get them to a safe haven. I want you to pile those young girls into that special bus of yours and drive it to Montana to Jack's cabin. This is the plan for the moment, and it will probably change, so don't get too comfortable with it. We'll be sending someone to stay with the girls there. Listen, Pearl, you might want to give some thought to changing your appearance once you leave Utah. I know, I know, you can disguise the bus and change the plates, but I'm talking about your physical appearance."

"Yes, yes, Annie, I understand all of that; but, I've never delivered a baby. Some of these girls are in their third trimester. You might want to think about sending a midwife and everything that will be needed."

"I'm on it, Pearl."

"Annie, I need to tell you a few things, so listen carefully." Pearl, her voice a little shaky, recounted the events leading up to her arrival at George Ellis's barn. "I'm going to be leaving as soon as I can get the girls together. You realize, of course, that I am literally kidnapping them, right?"

"All right, I understand. Don't worry about that right now. In the meantime, try and engage those girls in talk about how they live, what they believe, all the little et ceteras that make up their lives. After that, you won't worry too much about the kidnapping charge. Take pictures of them so that Maggie can use them if it becomes necessary. And drive carefully, Pearl."

Annie's eyebrows slid up to her hairline. She gave herself a mental shake and dived into the papers in front of her. Oh, she could hardly wait to get her hands on those bastards at the HOE compound and the guy—whatever the hell his name was—who ran the place.

The discussion continued, with the Sisters commenting and taking turns reading aloud from the information they'd printed out from the Internet.

Kathryn went first. "As we all know, because we saw it on satellite TV for weeks on end, that guy Warren Jeffs who was the head of the FLDS was convicted and jailed. I think he got ten years to life, and he has two more trials pending. If I remember correctly, they said he'll probably spend the rest of his life behind bars. So, we shouldn't have any qualms about invading that place. Okay, they rehashed all that until we were nearly brain-dead, then they hit us with all those women in their *Little House on the Prairie* dresses who carried cell phones. The ones who spoke like zombies about wanting their children back, etc.

"A while back, this guy Harold Evanrod stepped up to the plate, even though no one voted him in, if in fact that's how you get to be the Prophet. He splintered off and formed his own little group and started calling it the HOE, and, as we now know, that stands for Heaven on Earth, according to him and his followers. That particular compound is located approximately twenty miles from Sienna, where Pearl is right now.

"Jeffs and the FLDS people in Texas are a separate issue. There's nothing we can do about that, and we don't even want to go there since the authorities are making a mess of things as it is. Let them all stew in their own juice. What we can do something about is the HOE group.

"I have a little background, but not much because they practice secrecy to the nth degree in those places.

"There was an attorney named David Leavitt who prosecuted a guy named Tom Green. Green broke with tradition and went on the TV circuit with his seven wives and bragged that he'd married some of them when they were minors. At the age of thirty-seven, he impregnated a thirteen-year-old.

"Many of the spiritual/celestial wives register with the state as a single mother and draw welfare for their families. In one decade, Green and his dependents received more than $647,000 in public assistance. Do the math here, girls. He's just one guy. Multiply that by all those guys in similar compounds, and the amount of free money they get is mind-boggling. And it's the taxpayers who foot the bill.

"Leavitt considered Green a pedophile. He said little girls are raised from the cradle to marry as children and know only a life of polygamy. Leavitt said the children are victims of pedophiles and victims of the state of Utah, which turned its back on polygamy for sixty years. It appears it's a new ball game these days, with new rules.

"Long story short, Leavitt filed charges against Green and won convictions on charges of bigamy, criminal nonsupport, and child rape. Unfortunately, the judge was lenient and Green only served five years total in prison.

"After that, the voters turned on Leavitt and voted him out of office that same year, with many voters saying the publicity was distasteful to them. Try and figure that one out, girls."

Alexis took her turn and started reading. "What the polygamists were hoping was that the practice of polygamy would sink back into obscurity, but that hasn't happened. A few have gotten away to tell of the abuse and are, as we speak, providing the authorities with as much information as they can. Some of them are suing the United Effort Plan, which is a communal property trust held by the FLDS. A judge removed the trustees and appointed new ones. Believe it or not, police officers have been forced to resign because they practiced polygamy and refused to uphold the secular laws. They even forced a judge out of office for the same thing.

"Some of the states have tried to crack down on the endemic welfare fraud in polygamous groups. The fraud is even institutionalized as 'bleeding the beast,' by which church members mean taking from federal and state governments because the government has persecuted them or their Mormon ancestors.

"Two listeners paraphrased the polygamous priest James Harmston as preaching that God 'wants' them to take from every government program possible. God 'doesn't expect you to wallow in turkey manure. In another lifetime, we were persecuted and thrown out of our country by the government. We are entitled to everything we can get.'"

Alexis read on. "With God ordering up fraud, as argued by modern-day polygamists, there is plenty of it. Many plural wives claim they don't know the whereabouts of their children's fathers. As many as 50 percent were on public assistance in a place called Hildale, Utah, in 2001; 33 percent were on food stamps in 1998 compared to Utah's average of 4.7 percent. In 1997, every school-age child in Colorado City, Arizona, was living below the poverty level.

"That guy Jeffs got $2.8 million dollars from the federal government to build an airport for his chartered Lear jet. But that's Arizona, so you have to believe it's the same in the other states where they practice polygamy. Oh, another thing, Homeland Security gave that tiny little place a grant of $350,000, and it was the state's largest HS grant. The state of Arizona had to take over the Colorado City school system because of gross mismanagement of public funds."

Isabelle shuffled her papers until she found what she wanted. "Ah, here it is. I never heard of this, but since it's been reported, I have to believe it's true. The youngsters were called 'the lost boys.' They were kicked to the curb because they had a surplus of males. These kids were left to fend for themselves and didn't know how. There were four hundred of them. Those children were taught from the cradle up that the Prophet must be obeyed as God's representative, that the outside world is evil, and that anyone leaving will be ground to dust and damned in the afterlife. The youngsters didn't know how to cope, some committed suicide, some turned to drugs, they steal, and are homeless. Those poor boys live their lives like it's their last day on earth. They can't believe they won't have three wives as promised and are convinced that they're doomed. All they want is to go back to their mothers. There are just too many heartbreaking stories here to read," Isabelle said, tears in her eyes.

"Some of the boys, with some help, filed a civil suit back in 2004 against the FLDS. It's in negotiation now. The church is fighting it, saying that because they are a church, they have a constitutional right to set their own standards for excommunication.

"Some of the appointed lawyers are saying that the 'Babyland' cemetery in Colorado City has many unmarked graves, plus eighteen minor children, plus eight stillbirths.

"It's said that some women pray to have children with Down's syndrome because such children usually have docile temperaments and because the mothers get $500 a month in assistance for a handicapped child," Kathryn said in a cold, brittle voice.

"I don't want to hear any more of this," Annie said. "I think we're all getting the picture here. Young girls are being forced to marry old men, and their mothers do nothing to stop it, and even encourage it. Since the children don't know any better, they do what they're told. They're broodmares, nothing more. So, we're going to go to the HOE compound, somehow. We're going to take on those old men and the women who support them. Somehow we will get the children out of there to safety. Is that how you're all seeing it?"

"Damn straight," Kathryn said, speaking for the group. "But, Annie, what are we going to do with them once we take over?"

"I have a glimmer of an idea," Annie said, her eyes sparkling. "Tell me what you think. Remember when we were in Las Vegas, and we went to that abandoned nursing home down the road from Mr. Fish's property?" The women nodded. "Well, think about this. What if I buy that, add on a couple of wings, refurbish, and set it up to take care of all those people who want a better life? We can hire nurses and doctors and therapists. I even know just the person who I bet will jump at the chance to run the place. Paula Woodley. Remember her? I think she'll jump in with both feet, and she's loyal to all of us. Even after what we did to her awful national security advisor husband."

"Damn, Annie, that's a stupendous idea," Yoko said. "But it is rather like putting the cart before the horse. What if we screw up our mission?"

"Honey, don't think like that. We were all born to succeed. This time will be no different, and I, for one, am anxious to see if we can do it without Charles. Say the word, and I'll put the wheels in motion."

The chorus of ayes rang in the enclosed room.

"There you have it," Annie said happily.

Thirty minutes later Annie had those wheels in motion, and Paula Woodley was on board.

# Chapter 5

Nikki licked at her dry lips and worried her bottom lip with her teeth as she contemplated the stack of papers in front of her. She flexed her fingers before she started to sift and collate the inch-thick pile of printouts she'd just run off. How did Charles do this and not make mistakes? She'd lucked out, though, with Avery Snowden, a pal of Charles's from the old days. Like Charles he was a former British intelligence agent and only too happy to get back into the game. She had to admit that she was surprised at how much the man actually knew about the Sisterhood's activities, which meant Charles trusted him implicitly.

Nikki perused the papers in front of her one more time before she stepped away from the computers and marched down the steps and over to the round table, where the other Sisters were waiting for her.

"I think we're in business. Mr. Avery Snowden, Charles's go-to guy and the one who heads up the behind-the-scenes network Charles uses, is on board and will get back to me within the hour. In other words, we're going to see Annie's and Myra's money working for us. I will say this, Avery was a tad upset that we were not going to be compensated for taking on such a large-scale mission. He said money talks and bullshit walks, but whatever he could do, he would do.

"He explained it this way. It takes thousands of people to make the network function to our advantage, and if one of them just makes phone calls or lends a car or buys materials, they all have to be paid, and it adds up at the end of the month. He said this particular network has people waiting in line to help because our reputation is so sterling. We can always help ourselves to some of the HOE's funds when we're finished. Just enough to pay all those people for helping us. They're stealing it to begin with, so we'll just steal it back. Works for me," Nikki said loftily, as the others nodded to indicate their agreement.

"Our biggest hurdle right now is getting off this mountain and to Utah. When I told Avery this mission involved the polygamy sect, I heard him suck in his breath. The authorities, as we all know, are all over those people, especially in Texas and Arizona. He admitted he didn't know anything about the HOE group in Utah but said he would know everything there is to know by the time he calls me back."

Nikki turned to Alexis. "Is your Red Bag filled? Do you need anything? If so, make me a list, and I'll pass it on to Avery."

"I don't need anything, Nikki. I replenished what I'd used when we got back from Vegas. Everything's good to go."

"Did any phone calls come in while I was working on the computer? Yoko, any word from Harry?"

Yoko shook her head.

Annie's phone rang. The room turned silent as they tried to make sense of Annie's end of the conversation. Kathryn scribbled the word "speakerphone," and Annie pressed the button. Pearl's panic-stricken voice invaded the room.

"It's a huge white bus, no lettering on it that I can see. The girls are getting excited like they know who it is."

"Why are you traveling by day, Pearl? I thought yours was a nighttime operation," Annie said, her voice rising with anxiety.

"Things changed rapidly. There was a deputy who was a little too curious. I'm sure the Highway Patrol is monitoring my last stop or will be soon. You need to call and put my people on alert. By now I have to assume those polygamy people are looking for the girls. I just crossed the border into Idaho. You know what that means. They are gaining on me, and the girls are getting really excited. They keep saying the Prophet is coming to take them home. Don't even think of telling me to try and outrun them."

"Stay calm, Pearl, and leave your cell phone on for as long as you can so we know what's going on. Just put that ear bud in your ear and none of them will be the wiser. Help is on the way, but unfortunately you're all the way across the country, and it's going to take a while. If they just want the girls, give them up. You have no other choice. Do you have your gun?"

"Yes, in the you know what, under the you know what," Pearl responded. "Do you want me to . . . to use it?"

"God, no. Well, not unless you have to. My best advice is to play along, you're taking the girls to safety because they wouldn't tell you anything, and when you mentioned the police, they panicked. You're being a Good Samaritan, that's all. Make up some fictitious clinic that takes in unwed mothers in Idaho, and that's where you're headed. Remember, Pearl, they can identify you, the barn, and George and Irma."

"I know, I know. The people I just left have a plan in case something like this ever went down. Have someone call them right now to put that plan into effect. Oh, oh, the van is trying to cut me off. I have to pull over. I can't risk an accident with the girls on board."

"Okay, I'll stay quiet, but leave the phone open on the seat," Annie said.

The Sisters crowded closer to make sure they could hear everything that was going on. They heard Pearl downshift, heard the brakes on the bus start to catch. They could hear the excitement of the young girls as they whooped and hollered. Then they heard Pearl release the catch that would open the bus's doors.

"Who are you? What do you want? I'm going to call the police if you don't get away from this bus right now!"

A big man in his midfifties stepped up into the bus. His hair was gray as was his moustache. He was dressed—Pearl sought for the proper word and finally came up with it—nattily. She wondered if young people these days even knew what that meant.

"There's no need for hostility, ma'am. We just came here to pick up our property. We'll be on our way unless you give us a problem. We mean you no harm, and we are not carrying weapons."

"What property?" Pearl blustered. "I don't have anything that belongs to you. You can't just come aboard here and tell me what to do. These young girls need medical assistance. I'm taking them to . . ."

"No, you see, ma'am, that's where you're wrong, you are not taking these young ladies anywhere. These young ladies belong to me and these gentlemen behind me. They belong to us because they are our wives."

Pearl could feel her blood start to boil. "Stop with the nonsense, these are just young unwed pregnant women. They're not old enough to be married. If you take them, you are kidnapping them. I'll have to alert the authorities."

"No, you won't do that because you just crossed the state line from Utah into Idaho and our wives live in Utah. I'll be the one doing the calling, and I will press charges if you don't release these women to me right now."

"Let them go, let them go," the Sisters hissed. "Let them go and get out of there, Pearl, before those stupid goons make good on their threat."

Pearl knew when she was beaten. She nodded. "At least tell me where you're taking them. I want to know they'll be safe."

The big man, the spokesman of the

four-man group, smiled. "Why, ma'am, I'm taking them to Heaven on Earth, where we all live a satisfying, righteous, happy life."

The big man turned to the girls and shouted loud enough to be heard into the next county, "Come along, darlings, Daddy is taking you home. Say good-bye to the nice lady, and let's be on our way."

"Tell me something, how did you find us and who are you?" Pearl asked as the girls lumbered off the bus.

"My angels travel with GPS tracking devices. They're pinned to their collars. Or, I should say, there's one under the collar of my bride. As to who I am, I am the Prophet."

This last was said with such pride, Pearl felt sick to her stomach.

Pearl played dumb. She hoped she looked as poleaxed as she felt. "Of what?"

The big man drew himself up to his full six-foot height, fixed his calculating gaze on her, and said, "Of Heaven and Earth. Thank you for taking care of my wife and her sisters. Drive safely, now. There isn't much traffic around here, and if you break down, there won't be anyone to help you."

Pearl bit down on her tongue as she

slammed the door to the bus. "Did you hear that son of a bitch?" she snarled, the moment she was sure her voice wouldn't carry.

"Loud and clear. Be glad it worked out this way, Pearl. I'd hate to see your name plastered all over the morning papers. Not to worry, we'll get him and all the other ones out there. We have a plan. Well, we almost have a plan. Now that your immediate crisis is on hold, we have some breathing room. What are you going to do now?"

"I can't go back to George and Irma's. I'll double back and make my way to the next relay station. Listen, Annie, there's something you need to know. I don't think I'm wrong about this, either. The girl, the one named Emily, the talkative one in the bunch, she said she lost her baby. She referred to it as her 'bump.' She was going around patting the other girls' stomachs and saying she couldn't wait to get another bump. She's retarded, Annie. Not severely but she is definitely mentally challenged. She said she went to sleep and when she woke up her bump was gone. Now she wants another one. Actually, she's the only one who really talked.

None of them would tell me where their mothers were, they wouldn't tell me their names or where they were coming from. But, by God, at least one of them had a GPS tracking device pinned to her collar. The Prophet's bride," she snorted.

"Retarded?" Annie bellowed in shock. "And she had a baby?"

"A bump. She never mentioned a baby. Okay, I'm back on the road. Tell me I don't have to worry about George and Irma."

"You don't have to worry about George and Irma, Pearl. We'll take care of things on that end. Drive carefully and check in every few hours until you get to your next relay point."

"Will do," Pearl said as she broke the connection. She adjusted her wraparound sunglasses and marveled that she'd gotten out of that little mess intact. She couldn't help but wonder when her luck was going to run out.

Back on Big Pine Mountain, the encrypted cell phones and the three huge television monitors were working overtime.

Annie pressed a button, and a picture of what looked like a gigantic farm appeared on the screen. "Behold, ladies, you are now viewing the Heaven on Earth compound! Compliments of Google," she said dramatically. "According to the tax maps, this particular piece of property was purchased by some shell company out of Singapore. Not that we care. There are 120 acres. As you can see, there is a milk barn, another barn that, if you believe this, is used for winter food storage. They sell the milk in town. They have chickens for eggs. They sell those also. In the summer they sell their produce to local markets. They're the local pumpkin distributor, if that means anything."

Annie pressed another button. The scene was enlarged, and different buildings could be seen. "This is an aerial photo of the main house, where the Supreme Prophet lives. It's a five-thousand-square-foot house with front and back porches. These buildings," she said, using Charles's pointer, "are where the people, I guess you would call them 'disciples,' live. It's communal, dormitory style. No women actually live in the main house, according to one of the women who got away and gave all this information to the authorities. It was immediately posted on the Net." Annie moved the pointer. "This is the school. Rudimentary education at best. Eighth grade is as far as it goes. Most of the teaching, aside from math and English, is religion.

"No one in the compound owns anything. Only the Prophet can own things, and he owns a lot. He owns a penthouse apartment in Park City. He's into fashion, drives a Bentley. And according to what he told Pearl, he owns all the people who live at HOE. The word 'dictator' comes to mind."

"Okay, okay, now that we know all that, why are we going to get involved?" Isabelle asked. "Pearl is okay, she's back in business, and no one was hurt but the driver of the bus, who died. The girls are back where they're supposed to be. Or at least where they were headed. We all heard them, they sounded happy when they were 'rescued.' So, tell me, why are we putting our necks on the line for something we aren't involved in?"

In a shaky voice, Yoko spoke up. "Those men are pedophiles. Those young girls are nothing but baby-making machines. Some of them are only thirteen. That is not right. I really want to rescue them and show them a normal life. I was rescued and given a better life. I want to do the same for them."

"It's their religion," Isabelle said. "What right do we have to tamper with someone's religion? They didn't ask for our help. Pearl is safe and out of the mess. We could be going into a firestorm not of our making. I think we need to fall back and regroup."

"I want to know where the mothers are," Alexis said. "Do they just willy-nilly hand over their daughters when they turn thirteen? What kind of mother does that?"

"The kind of woman who has been brainwashed. That life is all they know," Nikki said. "Yes, Pearl is safe for the moment, and the young girls are safe, at least in a way. We have to decide if we want to get involved and show the world what those men are all about. The women, too. I think that business in Texas is a start, but I believe the authorities didn't think it through when they took those four-hundred-plus children. They were overwhelmed. That won't happen to us. We can go in there, take out the women and children who want to go, deal with those skanky men, and any uncooperative women, too. If we can wipe out just one of those places, maybe our notoriety will spur the authorities to close in and really do something about all those others and at the same time make those pedophiles run for cover."

"It's their religion," Isabelle protested.

"It's polygamy, and they live in a country where that's illegal," Annie snorted. "They're stealing taxpayer dollars. They're using children to give birth to children. The women have no options other than what that slimy so-called Prophet gives them. Do I need to remind you that the other prophet, Jeffs, is serving ten years in prison and probably looking at life in prison for the same thing this other Prophet is doing? What kind of religion is that? I'll tell you what kind it is," she said, answering her own question. "It's the kind where they use the word 'religion' to get them out of the messes they're in. They're pedophiles, they're tax cheats, they lie, and they brainwash their people. I say we swoop in there and take them all out. Let's vote. Right now."

Everyone but Isabelle raised her hand. She flinched when the other Sisters faced her down.

Only Annie spoke. "Okay, Isabelle, you stay behind on the mountain," she said in a voice that was colder than ice.

"By myself?" Isabelle shrilled.

"Damn straight by yourself, Isabelle," Kathryn said. "I don't want you covering my ass if your heart isn't in this." She looked around at the others, who were nodding that they sided with her.

"But . . ."

"There are no buts, Isabelle. If we can't depend on you, you're no good to us. You stay behind," Nikki agreed.

Isabelle fled the room in tears.

Her fellow Sisters looked at one another.

"Were we too hard on her?" Alexis asked.

Kathryn snapped to attention. Always the most verbal of the group, she pierced Alexis with her gaze. "You want to partner up with her, she's all yours. I hate to remind you of this, Alexis, but you were in prison once. Do you want to go back because Isabelle does something stupid because she's not watching and doing what she's supposed to be doing?"

"Good God, no. It's just that this is the first time one of us isn't 100 percent for the mission. I'm okay with it. Isabelle is entitled to her opinion and that's her right and she has to live with it," Alexis said.

Nikki turned thoughtful. "We did cut off our earlier discussion on how those people work. Let's download some of the videos on the Net showing how these folks brainwash their 'disciples' and keep their womenfolk in line. Hearing us talking about the evils of the HOE isn't the same as watching them practice what they preach. After Isabelle sees it, she might change her mind. Trust me, we'll know if she's 100 percent or she's faking it. Let's vote on it."

Five hands shot in the air.

"All right, Kathryn, the job is yours. I have to go back online now and contact Avery. Someone call Pearl to make sure she's okay." Nikki looked around. "I guess no one got a call from Myra or Charles, huh?"

They all shook their heads from side to side.

Nikki shrugged and climbed the three steps to the platform where the bank of computers waited for her.

Sometimes life was a bitch!

# Chapter 6

Kathryn started to pace, a sure sign of her agitation. It was clear that the issue with Isabelle was bothering her, perhaps more so than it did the others. While Kathryn wasn't exactly a hothead, she was clearly outspoken, sometimes to the point where the others cringed.

But, as Yoko said, coming to Kathryn's defense, Kathryn only said aloud what the others were thinking. Then Yoko reminded them all of the first days of forming the Sisterhood and how Kathryn was on her case twenty-four/seven, and how it all worked out in the end.

The others watched out of the corners of their eyes as Kathryn got more and more agitated by the moment. Finally, she whirled around, and shouted, "Annie, call Pearl and tell her to ditch the bus! Tell her to get off the road. They're going to come back for her. They can't let her get away. One of those girls had a GPS under her collar. I'll bet you my sunflower bikini that that GPS is now on her bus. Now, Annie, God dammit! Put her on speakerphone."

Nikki stopped what she was doing. The other Sisters heard her say, "Avery, I have to put you on hold for a moment." She looked at Kathryn and mouthed, "What?" Kathryn just shrugged.

Annie was already pressing the number that would connect her with Pearl. She didn't bother with a greeting but simply said, "Pearl, ditch the bus, take your gear, and get out of there. Stay off the main road if you can. Kathryn thinks those people planted a GPS tracker on the bus. Don't leave anything incriminating behind. Help is on the way. I can't give you a specific time frame, but they'll find you as long as you have your handheld GPS. Move, Pearl!"

The Sisters leaned forward, the better to hear the voice on the other end of the satellite phone. "I'm one step ahead of you. I had a bad feeling, so I ditched the bus thirty minutes ago, Annie. I tossed the distributor cap and I have everything I need. I'm moving. There isn't much traffic on this back road. My story will be, I'm hiking and had a falling-out with my friend, and I'm off on my own. What do you think is going to go down?"

Annie looked directly at Kathryn, then at the others. She nodded at Kathryn to indicate she should talk.

"This is Kathryn, Pearl. Just a gut feeling, but over the years I have learned to pay attention to gut feelings. You need to stay out of sight if possible until we can get help to you. Worst-case scenario is those people file a complaint with the cops, who go looking for you. From what I read, there are a lot of polygamists in law enforcement, even a judge or two. The children on the bus and the men who showed up to take them would have given an accurate description of you by now. And remember who you really are." Kathryn looked over at Nikki, who was talking a mile a minute to

Charles's second-in-command. She kept nodding as she spoke.

Pearl's voice came through loud and clear, almost as if she were in the next room. "I don't exactly look like the person who was driving the bus. My new name is Rosa Sanchez, and I look like a Rosa Sanchez. How will I know it will be your people if someone should accost me?" Kathryn looked over at Nikki, who whispered, "By her new name."

"They'll call you Rosa or Miz Sanchez. It's high noon, your time. Can you take the heat?"

"Not really. I can't be sure, but the temperature seems to be around a hundred. If not, it certainly feels like it. I have water. I'm going to look for some cover. I'll stay as close to the road as I feel comfortable with. Any suggestions?"

Yoko flapped her arms up and down. She shrugged her tiny shoulders. "She's between a rock and a hard place right now. Just tell her to stay alert and to drink plenty of water." She looked over at Nikki, her gaze quizzical.

It was Nikki's turn to speak on Annie's phone. "It's Nikki, Pearl. Ninety minutes, and that's being optimistic. Can you handle it?"

"I can. I will. If I'm caught, I'll leave the tracker so your people will find it. From there you'll have to find the nearest police or sheriff's department. If, and I say *if,* that's where they take me."

Annie reared up. "They won't be taking you anywhere near either place. They're going to take you back to that Heaven on Earth place and make you one of their slaves."

The Sisters as one gasped aloud. They all started talking on top of one another. "Yes, it could happen."

"No, it couldn't happen."

"Well, maybe it could happen."

Then, "Cross your fingers and hope for the best."

The connection broken, they turned once more to Nikki for their latest update.

Annie's cell phone rang. "Change of plans, Nellie. We're leaving the mountain. These are now your new orders, so listen up . . ."

Nikki handed Alexis a sheet of paper. Alexis scanned the sheet, and ran to fetch her Red Bag.

Kathryn picked up the sheet and read it aloud. "We're leaving here, one by one in crop dusters! That's how we're going to get to Utah? It'll take us a week to get there. We'll be so windblown we won't know what our names are when we finally land!"

Annie blanched. "Those little paper planes that look so . . . so rickety?"

Nikki nodded. "If you can come up with a better plan, let's hear it. Avery said it's the best he can do on such short notice."

Annie snorted. "I suppose if one is looking for adventure, one might surmise that flying in a crop duster is it." Ever the fashion guru, her next question came as no surprise to any of the Sisters. "What's the attire?"

"Camo, goggles, and one of those leather helmets the flyers used to wear," Yoko giggled.

Kathryn tried not to laugh. "I hesitate to bring this up, but does anyone besides me think we're a bit scattered at the moment? Usually things run a little more smoothly. Charles always had it laid out, and we just fell in line."

Nikki picked up a folder and threw it at

her. Murphy barked, uncertain if this was a new game or something else entirely. When he heard his mistress burst out laughing, he lay down, his huge head between his paws.

"For the moment, everyone in . . . our little . . . uh . . . group is going to Utah. Then we'll kick everything up a few notches and go on from there, but first we have to get there undetected and safe and sound. Charles has forty years' experience under his belt whereas I've had"—Nikki looked at her watch—"fifteen minutes. I rest my case."

"You're doing just fine, dear," Annie said. "I just wish I wasn't so worried about Pearl."

Three thousand miles away Pearl Barnes, aka Harriet Woonsocket, aka Rosa Sanchez found herself being eaten alive by sand fleas as she huddled in the scrub brush along the side of the road. Overhead, the sun blazed as it baked her surroundings. She was down to her last two bottles of water and had to pee.

The only vehicles she'd seen in the last hour were two farm tractors moseying down the road at ten miles an hour, one kid on a motorized scooter followed by a mean-looking dog, and a farm truck full of hay. She wondered if traffic would pick up once the heat of the day passed. What bothered her more than anything was that she was drenched in her own sweat and was sure she smelled to high heaven. God, if the other justices could only see her now they'd die laughing. Well, let them. That was her other life, and this was now. So what if she was soaking wet and smelled. She was alive and still had her reputation intact.

More minutes passed. More sand fleas. Pearl continued to sweat. She looked at her watch. Ninety minutes were almost up. Where was her help? She fished out her cell and was getting ready to punch in Annie's number when she heard it, the sound of a car. Not a pickup, not a tractor, not a kid on a motor scooter but the purr of a car's engine.

Pearl sucked in her breath as she scrunched down in the spiky, dry, crackly undergrowth. Her salty sweat dripped into her eyes, burning them unbearably. She swiped at her eyes as she tried to blink to clear her vision. She saw the flashing blue light but there was no siren. An unmarked police car. From the little she knew about police cars she rather thought they used Crown Victorias. The car was still too far down the road to make out what it was. It was moving slowly, as though the driver were eyeballing both sides of the road, looking for someone.

Pearl tried digging herself deeper into the ground, but the sand was too hot, dry, and packed solid to allow for any indentation. She prayed the driver of the approaching car had less than twenty-twenty vision.

Overhead, the sun continued to blaze. What looked like two buzzards flew overhead. "Just what I need, buzzards to pick my bones clean," she muttered.

She was so low to the ground that her ears picked up another sound. She flattened her head against the ground and listened. Two wheels. Maybe it was her help. Maybe it was the cop's reinforcements. Pearl's heart kicked up an extra beat. Her death grip on the handheld GPS tracker didn't slacken one iota.

The two wheels were closer, almost on

top of her. She heard the engine throttle back. Her help. She was almost sure of it. One hundred minutes. To gamble or not to gamble? She got to her knees as she waved her hand crazily. The engine stopped, idled, and she heard a voice that sounded all gravelly and hoarse. An old voice that had seen too much whiskey and way too many cigarettes. Like she cared.

The blue light came to a stop right behind the motorcycle. Oh, God, Pearl thought, a standoff.

"Okay, olly, olly out! Come on, Rosa, enough of this bullshit," the gravelly voice shouted so the officer, if that's who he was, could hear. "There's rattlesnakes out here and you know how afraid you are of snakes. Come on, Sweet Cheeks, climb aboard and let's kiss and make up. Rosa! I'm sorry I looked at that young girl. All I did was look. It's okay to look, honey, as long as you don't touch. Hey, there's a police officer here. Come on, honey, old Jess is just waiting to wrap his arms around you before he decides to run us in for something or other."

That was good, the man on the cycle had given up his name. Pearl straightened up and stepped out of the brush. She knew how to play the game. "Swear on the dog you won't look at another woman, ever again, Jess!" Pearl deliberately avoided looking at the officer in his spiffy uniform. This discussion was between her and her man.

"Okay, okay, I promise. Now get your skinny-assed butt on back, and let's go get us a little drink. I'm parched."

Pearl was about to swing one leg over the back of the ferocious-looking Harley when the police officer spoke.

"Not so fast, you two. Show me some ID, and, mister, I clocked you at ninety-seven miles an hour on that bike. That's a two-hundred-dollar ticket in these parts in case you're interested."

Jess, if that was his name, removed his helmet and lowered his Ray-Bans.

He stared at the cop for a full minute as he tried to take his measure. Mean little eyes, cocky as sin, Elvis on steroids was his final assessment. Jess knew without a doubt he could take that cop on, and with only one or two moves reduce him to dust, if need be. He slid off the bike in one fluid motion. "I'm going to reach into my hip pocket for my wallet, Officer. Is that okay? I guess maybe I was speeding but I was worried about my woman here. Like I said, she's afraid of snakes. Hell, she's afraid of just about everything but me."

He laughed to show what he thought of that statement. The patrol officer remained stoney-faced.

The officer backed up a few steps, his hand on the gun at his hip. "Do it. Nice and slow. Have the woman hand it to me."

Jess swiped at the sweat on his forehead before he pulled the wallet from his pocket. He handed it to Pearl who in turn handed it to the cop.

The officer flipped open the wallet and said, "You're Jess Dewey, aged sixty-six, and you reside where?"

"Yuma, Arizona. At times. Other times I'm on the road. I head up biker conventions. Me and Rosa, that's what we've been doing until she got all prickly with me and lit out on her own. Plan is to go on up to Montana and spend some free time before the next event. Something wrong with that, Officer?"

The policeman ignored Jess. "Ma'am, I need to see some ID." Pearl dug into the pocket of her cargo pants and came out with a wallet and a cruddy-looking passport that looked too shoddy to be a fake. The stamps showed she went back and forth to Juarez, Mexico, once a month.

"You two stay put. Give me those keys until I verify this information."

Jess tossed the key to the officer and turned away. Pearl followed him.

"He's a cop, but he's also a polygamist," Jess told her. "I saw his picture in the paper about two weeks ago. He wants to run us in so bad he can taste it. I don't know about you, but I think our best bet is to cut and run. I can take the guy with no sweat. What do you want me to do, ma'am?" Jess asked.

"Exactly what you just said, and get me someplace safe. I don't think either one of us should use a cell phone right now. What do you think?"

"I have to use mine. I might do free-lance work, but I have people I have to account to. If I'm going to take this guy out, those people have to be able to pick up the pieces. *Capisci?*"

The cop was walking back toward them, Rosa's passport and both their wallets in his hand. "I'm going to have to ask you to come along with me back to the station. The chief has a few questions he'd like answered."

Jess's eyes swept the cop. He was smiling, but it did not reach his mean little eyes, and Jess wasn't about to take any chances. As Jess reached for his wallet, he grabbed the man's wrist at the same time and bent it backward while his other hand chopped at his throat. The man went down, gagging and gasping for air. "Watch him," Jess hissed, as he ran to the patrol car. Quicker than a snake he removed the flashing blue light and disabled the two-way radio. He pocketed the cell phone that was on the seat as well as the road map. He rummaged until he found a set of FlexiCuffs. He carried them back to where the cop was still gasping for breath.

"Listen to me, you child-abusing son of a bitch. I know you're one of those damn polygamists because I saw your picture in the paper along with those of six or seven other cops. You have eight wives and about twenty kids if I remember correctly. No way were you taking us back to your little jail. You were going to drop us off at that hellhole where your polygamy people live. Well, Mister Law Enforcement, that ain't gonna happen today."

A second later the cop's gun was in Jess's hand and he was dragging him back to the unmarked car, where he shoved him inside and hooked him up to the door handle with the FlexiCuffs. He rolled down all the windows and let the engine idle so the AC could operate. He glanced at the gas gauge. A quarter full. The AC would eat that up in fifteen minutes. Oh, well. Then he shot out all four tires, the sound ricocheting across the flats.

Jess turned to Pearl to see how she was reacting to what was going on. He decided she was okay with everything that was playing out in front of her. The lady had guts, he had to give her that. "The reason I remember this guy so well is, his eight wives are on welfare. The local paper got feisty a few weeks back and did a big spread on the sect; then the paper clammed up, and there was no follow-up. You and me and all the other citizens are paying for all his kids and wives. There's something wrong with that picture. Look, I'm expecting a new ride any minute now, so I'm going to have to knock this guy out cold before they arrive. Much as I hate to do it, we have to leave this bike behind even though it's untraceable."

Pearl flapped her hands in the air to show she didn't care one way or the other. All she wanted was to get out of there to someplace safe. She took a few seconds to wonder if she was getting a little too old for this life she'd chosen over finishing out her days on the Supreme Court.

Jess walked back to the unmarked car, reached in the window, and delivered a bone-crushing slam to the polygamous cop's face. He felt an unholy satisfaction when he saw blood from a broken nose spurt all over the car. The policeman fell back against the seat. "That," Jess said, "is for all you damn welfare cheats."

Then Jess reached down in his pocket for the key to the Harley and tossed it as far as he could. He dusted his hands dramatically as he made his way back to where the Harley waited.

Pearl pointed down the road. Off in the distance a motorcycle could be seen traveling fast. Then she saw two more cycles. Jess quickly shot out the tires of his Harley and grabbed the saddlebags with his gear. Putting on a pair of skintight latex gloves, he reached inside the crankcase and did something Pearl couldn't see, after which he dusted down the Harley's sur-faces.

The three Harleys ground to a halt. The roar of the idling engines was deafening. Jess motioned for Pearl to climb on the back of the lead bike, while he climbed on the second in the three-vehicle convoy. Engines revved and off they roared, the sound almost more than Pearl could stand, but she hung on for dear life.

Well, she'd always wanted to feel the wind in her hair and face. While a convert-ible would have been more to her liking, she accepted what she was given because she was safe—at least for the moment.

# Chapter 7

Maggie slid her cell phone into her pocket. She looked from Jack to Harry to Bert. "You all need to get to Utah. Annie's Gulfstream is being readied as we speak. Things keep changing by the minute, that's why you need to keep your cells fired up. Ted will be with you. You'll stop in Vegas to pick up Lizzie."

"I'm due in court today," Jack said, his stomach rumbling at this sudden order. "What's going on?"

"Well, if you'd left your damn phone on, you'd know. Everyone under the sun has been trying to reach the three of you."

Maggie quickly gave them a rundown on the current state of affairs.

The trio looked at her, bug-eyed.

"Bert, I'm sure there's something you can do in regard to the FBI. But you have to get there under your own power. We can't take a chance of you being tied to any of us."

Bert nodded. "You bet. The truth is, we're already involved with the Jeffs case. We have agents in place already. As director, I have every right to go there to check on what's going on. Don't worry about me, Maggie."

Jack looked dubious. "I feel a root canal coming on. My assistant can handle my motions today. Damn good thing it's Friday. Is this a quick and dirty, or do you see days of this, whatever the hell *this* is?"

"Annie said they're winging it, but we all know about Murphy's Law. I'm a little concerned because no one will tell me what's going on with Myra and Charles other than that the two of them went off to England. How they made that happen is beyond my comprehension."

Jack snorted. "Charles has a powerful

ally across the pond, that's how it happened. The question is, what is the problem?"

"I don't know, Jack. What I do know is
that the others aren't focused. I want you
all to keep that in mind. Harry, you haven't
weighed in. You on board?"

"Yes, I'm on board. Wheels up. When?"

Maggie looked at her watch. "Ninety
minutes. Look, I have to go. I'm going to
try and get a special edition out to pave
the way for all of you. Once it hits, Utah is
going to be overrun with media, so be
prepared. I know you all have questions,
save them and call instead. Ted will fill
you in on the way."

"What about the girls? How are they
getting to Utah?" Jack asked.

"Crop dusters!"

"Jesus," was all Jack could think of to
say. What he wanted to ask was, *"How is
that possible?"* But he didn't. With the vigilantes, anything was possible. He looked
over at Harry, who appeared to be in a
daze.

"You're still sitting here!" Maggie barked.
"Dulles! Move!"

The men moved.

Maggie moved.

The *dojo* turned deathly quiet.

Maggie turned around in time to see Harry flip the window sign. She didn't have to go back to read it. CLOSED UNTIL FURTHER NOTICE. Harry didn't believe in giving explanations, and his clientele, mostly law enforcement students, would be only too glad to get a reprieve from the grueling training.

Maggie walked to the corner and hailed a cab. Her mind raced with what was going down all around her. Her adrenaline kicked in, and she was in high gear within seconds as she text messaged her colleagues. To Annie she wrote:

"Tonight's headlines will be a tsunami. N&E flying commercial."

Meaning Nellie and Elias.

"Big Boy flying on company time."

Meaning Bert was heading southwest on the FBI's dime.

"All others on your flying machine."

And the last bit that she couldn't resist.

"Be sure to lather up with Vaseline so your skin doesn't peel off."

Back at the *Post,* Maggie flagged down Ted Robinson and Joe Espinosa. "Look alive here, you two. Ted, you'll be flying out of Dulles with Jack and Harry. Report in on the hour. Joe, get me everything, and I mean everything, on those polygamy people. I already have all of the pictures I need to run on the front page. Boy, this is going to be Pulitzer fare, I can feel it in my bones. C'mon, c'mon, you're as bad as Jack and Harry. You're still standing here. We have a special edition to get out.

"Move!"

Joe moved at the speed of light, but Ted stayed rooted to the floor.

"You know what you're doing, right?"

"God, I hope so. The shots Pearl took of those young girls will fill the entire front page. They don't look any older than twelve or thirteen. What's that tell you?"

Ted's first rule was never to question anything Maggie said. He corrected the thought. *She'd let him get away with one question,* and that was it. He'd already asked it, so he turned on his heel and started for the door. "I guess I'll see you when I see you, huh?"

"Yeah," Maggie said, her mind a million miles away. Suddenly she looked up, and said, "Hey, Ted!"

Ted turned around. "Yeah?"

"I love you."

Ted hopped and skipped all the way to the elevator, a sappy look on his face.

Maggie shifted her mental gears one more time as she scribbled what she thought was the perfect headline for the special edition. Inch-high, heavy black lettering should do it. She blocked out the numbers on her computer before she pushed back her chair to view her handiwork.

**HEAVEN OR HELL?**

Maggie's fist shot in the air. "That'll do it! Get that Pulitzer ready!"

* * *

Isabelle Flanders, her shoulders stiff, her body ramrod straight, marched across the compound, her eyes red from crying. She stomped her way into the main building, her red-eyed gaze seeking out Kathryn. "Okay," she said before she could change her mind, "you were right, it's a cult and not a religion. They hide behind the Word. I wish you hadn't made me watch and read that junk. But I did. I'm on board if you still want me. And I apologize for acting like such a . . ."

"'Jackass' is the word you're looking for. Apology accepted." Kathryn took a full minute to observe her Sister to see if Isabelle was putting her on or if she had really come around to their way of thinking. Whatever she saw in Isabelle's eyes seemed to satisfy her because she said, "Not to worry, we all get a terminal case of the stupids from time to time. We leave in an hour."

"What about the dogs?" Isabelle asked.

"Avery is sending someone to take care of them and the mountain. We have it together, Isabelle." Kathryn cut to the chase and gave her Sister a quick rundown as to their current plans. "Maggie says we should lather up with Vaseline to protect our faces."

"Crop dusters! How long will it take us to get to Utah in a crop duster?"

"Like forever," Kathryn said cheerfully. She could afford to be cheerful at the moment because Bert had just sent her a text message that he would see her in Utah.

Isabelle digested the information and laughed. She could read Kathryn like a book. "Any news come in from Myra or Charles?"

"Not a word. I don't expect we'll hear much, either. At least for some time. Right now we can't afford to worry about either Myra or Charles. They're in good hands, whereas we are flying this mission by the seat of our pants."

"Pearl's safe." While it was a statement, it was still a question.

"For the moment at least. Maggie is simply going to refer to her as a 'Good Samaritan' in the special edition. The pictures she sent are crystal clear. Maggie's going to spread them all across the front page. I don't know much about the newspaper business, but I'm thinking this is a Pulitzer for someone at the *Post.*"

Kathryn moved off to take the dogs for a run while Isabelle joined Alexis and Yoko. On her way out Kathryn could hear Annie mumbling to herself about Myra and Charles not answering their cell phones.

If Annie had known what was going on in London, it was possible her thoughts might have been a little more charitable. Then again, maybe they wouldn't have been. Annie, as they all knew, was mercurial.

Across the pond, cranky and out of sorts, Myra Rutledge was the first one down the metal stairs. She waited at the bottom for Charles, her facial features hard and cold. She wore sunglasses even though the day was dark and gloomy. Just the way she felt. It was raining—a cold, wet, steady rain. She felt chilled to the bone.

She stepped into the waiting car and settled herself as far away from Charles as the seat would allow. She had never been angry with Charles. Never *ever.* But that had changed. She didn't bother to try to hide the anger. What was the point?

"Where are we going?" she asked with frost in her voice.

"The Renaissance Chancery Court Hotel in Soho," Charles said wearily. "I'm sure there will be some shops where you can pick up some clothing and essentials. Myra, if you want to go back, I'm sure I can arrange something."

"What is the point? I'm here. Why would I go back?"

"Because you're so miserable. Right now you hate me, hate sitting next to me. I can't make any promises to you about anything. I understand if you . . . What I mean is . . . Bloody hell, I don't know what I mean." Charles turned to look out the window at the pouring rain.

Myra's stomach clutched itself into a tight knot. She knew she was being hateful, and she hated herself for acting that way. She tried once again to explain. "Charles, I wasn't angry over the fact that you have a son all of a sudden that you knew nothing about. What I was angry about, and am still angry about, is that you were going to sneak away like some thief in the dark of night and just leave me a note. A damn note! I think I deserve more than a damn note. I never thought of you as a coward, but I do now. What in the world did you think I was going to do? Turn on you? That would never have happened. Never. I would have understood."

Myra's voice turned so sad, Charles turned around to stare at her, the love of his life.

"I guess you don't know me at all, Charles."

"Myra, I couldn't . . . I didn't know . . . I panicked. How many times, how many ways do I have to tell you how sorry I am? I'm a basket case, can't you see it? The way you were after Barbara died. I was there for you. I understood. You don't remember how ugly and cruel you were to me, to Nikki. We understood.

"My God, Myra, you looked right at Nikki and said, *'Why wasn't it you instead of Barbara?'*"

All color drained from Myra's face. "I never . . . I would never . . . Why are you lying to me like this? You are lying, aren't you, Charles?"

There was such desperation on her face, Charles felt sick.

The pitying look on Charles's weary

face told Myra the truth. "Dear God in Heaven! And you . . . Nikki . . . you never said . . . I must have been out of my mind. That poor child!" Myra sobbed, her shoulders heaving.

Charles wanted to wrap his arms around her, but he simply couldn't make them move. "We were there for you because we both loved you, and we both understood. No matter what. That's all I'm asking of you now, to understand and be my rock. I desperately need a rock, Myra. Please." Charles reached across to take Myra's hand in his own.

Myra clutched at it, tears rolling down her cheeks. All she could do was nod because she didn't trust herself to talk about those dark, ugly days Charles was referring to. She squeezed his hand. Then she threw herself against him. Charles's arms moved on their own and they were clinging together like two survivors on a raft at sea.

It was Myra who finally spoke first. Her voice was filled with tears but hopeful when she asked, "Do you have a plan, dear?"

Charles sighed. "Not really. My instructions were to settle in at the hotel and someone would come around and brief me. I know nothing more, Myra." There was a catch in his voice when he said, "I don't know what I feel. I'm back on British soil. I never thought that would happen. I certainly never expected to return under these circumstances."

Myra was saved from a reply when the special government car slid to a stop in front of the hotel. A doorman held the door for Myra. He looked her up and down and sniffed his disapproval at her attire. Myra straightened her shoulders, touched the glistening pearls at her neck, and swept by him and through the door that was being held open for her. She looked around to see if she could see a shop that would have something appropriate for a change of clothes. She turned to see Charles engaged in conversation with a man who looked official. Obviously, they were not going to have to check in. People behind the registration desk were openly staring, wondering who these two important people were who didn't go by the rules.

Within seconds they were whisked into a private elevator and taken to what had to be the most impressive suite in the hotel. Myra took her own tour and then headed immediately to the phone in the bedroom, where she called down to the desk and asked them to send someone up from the Hermès shop with a variety of outfits, then rattled off a list of sundries to be brought along as well.

With nothing else to do, she decided to run a bath while she waited. The minute she heard the door close, she ran out to the main part of the suite. "Who was that man? What did he say? Is there news of your son? Talk to me, Charles."

"The man's name isn't important, Myra. He was sent here by . . . by a friend. He ordered food and said he would give us time to freshen up, then he would come back and take us to the hospital. That's it in a nutshell. It won't do you any good to pick at me because there is nothing else to tell.

"I'm so glad you're here, Myra. I did say that before, didn't I?"

"Yes, dear, you did. I'm sorry, too, that I was such a . . . I guess Kathryn would say, bitch. Speaking of Kathryn, we should call the girls."

"You can do that while you're soaking. I'll leave it up to you as to what to say."

A knock sounded on the door. Room service. Charles paused while the waiter set out the food: thick ham-and-cheese sandwiches, American-style potato chips, pickles, and a huge pot of strong black coffee. American food. He suddenly realized he was hungry. Charles hesitated to see if he was going to be given a bill. He looked over at the waiter, who shook his head and said, "There is no charge, and I cannot accept a gratuity. Enjoy your meal."

Myra finished her own sandwich and the last of her cup of coffee. Nothing that she could remember had ever tasted as good as that particular sandwich.

A second knock sounded. The manager of the Hermès shop, followed by two assistants, entered the room, their arms laden with clothing. Myra wasted no time. She pointed a finger. "I'll take that, that, and that." She shrugged at the colorful box of lingerie and left the room.

The three women discreetly backed away toward the door. Charles could see the curiosity in their eyes, no doubt wondering about these two strange people who were occupying the best suite in the hotel. And apparently the woman had brought no clothing, not even cosmetics.

Myra slid down into the slick wetness of the huge tub and sighed. The water felt wonderful—hot and steamy. She'd been chilled to the bone, but now, with food and hot coffee in her stomach, she felt like she could take on the world. Five minutes of luxuriating in the fragrant water was all she allowed herself before she reached over to pick up the satellite phone to call Annie. Her end of the conversation took all of two minutes to bring Annie and the others up to speed. Annie's response took twenty minutes, with Myra gasping in surprise.

"Annie, can you all handle it? Are you sure Pearl is safe? Crop dusters all the way to Utah. Mother of God! I should be there! But, I need to be here! Oh, Annie, I am so torn. I know, I know, you can all handle it. I'm going to worry. Well, Annie, I don't see how you can stop me from worrying. I was born to worry. Listen, I want you to stay in touch as often as you can. Every few hours if possible. Crop dusters! No, no, Annie, it is not a lark." She stopped talking to listen. "What in the name of God is a PW? Point Woman! All riiiight!" She listened again. "You're going to invade the Heaven on Earth compound! Dear God!" Myra listened again as she wiggled her foot, hoping she could manipulate the hot-water faucet. "Lizzie is meeting up with Ted, Jack, and Harry. Well, that makes me feel better. Nellie and Elias are flying commercial and will be available, as will Bert, who has both feet in this mess. What about Maggie?"

Myra finally managed to turn the faucet with her big toe but it made her toe hurt. Steaming water rushed into the tub. She wiggled her shoulders to better adjust the satellite phone at her ear. She continued to listen and, in spite of herself and the circumstances, her fist shot in the air. "I'm sure I can find a computer in this hotel, and I'll go online to see the *Post*'s headline in the morning. Remember, we're five hours ahead of you, and keep in mind that as you go west that difference will increase. But just call whenever you can. Good work, Annie, and tell Maggie I know there is a Pulitzer for her in this somewhere. Promise me something, Annie.

Promise you will watch out for the girls and keep them all safe." She wanted to say, *"Especially Nikki because I have so many things to make up to that young woman."* But she didn't because her eyes filled with tears, and she didn't want her best friend to know she was crying.

"Good-bye, Annie. Remember to call and give our regards to the girls, and to Murphy and Grady, too."

Myra raised her foot again to push the lever that would drain the water from the tub.

She stood up and wrapped one of the hotel's luxurious robes around her. She gave herself a mental shrug. *As Kathryn would say, time to get this show on the road, kick some ass, and take names later.*

"Damn straight," Myra snapped, using another of Kathryn's pet phrases.

# Chapter 8

It was still raining when Charles and Myra were whisked from the hotel into a waiting car. Myra wasn't sure, but she thought it had some kind of official-looking gold seal on the door. The forty-five-minute drive was made in silence, the only sound to be heard was the pounding rain on the roof of the car. From time to time, either Myra or Charles would squeeze the other's hand.

Myra looked down at the watch on her wrist to see the glowing numbers and wondered again why they were making the trip in the middle of the night in such secrecy. Surely few would remember

Charles's long-ago days as a British intelligence agent. Who would even recognize
him these days? Then she realized it was
she who was being protected. She was the
visible one, the one whose picture had
been plastered around the world as a
member of the infamous vigilantes.

Myra felt the huge car slow, then come
to a stop. Charles squeezed her hand so
hard she thought he'd broken her fingers.
She winced but didn't make a sound.

The door opened, and Charles stepped
out. Then Myra. She tried to see through
the pouring rain, but all she could make
out was a dim yellow light.

"It's a private clinic, Myra. I rather
thought this might be where we were
going. It's a . . . What it is is . . . a special
place where the royals are brought when
they don't want the media to know about
what's going on. The chief physician here
has only one patient. There are separate
doctors to tend to the others if they
become patients."

"How do you know all this, Charles?"
Myra whispered.

"I know because I was brought here
once a very long time ago. The people

who work here saved my life. It looks the same," he said once the driver of the car had inserted a special keycard to open the door. Charles stepped through what looked like a regulation doorway, followed by Myra, and into a small foyer. "It rather resembles a country house, don't you think?" When Myra nodded, he said, "That's what I thought when I was brought here that first time."

Myra looked around. There were two chairs, a tiny desk, and a colorful carpet. The foyer was crowded with three people. The only picture on the wall was of the queen.

Myra had the insane urge to curtsy, but she knew her bad knees wouldn't allow it. She smiled inwardly, the chance of her ever having to curtsy before the queen was so remote she almost laughed aloud. She shivered. Charles's hold on her arm tightened.

The man who had driven them there, the man who opened the door for them, and who was talking into his sleeve, had to be an MI6 agent. Annie was going to love hearing about all this. Myra couldn't help but wonder when that time would come.

They were moving down a long, sterile-looking hallway. They turned the corner and saw a small waiting room with a beige-colored love seat and three chairs. A different picture of the queen graced the one solid wall. Although the lighting was dim, Myra was able to make out a blanketed figure curled up on the love seat. She watched as Charles looked over at the sleeping figure. She wished she knew what he was thinking.

The agent led them around another corner, and Myra realized they were being taken to what would have been an intensive care unit back in the States. She heard Charles suck in his breath, or was it herself she was hearing?

Two nurses dressed in starched white looked up and nodded. The older of the two got up, walked around the desk, and motioned for Myra and Charles to follow her. The agent stayed behind, his eyes glued to their backs. The nurse paused at the door for a moment before she opened it.

It was a private room, with a hospital bed, a service table that stretched across the foot of the bed, and a private-duty nurse sitting in the one chair. Machines hummed and whirred.

The private nurse looked up but immediately looked away to concentrate on the machines she was monitoring. The room was dimly lit, but Myra could see clearly the man lying in the bed. She flinched as did Charles at the tubes going in and out of the patient's body.

Myra and Charles inched closer to the bed. Tears rolled down Charles's cheeks.

"Dear God," Myra said, "he looks just like you did when you were his age. Do . . . Do you know his name, Charles?"

Charles heard the question but at the moment he couldn't have spoken even if his life depended on it. His son, Geoffrey Barnstable. He'd been a crack pilot in the RAF, the Royal Air Force. What was it his friend had said? *"Like your Top Gun back in the States. He distinguished himself many times, Sir Malcolm. Because of some health problems, none of them deadly serious, Geoffrey had stopped flying and was training pilots for the RAF. The plane malfunctioned, crashed, and*

*killed the rookie pilot. Geoffrey was heli-*
*coptered to that hospital, where his prog-*
*nosis is less than encouraging."*

Charles couldn't take his eyes off his son. He struggled in the dim light to see a likeness to himself or to the man's mother. He hated that he couldn't remember what Beatrice Barnstable looked like. Forty years was a long time, but still, he should be able to remember something other than her wild mane of dark chestnut hair. He shook his head to try to clear it. Later he would struggle to remember what his son's mother looked like. All that was important just then was that he had a son, and he was looking at him right that second. Would God take him away just hours after Charles had found him so many years later?

Charles looked over at the nurse. "Is he in a coma?"

"A medically induced coma. Doctor is to bring him out of it today. Five more minutes, then you must leave, as we have some work to do here. You can wait in the private waiting room, or you can visit the chapel. There's a small kitchen to the left of the waiting room where you can find tea, scones, and, I believe, some chocolate cake."

Charles wanted to reach out to touch his son but couldn't make his arm move. *Another time will present itself,* he thought. At least he hoped so. He allowed himself to be led to the doorway.

In the waiting room, Charles and Myra sat down in the two chairs across the room from the love seat where the blanketed figure still slept. Charles wasn't sure, but he rather thought the sleeping figure might be his son's wife.

Myra reached out to take Charles's hand in her own. "He looks like you, Charles," she whispered. "I'm sure he's a fine man just like you are. Can I ask you something, Charles?" Charles nodded. "How is it the queen knew about your son, and you didn't? If this," she said, waving her arm about the small waiting room, "is just used for royalty, why is he here? Is it because of you?"

Charles leaned his head back and closed his eyes. What to say, what not to say? And did it really matter what he said at this point? "I was told that when Lady Beatrice was dying, Liz found out. 'LB,' as

Beatrice liked to be called among friends, swore her to secrecy. They were childhood friends, that kind of thing. She asked that Liz look out for her son, as any mother would have done. Keeping a confidence, Myra, is sometimes a terrible thing. I know Liz was tormented over it, but she'd given her word, and the young man simply wasn't interested in hearing anything about me. I was told LB never said a negative thing about me, but the young lad wanted no part of knowing about his father. All he knew or thought was that I abandoned his mum to go it alone. He's carried that with him his entire life."

"And now you show up out of the blue at the eleventh hour. Oh, Charles, what will that young man think when he wakes to see you? Perhaps we . . . you should wait until he is a bit stronger before you present yourself. What if he goes into shock, or something equally bad?"

"I've been thinking the same thing. I rushed here because it seemed the thing to do. I've had nothing to do but think since I received that phone call. The call was so urgent—life-or-death. I reacted. I suppose when he comes out of the coma,

I could make the decision then to see him or not see him. The last thing I want is for him to have a setback. I think I should wait until the doctor comes in before I make any decisions. Trust me, Myra, I will do whatever is best for Geoffrey."

Myra looked over at Charles. He'd said, "Geoffrey." Not "my son." She knew Charles well enough to know that it was not a slip of the tongue. He was mentally preparing himself to walk away. Better to think of the young man as Geoffrey rather than as his son, his flesh and blood, the son who wanted nothing to do with his father. But what would it cost this dear man sitting next to her?

Across the room the blanketed figure stirred, the blanket slipping to the floor. The huddled figure squirmed, then sat up and looked around. Myra stared hard at her, as did Charles. Even in the dim light Myra could see a mass of freckles marching across the bridge of the woman's nose. She had shoulder-length curly brown hair. She appeared to be slight of build and was dressed in jeans, sneakers, and what looked like a woolly sweatshirt. Myra judged her to be in her mid- to late thirties.

The young woman murmured something that sounded like hello. Charles and Myra murmured hello in return. The woman reached for the blanket and covered herself. She was wide-awake, staring at nothing, her hands folded in front of her. Myra wanted to cry for the woman's loneliness, for every emotion that was obviously rippling through her.

"I think I'll go to the kitchen and get some tea," Myra said.

Charles nodded, his thoughts far away.

In the kitchen there was a pot of hot water simmering on a burner. She fixed the tea the way she knew Charles liked it and, at the last moment, fixed a third cup and added it to the tray, along with honey, lemon, and milk. Charles liked milk and three spoons of honey in his tea. He had a sweet tooth without equal.

Myra carried the tray into the waiting room and handed Charles his cup of tea. He accepted it, looked at it, and returned to stare out the one small window at the darkness outside. She moved over to the lonely figure on the love seat and held out the tray. The young woman tried to smile and gratefully accepted the cup Myra offered.

"Just some honey," she said, twirling the honey stick into the small bowl. "Allison Barnstable. My friends and family call me Allie," she said, holding out her free hand.

Myra panicked. She had to give a name. "Jane. Jane Featherstone." She picked up the tray and was about to turn around when Allison Barnstable reached out a hand to her.

"Do . . . do you have someone *here?*"

The panic stayed with Myra. "In a manner of speaking." She motioned in Charles's direction. "I'm here with a friend," was the best she could manage.

"Then you are in good hands. This place is special. I don't know why that is, but that's what someone told me. I think my husband is the only patient here. Someone else told me that my husband was injured in a flight-training exercise. They brought him here, then they came and got me. I've been here three days. I wish my mum was here, but they told me she's taking care of the children. Visitors are not allowed. I just get to see Geoff through the glass. I don't even know if he knows I'm here. I never met the doctor, either. I told them who our family doctor is, but they didn't call him. I wish I knew what this place was. Do you know?"

Myra thought Allison's voice sounded bitter and cold even though the words themselves sounded caring.

Myra shook her head. Her heart was breaking for the young woman. Fearful she might say the wrong thing, Myra walked back to the kitchen. After tidying up the mess she'd made, she was about to leave when she turned to see Allison Barnstable in the doorway.

"Since there is only one patient here in this special place and visitors are not allowed, you and that man in the waiting room must . . . Are you here about Geoff?" When Myra didn't answer her, Allison pressed her. "You are, aren't you? Why? Who are you? I know you said your name was Jane Featherstone, but what is *his* name? Oh, my God! That man is Geoff's father, isn't he?" Allison backed up, an ugly look on her face. "You can't come here now. Not now when my husband . . . No, no, this isn't right. You can't discard a baby, then show up forty years later and . . . and . . . oh, God, no! You have to leave. Right now. How dare you! How dare he . . . You need to leave. I don't want you here, and when and if Geoff wakes, he won't want you here, either. He hates that man for abandoning him and his mother."

Myra clutched at her pearls as if they were a lifeline. What she really wanted to do was gather the tormented woman into her arms and hug her. "It wasn't like that, Allison. You need to talk to . . . to . . . Sir Malcolm. There are two sides to everything. Surely you know that."

"*SIR* Malcolm!" Allison spat. "*SIR* Malcolm! Bloody hell if that doesn't take the cream!" Allison turned on her heel and ran back to the waiting room, where she went to the love seat and buried her face in the blanket.

As Myra walked from the kitchen to the waiting room, she could hear the young woman sobbing. From the doorway, she noticed that Charles was oblivious, still staring off into space.

Myra grappled with her thoughts. What should she do? What could she say?

Should she just sit down next to Charles and hold his hand? Or should she go back into the kitchen and call Annie and the other Sisters? The latter, she decided. She walked to where Charles sat and patted his arm. If he noticed, he gave no sign that Myra had even come back into the room.

Before returning to the kitchen, Myra glanced at the angry-looking young woman. *I'd be angry, too,* she decided, *if I were in her shoes.*

In the kitchen, under the bright lights, Myra calculated the time difference between England and the States. She wanted to cry when every single phone she dialed went to voice mail. There was only one number left to call, Maggie at the *Post.* If Maggie didn't pick up, the switchboard would certainly answer.

Being put on hold nine times forced Myra to rethink her immediate problem. Somebody, somewhere had to have a phone that was turned on. Nellie! Nellie always answered her phone. She hit the speed dial and was rewarded only with Nellie's voice mail. They all must have been en route or had had to shut down their phones for one reason or another. There was no reason to panic, she told herself. She was on her own for now and would have to rely on her own common sense and offer the best advice she could for Charles, advice that he would probably ignore, anyway. At that moment, Myra knew, she barely existed for Charles. Hot tears burned her eyes.

Myra walked back to where Charles was sitting. She leaned over and tugged at his arm. "Charles," she whispered, "I need to talk to you. Come into the kitchen with me."

Charles looked up, his gaze vacant. "Is something wrong, Myra? Is the doctor here? Where is he? I need to talk to him."

"No, Charles, he isn't here yet. I'm sure he'll be here as soon as it turns light out. Doctors always make early-morning rounds. I need to talk to you. Please, come with me."

Charles got up, his gaze going to the young woman on the love seat. He knew he was staring at his son's wife. His daughter-in-law. She couldn't be anyone else.

# Chapter 9

Maggie Spitzer's fist shot in the air for the tenth time in as many minutes. She looked down at the slash-and-burn headline, and her fist shot forward again. Joe Espinosa laughed out loud. "We did it and scooped every other paper and media station! The switchboard is on overload."

"Who knew?" Espinosa quipped.

"You want to join me for some dinner, Joe? It's the least I can do for this great front page. Don't worry, Ted won't kill you if he knows we're going out to eat together."

Joe pretended fear, then laughed so hard he almost fell off his chair. Finally, he was able to come up for air and managed to gasp, "What headline are you going with for the early issue?"

Maggie chewed on her nails. It was the one fault she couldn't conquer. Even when she'd had acrylic nails, she somehow managed to chew the horrible stuff down to the quick. "I'm working on it. I have a few hours yet, but I'm leaning toward HELL ON EARTH! You have enough material to point out the HELL side, don't you?"

"Damn, Maggie, the more I dig, the more I come up with. What we really need is a witness, a snitch, one of the followers who got away. I'm working that end and have calls out to everyone I know. I have a hot lead, and, believe it or not, our squealer lives in Landover, Maryland, just a hop, skip, and a jump from here." Joe looked down at his wristwatch, which was big enough to pass for a hockey puck, and said, "I'm heading out there in a few minutes so, no, I can't celebrate with you. If I can get her to agree, I'd like to bring her back here so you can have a go at her."

Maggie chewed on her lower lip. "Okay, I can order in. We don't have much time, Joe, so text it in as you go, but yeah, bring her in. We can make her famous if that's what she wants. Go!"

Maggie looked around at her empty office, then down at the fiery headline. "Sometimes," she murmured to herself, "I am just so smart I can't stand myself!" She looked up to see her weary-looking secretary, who was holding out a stack of pink slips.

"Everyone in town wants to talk to you, Maggie. You're the woman of the hour!"

"Hold them off, Sally. How do you like this headline for the morning edition?" Maggie held up a huge cardboard mock-up of a front page with the heavy black headline that read, HELL ON EARTH!

"That'll do it!" Sally said, laughter ringing in her voice. "In case you don't know it, the newsroom is fully staffed. No one went home."

"You're kidding! Okay, order in for everyone, and don't go chintzy on the beer and wine. Make sure they all know they're off the clock. We'll make up the hours some way."

"You got it, Maggie. Congratulations!"

"Thanks, Sally. Hey, is your mom okay with you staying on late?"

Sally Duval, a minimum-wage employee, was one year out of college and desperate to go on the real payroll but knew she had an uphill road to get to that exalted position of reporter. She'd started in the mailroom, graduated to the position of switchboard operator, and from there to Maggie's inner sanctum, where she watched over her boss with an eagle eye.

"She told me to spend the night at the Hay-Adams if it was too late to make the trip home. But I could also bunk on that blowup mattress we keep available for the late-nighters. Don't worry about me, Maggie. I'm here until you don't need me anymore."

Since taking over the helm of the *Post,* Maggie, through trial and error, had managed to surround herself with the best, the most loyal staff in the business. There wasn't anything her crew wouldn't do for her, and there was nothing she wouldn't do for each and every one of them. Plus, thanks to Annie's generosity as the hidden owner of the *Post,* her people were the highest paid in the nation and had the best benefits. To get a job at the *Post* was equivalent to being hired by the White House for top secret work, except that Maggie's staff had a much more competent boss, who hired only the best of the best.

Tears sprang to Maggie's eyes when she held up the paper to look at the sweet faces of the fourteen young girls on the front page of the paper, thirteen of them pregnant. Pearl Barnes, the Good Samaritan, had managed to get exceptionally clear shots of all of them in their old-fashioned clothing, their pregnancy obvious to the dumbest of the dumb. Every parent worth his or her salt had to be outraged that something like that could be going on and that the authorities were looking the other way, according to the calls that were flooding the *Post* and the television stations. At the last minute, Maggie had their resident artist draw a sketch of the Good Samaritan that purposely didn't even remotely look like Pearl Barnes—to be added to the front page.

"Time to step up to the plate," Maggie chortled as she buzzed Sally to ask her to call the local sheriff's office in Sienna, Utah. "Yes, I know what time it is. It isn't *that* late in Utah. Get a number and wake him up. We want a comment for the early edition. 'No comment' is as good as a comment. We want his ass on the line, and our first question is: Is he a member of that sect? The second question is: What is he going to do about those girls? And I don't want to hear any crap that we're trampling on their religious freedom, either."

"Got it! I'm on it, Maggie."

And Maggie knew she would be. Sally never gave up. One way or another, Sally would track down the sheriff and have him on the line as quickly as she could.

Maggie went back to work for another hour until Sally buzzed her to say that the food had just been delivered to the newsroom. Maggie hightailed it down the hall and was the first to hold up her bottle of beer to a resounding cheer. The crew fell to the pizza, the burgers, the fried chicken, and everything that had come with them.

Maggie was on her way back to her office when her special phone rang. It was Pearl Barnes.

"Don't say anything, just let me talk."

Maggie felt her shoulders tense up at the panic she was hearing.

"I'm okay for the moment, but someone is on to me. That man Jess had to dump me for his own good and the safety of the other two he was traveling with. He said he was too important to the cause—that's what he called it, Maggie, 'the cause.' I couldn't argue with that. I hitched a ride with a trucker, gave them Kathryn's name and handle, and they got me this far. Tell Kathryn some guy named Lucky Louie says hi. I've been followed, but I think I eluded whoever it was at the last truck stop. Lucky Louie met up with some fellow truckers and they . . . uh . . . took matters into their own hands. They found a trucker going my way, so I hitched a ride.

"Those polygamy people are like snakes, Maggie. This is exactly where I am right now, so listen carefully. Just for the record, George and Irma Ellis are long gone. I doubled back because something wasn't feeling right to me. I'm the only link to those girls, and once you ran your special edition, even with that doctored-up picture of me, I wasn't safe. I saw the paper in the truck stop. That's all anyone was talking about, all the way here from Washington, Maggie.

"I'm actually thinking about pulling George's motorcycle out of the barn and taking off, but let's face it, I'm old, and I don't have the spit and the nerve I once had. If it comes to that, I'll take a shot at it, but it won't go well."

Maggie wanted to ask a million questions, but she bit down on her tongue. For someone as savvy as Pearl, why hadn't she stayed with the men Avery sent to take care of her regardless of what Jess had said? Maggie had long ago given up calling Pearl 'Justice Barnes.' When you were breaking the law, somehow a title, no matter how important or distinguished it was, didn't seem to matter. More importantly, Pearl didn't care.

"Listen, Pearl, Lizzie Fox is due to land in Utah any minute. She's with Ted Robinson, Jack, and Harry. I'll call them now. Stay put. Exactly where are you—at the Ellis place?"

"In the damn root cellar." Pearl quickly explained about the spiked road and warned Maggie to tell the others. "It's a little tricky if you don't know exactly where the switch is. I'd do it, but then I open myself up for visitors. That man Jess gave me an education on what goes on around here, and it isn't pretty. He said no one is who they seem to be, and that goes for the cops and the judges."

Maggie copied down the exact location of the switch, how to operate it, and how to turn it back on from the barn.

"For whatever it's worth at the moment, Maggie, I am Rosa Sanchez from Juarez, Mexico."

"Got it. Go back to the root cellar and keep your cell on. Can you keep it charged?"

Pearl laughed, or made a sound that sounded to Maggie like a laugh. "Believe it or not, this root cellar has electricity, so I can do that. George thought of everything when he built this place. He's a good man, I hope he's safe."

Maggie didn't know what to say about the Ellis couple, so she simply said good-bye and cut off the call. She started to text message then, faster than a drug addict on speed, even while she chomped on a cold pizza crust.

And that was when all hell broke loose as Espinosa's texts started coming through. Maggie screamed for Sally, who then yelled to the crew in the news-room. They worked like the well-oiled, well-paid team they were. Not only did they have a full interview with a young woman named Marion Jennings, they had a picture of her—actually, they had two pictures of her—one in her Heaven on Earth garb and one of her in regular clothing. Maggie thought Marion was beautiful, but she had the saddest eyes of anyone Maggie had ever seen. Espinosa had captured the young woman in a vulnerable moment.

Marion Jennings was eighteen, with three children—the oldest was five years of age—all of whom she'd had to leave behind. Not because she wanted to leave any of them, Maggie discovered as she read Espinosa's interview. The children were taken from her and passed on to the group mothers. The reason she had cut and run was because the Prophet issued a declaration that she was to marry her cousin and produce three more babies if she wanted to earn eternal salvation.

Maggie was so furious at what she was reading, she wanted to reach out and strangle someone. How could something like that happen? Right there in the Southwest. The country's heartland.

An hour later, with no answers to any of her questions, Maggie wrapped up the front page and put the paper to bed.

Maggie looked up, her eyes half-closed, when Sally rapped on the door.

"I'm going if that's okay. I couldn't locate that damn sheriff. I'll keep trying, and I'll do my best to put the fear of God in him. I'll be at the Hay-Adams if you need me. Just call my cell. Everyone else is gone. You should go home, Maggie, and take a long, hot bath and have a big glass of wine. You deserve it."

"Yeah, I guess it's time to wrap things up here. Sometimes I feel like I'm married to this place. I love it, though. Thanks, Sally. Take a cab to the hotel and bill the paper for it and the room. See you in the morning. Take your time coming in, and be sure to have a good breakfast. I have a feeling things are going to start happening even faster around here when the morning edition hits the street."

Maggie reached for her purse and jacket. That was when she realized how tired she was. She eyeballed the sofa in her office with deep longing. Should she go home, or should she stay here? She had a change of clothes, her own private bathroom where she could shower. It was a no-brainer. She tossed her jacket and bag onto a chair and made it to the couch, her eyes closing as she lowered herself and pulled up the blanket she kept for just such an occasion.

Joe Espinosa, with Marion Jennings at his side, took one look at Maggie asleep on the sofa and backed out the door. "I'll drop you off at the *Post*'s apartment" he told her, "and pick you up around nine. Things will get wild once the paper hits the street. Every news channel and reporter in the business will be after you. Everything you need will be at the apartment. Is that okay with you?"

The pretty young woman with the sad eyes nodded.

"Good, then let's hit the street. It's late, and you look tired. I am, too, it's been a hell of a long day. God alone knows what tomorrow will bring."

# Chapter 10

Jack Emery looked left, then right, before he steered the SUV onto the gravel driveway that would take him to George Ellis's barn, where Pearl Barnes was waiting. "This has to be it," he said, but his voice sounded dubious. "This is in the middle of nowhere. The mailman must get paid overtime to deliver all the way out here, wherever *here* is."

Ted Robinson climbed out of the backseat the moment Jack steered the SUV through the dense shrubbery. "Where's the switch? I don't see anything that looks like a lever. Don't move that truck unless you want your tires shredded."

Both Harry and Jack climbed out and gingerly walked around, looking for the switch. Pearl had said it was underground, by an ancient Joshua tree. Meanwhile, Ted examined the road to find the raised spikes.

"Holy shit!" Ted said when he found them, then snapped a picture of the deadly spikes. "Wonder how that guy did all this. Maggie said that Pearl said there's a grid every eighth of a mile for the first mile and a half. Must have been a labor of love."

"Found the switch!" Harry shouted triumphantly.

Five seconds later, the mechanism that controlled the spikes had been switched off, and the spikes were back underground. The three men climbed back into the SUV and made their way down the winding road.

"This is some spread," Ted said as he leaned out the window, snapping picture after picture. "I can't believe people actually *choose* to live like this, cut off from the world. No neighbors, no takeout, no drug-

stores, no bookmobile, and no one dropping over for coffee or a beer. Perfect hide-
out, though. Those spikes, though, that
bothers the hell out of me. Law enforcement must know about them. I'm not trying
to rain on anyone's parade, but there are
other ways to get to this place besides
driving a vehicle. Like what my grandpa
would have called 'shanks' mare'! Your
own two feet," he explained, seeing Jack's
puzzled look.

Jack snorted at Ted's words. "And you
think the rest of this place isn't booby-
trapped? Hell, the guy probably has clay-
more mines all over the damn place. Or
those snares up in the trees that drop and
haul your ass right up into the foliage
where you stay until he decides to let you
down. I think old George, whoever the hell
he is, had it going on here. Look, there's
Pearl by the barn door."

Jack cut the engine and climbed out of
the SUV, followed by Harry and Ted. The
first words out of Jack's mouth were,
"Jesus, Pearl, you look like hell. Are you
okay?"

"Thanks, Jack. Hell, no, I am not okay. I

have to get out of this place. Come inside. Who knows what kind of long-distance listening devices might be trained on us."

Inside the massive barn, the three men looked around in awe. Pearl went over to the far wall of the barn, opened the electrical panel, and yanked at a lever. "The road is armed now."

She gave them a guided tour that took only five minutes. "Now you see why I have to try and protect this place. George is crucial to my operation. This is by far the best safe house/barn on my underground railroad route. Where's Lizzie?"

"Back in town, trying to get the lay of the land. It's pretty dismal out here, Pearl."

"Nellie and Elias?"

"I think they're on their way and will meet up with Lizzie in the next few hours."

Pearl shook her head. Too many strangers in a small town, especially that small town, won't be good. Strangers stood out like white elephants in a black room. "Any news on Myra and Charles? I've been trying to reach Annie and the girls but haven't been able to make contact. With everyone unavailable, who's running this operation?"

"Maggie Spitzer." Jack laughed. "And she's doing a hell of a job, I have to say. I haven't seen today's edition, so if there's a computer here, I'd like to hook up and check it out."

"George took it with him. This place has been sanitized." Pearl held out her hands so the men could see her skintight latex gloves. "Don't touch anything," she warned. "There are some soft drinks in the refrigerator if you're thirsty. A few boxes of crackers and such. Help yourself, but be sure to take the trash with you. Here," she said, reaching into her pocket for spare gloves to hand out. "They're surgical gloves, so they won't be awkward on your hands. Just be careful not to rip them."

Ted popped three colas and distributed the gloves. "Tell us about the town of Sienna. I need to get a feel for it so I can report in to Maggie for tomorrow's paper. Exactly how far is the Heaven on Earth compound from here?"

Pearl took a mighty breath. "The compound is about twenty miles due east of where we're standing. Population of Sienna is about eleven hundred, give or take a few. There are 650 houses, some of them farms. On some of the farms there are other houses where the offspring live. There are a sheriff and two deputies. George says that ever since the death of his daughter they've left him alone. They think he's a little off in the head. In other words, he doesn't bother them, and they don't bother him.

"The town has a small police station: two rooms and a bath, and two cells for overnighters. There's a general store that sells everything including groceries and medicines. It doubles as a post office. There's one country doctor, who is also the dentist. God only knows if he's licensed to do either. The sheriff is also the judge. George said he's a lawyer, but since there was no lawyering business, he does other things. Then there is the rooming house with six rooms to let for any visitors who find their way here. According to George, visitors are not made welcome and aren't treated very well. It's pretty backward. Even for a small town, it's not a happy place. Way too many secrets, according to George.

"And before you can ask, the sheriff, the deputies, and the doctor are polygamists but live outside the compound. What that means is that whatever goes on at the HOE compound doesn't make its way to the outside world. It all stops in Sienna." Pearl stopped speaking and ran to the barn door. "It's some kind of plane," she shrilled.

Jack grinned. "I think it's your ride to safety, Pearl. It's the girls, they're coming in on crop dusters and you're going out on one of them. And I can guarantee as soon as they land, the sheriff and his two deputies will be paying this little farm a visit."

"How much time do I have?"

Jack craned his neck to see out one of the barn's windows. "Five minutes, give or take a minute, depending on how fast you can run. Stay safe, hunker down till we give the all clear. That's an order, Pearl."

Pearl nodded, and ran as fast as she could. She waved to Isabelle, who jumped out of the plane's doorway. Strong hands reached down for Pearl. A second later she was gone from sight, and the crop duster was kicking up dry earth as it rocketed across the field and went airborne. The pilot dipped his right wing in a salute.

Isabelle ran like the Hounds of Hell were on her heels. She literally fell into Jack's arms. "Nikki is in the third plane. Kathryn lands next. Alexis is after Nikki. Then Yoko, and Annie is last. She insisted on being the last, captain of the ship or something like that."

Ted Robinson looked at the windburn on Isabelle's face. He popped a cola for her and showed her where the bathroom was. He handed over a set of latex gloves, and said, "You know the drill. Don't touch anything."

Isabelle downed the cola in two long gulps and asked for a second. Ted obliged just as the second crop duster came in for a landing. And then the third came in, followed by the fourth, then the fifth. Within fifteen minutes, all six planes were airborne and gone from sight. The only indication they had landed at all were huge bags of insecticide that had been dumped there in case anyone asked questions about six planes flying into the same location.

The reunion was everything everyone wanted it to be. Nikki clung to Jack, her grip so fierce, he had trouble breathing. But he didn't move. Harry just kept swinging Yoko around and around until he got dizzy. Alexis sat down in the middle of the floor and cried. With relief. Annie, full of spit and vinegar, looked around the barn and said that it wasn't the Ritz, but she knew she could acclimate, and that she'd just had the most exhilarating experience of her life but she'd never want to do it again.

"Report in, everyone," Jack said. "I need an update. What's going on? Any word from Myra and Charles?"

The others groaned.

"If you say one more word, Annie, I am going to kill you," Kathryn said, glaring. She rolled over on the floor next to Alexis and pounded the floor. "God, we stink! Almost two whole days in the air! Has anyone heard from Bert?"

Then they were all talking at once. Isabelle joined them, her wet hair slicked back, smelling of Johnson's Baby Powder. She was wearing Irma Ellis's clothing, and latex gloves. In one gloved hand was her third cola.

"Move, ladies, we're going to be having company soon," Jack said. "There are four showers in each bathroom. Clothes are in the closet on the left. Make it snappy." He looked down at Nikki, who was still clutching him so tight he was gasping. "You have to let up and hurry, babe, or you're going to be left behind. I'll be here when you get out."

"Promise," Nikki said in a jittery voice.

"I promise."

Nikki trotted after the others, but twice she turned around to look at Jack before she disappeared from view.

Annie was untangling herself from the chair she was sitting on.

"How bad was it?" Jack asked.

"Bad. There's no way you could handle it, Jack, so I'll spare you the details." Annie offered up a sloppy salute and wobbled down the hall to the bathroom.

"What the hell does that mean?" Harry asked anxiously.

In a voice little more than a croak, Jack said, "I think she meant wind, rain, turbulence, jets flying low coming in for landings, dust flying at them from all angles, that kind of thing. She's right, you and I wouldn't have been able to handle it. We would have been puking our guts out the windows. If crop dusters have windows, that is. You're getting all glassy-eyed,

Harry. They're here. They're safe. Jesus, can't you hear them in there? They're singing that song 'Dancing Queen.'"

Harry cocked his ear toward the hall leading to the bathrooms. Sure enough, the Sisters were singing, loud, off-key, and laughing like lunatics. In spite of himself, Harry laughed when Yoko's voice blasted from the shower.

"It's her favorite song. She can't sing worth a damn."

Jack's foot tapped to the nonexistent rhythm. "That little whippersnapper can wipe up the floor with you, Harry. If they'd been in trouble, Yoko would have been dancing on the wing making sure the plane landed safely so she could get to you. And you worried about her! Why the hell do you think they're singing that song in there? You're so stupid, I don't want anyone to know I know you."

"Yeah, Harry, you're stupid," Ted volunteered. "Even Maggie said you're stupid."

"It's okay, Ted, Harry is in love," Jack said.

"Yeah, well, so am I, but I know better than to let Maggie think I'm smarter than she is."

"Yeah, yeah, me, too." Jack guffawed.

"Both of you, eat shit," Harry said.

Jack and Ted laughed louder. Then they all suddenly noticed Isabelle on the floor. She was laughing so hard she had to hold her sides.

"Listen, Isabelle, you aren't going to . . . you know . . ." Ted stuttered.

Isabelle's head wobbled back and forth. "Your dumb-ass conversation is safe with me." She went off into gales of laughter again as she, too, started singing the words to "Dancing Queen."

Ted's sudden whoop of elation startled the others as they closed in around him.

"Maggie scooped every paper in the country. Espinosa got a live interview with one of the departed followers of the HOE. She's on the front page with before-and-after pictures. Espinosa has her in hiding at the *Post*'s apartment. The good stuff is above the fold. Like mine and Joe's names. Man, it doesn't get any better than this! Those slash-and-burn tactics of Maggie's are really paying off. That was the good news. The bad news is the whole world is about to descend on this little town

and that damn compound. Maggie is saying we don't have a whole lot of time."

"I get that part about the time," Jack
said. "What I don't get is what are we supposed to do now that we're all here?
Where the hell is our fearless leader, and
what's our game plan?"

"I'm right here, Jack," Annie said, coming up behind him. "Believe it or not, I do
have a plan. Of sorts. Actually, it's more of
an idea than a plan. Considering our circumstances."

"Let's hear it," Isabelle said.

"With the world's media about to
descend on the HOE, I think it would
behoove all of us to get inside that compound *before* that happens. I'm sure with
all that acreage out there, there have to
be some hidden entry points. I'm just as
sure there will be some kind of gate that
opens and closes that would be under
surveillance. We should do it as soon as it
gets dark."

"We, as in the guys and us, or just us?"
Kathryn asked.

Annie sniffed. "I didn't get that far in my
planning." "I think it's an either/or. Bear in

mind, we are only six, and there are a lot of people in that compound. We don't know what kind of communications system they have. All of us," she said, making a snap decision.

Jack's cell rang. His eyebrows shot upward as he mouthed the word "Bert."

"What's up, Mr. Director of the FBI?" Jack listened, then he whirled around to look out the window to see if they were being invaded. "No shit! Okay, okay. Give me five minutes."

"Turn the grid off. Bert's up at the end of the road with the two deputies from the sheriff's office. I think it's almost showtime."

Annie ran to the electric box to retract the dangerous spikes before she ran to the window where everyone else was clustered.

At the end of the two-mile-long driveway, Bert Navarro was holding court. He stepped out of his rental Mustang, his FBI credentials in hand. The two deputies, creased and polished, looked at the ID Bert was holding.

"Deputy Clyde Reeves, and this is my partner, Sam Nesbit. What can we do for the FBI today?"

"For starters you can call in to the sheriff and ask him to join us, then you will do exactly what I tell you to do from that point on."

Nesbit appeared to be the bolder of the two. He was sloppy and beefy, which the creased uniform couldn't hide. He was jowly, with a set of nicotine teeth and a dirty-looking mustache. "And why would we be doing something like that? We don't take orders from strangers, FBI or not. In case you haven't noticed, there are two of us and one of you."

Bert laughed as he thought about the brown belt Harry had presented to him the previous day. Or was it the day before? Not that it mattered. The brown belt said he could take these two within a minute and have time left over.

Deputy Reeves suddenly looked uneasy. He looked over at Nesbit, who was suddenly looking everywhere but at him and Navarro, his bluster all but gone.

"Call the sheriff." Bert looked at his watch. "Siren blasting, ninety miles an hour, he should be here in about . . . four-and-one-half minutes. Tell him the FBI requests his presence immediately. Do it!"

Reeves reached into the cruiser, pressed a button, listened a moment to the squawking on the other end, and delivered the message verbatim.

"So, tell me, what are you two fine deputies doing way out here?"

"Checking on George Ellis. Six or seven planes just landed back there, and we want to know what's going on. A lot of strange things have been happening around here the past day or so. Found a man dead in a bus yesterday. Some woman kidnapped a bunch of young girls, then ran off with a couple of men on cycles. All leads point to this place. Sheriff asked us to investigate. What's the FBI's interest in this little place?"

Bert looked at his watch again. He could hear a siren in the distance. "The thing about the FBI, Deputies, is, we ask questions, we don't answer them. Do you have a problem with that?"

"No, Mr. Director, I don't. I don't think Nesbit here does, either, but the sheriff might. He's pretty prickly about people invading our little town."

"Really. The way I see it is this: If you aren't doing anything wrong, you have nothing to worry about. The other thing is,

I don't personally give a shit what your boss thinks or feels. Now, if you want an experience from hell, I can deliver that with one phone call. All the resources of the Utah, Nevada, and Arizona FBI can be here within hours. You deputies outside members of the HOE?"

Both deputies looked off into the distance. Bert had his answer.

Thirteen seconds later, a cruiser pulled into the rocky driveway. A tall man who looked exactly like Clint Eastwood when he was fifty stepped out of the car. He reached back into the car to turn off the siren and flashing light.

"Sheriff Ron Finn," the sheriff said, holding out his hand.

Bert gripped the man's hand in a vise-like grip and enjoyed the pain he saw in the other man's eyes.

"What brings the FBI to this sleepy, off-the-map little town?"

"Like I told your two deputies here, Sheriff, the FBI does not answer questions, we ask them. Being in law enforcement, I'm sure you know the FBI takes precedence, so whatever you and your people are doing here at this farm has to cease now. The Bureau is stepping in. But in the interests of fairness to you and your two men here, I will allow you to follow me down this road so that you can see we're serious about all of this. Before we head that way, are you an outside member of the HOE?"

The sheriff's face closed tight. All signs of affability disappeared. "Is that what this is all about?"

"I guess you weren't listening, Sheriff. I said the FBI doesn't answer questions, we ask them. I'll ask you again. Are you an outside member of the HOE? Your deputies here declined to answer the question when I asked them a few minutes ago. I'm waiting."

The sheriff didn't look so much like Clint Eastwood at that moment. His eyes narrowed, and his hand went to the gun at his hip. Bert's foot lashed out faster than the breeze that rippled through the scraggly trees, and Sheriff Finn was staring up at the last of the afternoon sun and Bert's foot, which was hovering about twelve inches above his face. Reeves licked at his lips as Nesbit smirked.

"You want me to ask again, or do you want to volunteer the answer?"

The Clint Eastwood lookalike said, "My religious affiliation is none of your goddamn business. I don't give a damn if you're the FBI or not. That goes for my men, too."

Bert cocked his head to the side, looked at both deputies, who looked away, then down at the man on the ground. Bert's foot was steady, with no sign of a tremor. "I'm going to take that as a yes." His foot moved then and came down, not on the sheriff's face, but on his shoulder. The sound of crunching bone was so loud even Bert flinched as he whirled around, and with two quick jabs, both deputies were lying next to their boss. *Oh, Harry, if you could see me now, you'd be so proud of me, you'd bust wide-open.*

Bert laughed at his own wit. "You just don't mess with the FBI, guys. I was nice, I was polite, just the way the manual tells me to be. This is the result."

Bert reached down and hauled Nesbit to his feet. "Put your boss in his cruiser and drive down that road. Reeves, you drive the other cruiser."

Bert climbed into his car and followed the two cruisers until they reached the barn. The door opened, but no one came outside. Just for the hell of it, Bert pulled his gun, fired into the air, and yelled, "FBI! Everyone out with your hands in the air!"

Kathryn ran out, her hands in the air for the barest of seconds before she hugged the director, then planted a liplock on him that made the others dizzy.

Annie was next, her arms flailing the air. "This is our answer. This is how we get into the HOE! Police cruisers! Genius! Pure genius! This dear, sweet man just provided us with what we need. Oooh, oooh, that one looks like he's hurt. Is he going to die? Well, there certainly is a lot of land here to bury him," she rattled on as she peered into the two cruisers.

Without being told, she removed all the weapons, even the shotguns. Annie's fellow Sisters raced over to help her.

"We now have *firepower!*" Annie chortled as she checked out one of the shotguns, racked it up, and pointed it at the two deputies. "Bang!" she said playfully. Both men turned as white as Annie's hair.

Bert, his breathing back to normal,

looked around. "Someone get a towel and make a sling for this guy's arm. Give him a couple of aspirin."

Yoko ran into the barn and returned with a fluffy yellow towel that looked as big as a blanket. She wasn't gentle when she fixed the sling. She then danced her way over to Harry and reached for his hand. Harry looked so sappy at that moment, Jack wanted to kick him—until he felt Nikki's hand in his own. He just knew he looked as sappy as old Harry.

"Hook these guys up to the door handles and let's go inside. We need to talk," Bert said as he led the way, leaving Harry and Yoko to take care of the deputies.

Ted took center stage and started to report Maggie's findings. He ticked them off on his fingers. "She wants to know if Lizzie will represent Marion Jennings. And, she wants to know if we want her to send the young lady out here. She, Marion, is willing to make the trip. "She has stayed in touch with a few others who got away. She says they all need help. She's willing to do whatever she can to help us. Maggie thinks the getaways should be compensated for their life in hell while residing with that sect. For whatever it's worth, I agree. Plus, Marion wants her kids. I think Lizzie will take it on, but I was told to ask. The next thing is Maggie says we should infiltrate and get as many pictures as we can. As quick as we can. And, last, and most important, Joe Espinosa said the papers should be hitting Sienna and the HOE compound by dawn's early light. He hacked into the rental car companies and got all their delicious renters' arrival times. Then he screwed them up to give you guys extra time.

"The boardinghouse in Sienna, where Lizzie and Nellie are, is booked solid. The owners are putting up cots, and some townspeople are agreeing to rent out spare rooms in their houses. Joe fooled around with the visitors' charge cards, so even there you might get a few minutes' reprieve. There is not a recreational vehicle between here and Provo or Park City to be had. That, people, means we have the inside track if we move our asses. I think waiting for darkness is a good idea. If we go with the cruisers and our own rental cars, we can be our own force. We take the sheriff's cell phone and we'll have his squawk box. Win-win, ladies and gentlemen!"

"Huddle!" Bert said, dropping to his haunches.

The others followed suit until they formed a tight circle in the middle of the floor.

"Let's hear it! I don't care how stupid it sounds, just spit it out and we'll deal with it."

# Chapter 11

"That was a little too close for comfort," Lizzie Fox said as she slid behind the wheel of her rental SUV. She looked over her shoulder at Judge Nellie Easter Cummings, who was sitting in the backseat, kneading her arthritic hands. In the front passenger seat, Elias Cummings, retired director of the FBI—and Nellie's new husband—simply nodded as he craned his neck to stare through the tinted windows at the hordes of newspaper people descending on the rooming house the three of them had just vacated.

Lizzie yanked at the bill of the baseball

cap that hid her wild mane of silvery hair. Oversized sunglasses and the high collar of her denim jacket shrieked tourist—perhaps a daughter vacationing with her retired parents. A family. She hoped.

Lizzie knew she was news. Simply because she was once the attorney of record for the vigilantes. Things happened when she was around, that was the bottom line. Getting away now meant she had a window of time to do what she had to do without the media dogging her every step.

Within five minutes she was out of Sienna and on the highway. Her destination was the airport in Provo, where she was to pick up Marion Jennings and Joe Espinosa. From that point on, depending on how things went, she'd make the decision if she should head for Salt Lake City or not.

"Nellie, call Annie and see if everything is still on schedule. Be sure to ask if there is any news on Myra and Charles. Damn, will you look at this traffic! All those satellite trucks. Big doings back there in Sienna," she said, laughing. "We got out just in time." Lizzie looked over at Elias and laughed again. "C'mon, Elias, admit it, your adrenaline is pumping."

The big man in the passenger seat grinned. "Retirement for the most part is rather boring. A little action on the side does make for interesting conversation. I hope our cover story of looking for investment property works, if it comes down to that."

Lizzie heard the snap of the phone and knew Nellie had ended her call. "What'd they say?"

"No real news on Myra and Charles. Myra did call Annie and said it was all very hush-hush, and that people, friends of other people, were helping Charles and Myra. The young man is in a medically induced coma, but they were to bring him out of it today. It's touch-and-go. That's it on that front. Annie says they're waiting for darkness, then the plan is to head out to the HOE compound. They have two police cruisers, and the sheriff and his two deputies are handcuffed to an old snow-plow in one of the working barns. The girls all landed safely, along with the supplies that someone named Avery Snowden sent along in the crop dusters. I think Mr. Snowden is Charles's go-to guy.

"Annie wants you to go to the biggest newspaper in Salt Lake City or Provo, she doesn't care which, or have Ted do it, to arrange for an interview with Marion Jennings. That will speed things up when the locals, the ones who don't read the *Post,* see what's going on.

"Maggie says you have to convince Jennings to call in to the FBI and file a complaint. Bert is already here, but he can't do anything until a call goes through, at which point he can file for a federal warrant. He's going to be going to Provo shortly. He'll wait to make his appearance."

"What about the sheriff and his deputies? Didn't they see Bert?" Lizzie asked as she maneuvered the SUV around two stalled pickup trucks. The moment she was in the clear her foot hit the gas pedal.

"I believe Mr. Snowden and his people, Annie called them 'the sweepers,' will come in and . . . uh . . . tidy up. I take that to mean the men will simply disappear for a very long time."

"Do those men know the vigilantes

were there? Did they put two and two together?"

"I don't know, Lizzie. Annie didn't say. At this point, I don't think it matters. Who are they going to tell? By this time tomorrow, they'll be long gone." *I hope,* she said to herself.

After dropping off Nellie and Elias at the hotel, Lizzie made the rest of the ride to the Provo airport thinking about what the immediate future held for all of them.

Two hours later, Lizzie was standing alongside the SUV in the broiling sun as she waited for Espinosa and Marion Jennings. With nothing else to do but wait, she called Annie to see if anything had changed since Nellie's last call.

"Nothing other than that Bert is on his way to Provo. The boys," Annie said, referring to Jack, Harry, and Ted, "are talking to the sheriff and his two deputies. I think it's fair to say the boys are doing all the talking. The sheriff is pretty tight-lipped, at least for the moment. Harry was talking about inflicting a little pain without leaving any marks. I think that got the deputies' attention, but the sheriff is a pretty tough nut. I could be wrong on this, Lizzie, but I think he thinks that the cavalry is rushing to his aid. I hope he doesn't know something we don't know."

"Me, too. What role, if any, do the state police play around there?"

"I'm not sure. Ted seems to think it's pretty much hands off unless the locals request their help, which, according to Ted, never happens. Sienna and the compound are off-limits. In other words, let sleeping dogs lie unless those sleeping dogs rear up and growl. That's why we have to get away from here and inside that compound before that can happen. If we can take charge, then we can control what goes on."

Lizzie digested Annie's summary, but she wasn't so sure it was going to be as easy as Annie thought it was going to be. "What happens when that federal warrant comes through? Bert will have to act and go into the compound. What's your window of time, Annie?"

When there was no immediate response to her question, Lizzie knew Annie was worried. She prodded her.

"It depends on how long it takes to get the warrant," Annie said. "So, if the Jen-

nings girl is going to call in the complaint,
check with me first. There won't be any
locals showing up, and by locals I mean
the sheriff and his two deputies. It's going
to be a circus, that's a given."

Lizzie wished she knew more about the
inner workings of polygamy and what she
could expect to go down. She perked up a
second later. Why was she so worried?
Marion Jennings had lived the life and
would be able to tell her everything she
needed to know. "Is there anything else I
need to know, Annie?"

"Not right now. I'll call if something
crops up."

The phone call ended just as Espinosa
and a tall young woman, who could have
passed for a model, approached Lizzie's
parked SUV. Introductions were made,
then Lizzie drew Espinosa aside and said,
"You're to go back to the Ellis farm, where
everyone is waiting for you. I reserved a
rental car for you. All you have to do is pick
it up. This," she said, handing over a slip of
paper, "has the directions to the farm.
Whatever you do, do not start down that
driveway. Call Jack or Ted and make sure
the grid is turned off, or your tires will get

shredded. Tell me now if there's anything else I should know."

"Well, if there is, Marion can fill you in. There is one other thing. The minute I got off the plane I called the Provo *Daily Herald* and the *Deseret News* in Salt Lake City. Both reporters are going to be calling you for a one-on-one with Jennings. But only do one interview, so whoever calls you first is the one you go with. That's straight from Maggie. Okay, I guess I'll see you when I see you. She's got a hell of a story for you, Lizzie. I hope you can help her and her friends."

Even though she was wearing wraparound sunglasses, Lizzie held up her hand to shield her eyes, that was how bright the sun was. She watched as Espinosa loped over to the line of rental cars waiting to be picked up. When she saw him hand over his paperwork and slide behind the wheel, she climbed into her own SUV and headed to the nearest Holiday Inn Express, where she was setting up shop.

It was five thirty, two hours till twilight, when Ted Robinson's cell phone rang. All he heard was, "Turn that damn thing off. I'm at the road. I'll be there in a few minutes." Ted raced over to the switch and turned it to the off position.

"What? What? Espinosa is coming here!" the Sisters shrieked.

"Whose brilliant idea was that?" Alexis demanded.

"Maggie's idea," Ted shot back. "What, you're all idiots all of a sudden? You think he doesn't know who you are and what's going on? Get real. Maggie wouldn't have sent him if it wasn't okay. The guy has worked with me for years and never once gave you up. That has to say something, don't you think?"

The Sisters huddled, to Ted's dismay. He wished Jack and Harry were there, but they had gone out to the old barn to check on their prisoners. "Hold on here, ladies. Before you make any hasty decisions let me tell you something about Joe Espinosa. He's one of eight kids, the only son. His father died early on, leaving his mother to take care of all of them. He's the youngest. They managed to scratch out a living somehow, and as the girls got older and went to work, they found a way through sacrifice to send Joe to college. He's the only one in that very large family to get a college education. Joe is a United States citizen. He sends every cent of money he can back to his people in Tijuana. Go visit anytime. Their shop is the third one on the street on the right side after you cross the border. It's not much, but it works for them. Joe has lived in a one-room dump for as long as I've known him because he can't afford anything else. There are thirty-seven members in his immediate family. Thirty-seven!

"Joe's mother is the vigilantes' staunchest supporter. Along with her daughters, she opened a shop right across the border and sells all kinds of stuff with your names on it. She's eking out a living of sorts. Everyone in Tijuana knows who you girls are. She has posters everywhere. You even *think* about tossing him out, and I'm going with him."

Annie stepped forward. "Joe supports thirty-seven people? On his salary? How can that possibly be?"

"It works because it has to work. He moonlights sometimes for extra money. Some of his family work if there's work to be found. They aren't lazy, Annie. It's the economy down there. His money helps, but it isn't nearly enough."

"Well then, we'll have to do something about that, now, won't we?" Annie turned to the others, and said, "You all know my motto. Money talks and bullshit walks. Let's see if that's true. Girls, welcome Mr. Espinosa to our small but growing organization while I . . . uh . . . take care of a few things."

"Guess that says it all," Kathryn announced as she followed Annie to the back door. She watched as Annie opened it to get better reception. Kathryn stayed inside and listened unashamedly. She wished she could hear the person on the other end of the phone, but Annie's end of the conversation told her enough to make her grin from ear to ear.

"Conrad, I need you to do something for me, and I need you to do it quickly, and I don't want to argue with you. Now listen to me. I want you to bring some people across the border and . . . and what I want you to do is . . . find a way . . . to . . . make them legal. No, no. No green cards. I want *citizenship*. What difference does it make how many? A number is a number. Don't go getting pissy on me, Conrad, I pay you handsomely. Think what it would be like if you were on the unemployment line. Think of the humiliation. Your wife wouldn't be able to get pedicures, your grandchildren would have to go to public school, and you'd have to mow your own lawn.

"All right, all right, thirty-seven people total. Stop screaming, Conrad. I'm talking push mower, not the kind you ride around on. Send someone to get all the details, exact names, that sort of thing. No trail left behind. Of course, I know it's illegal. I do illegal things, that's my life now. Why would you think housing for thirty-seven people is a problem in this horrible economy? Conrad, why with all the money I pay you, do I have to think for you, too? Send them all to my plantation and let them take it over. Give everyone a job. Hire tutors for the children, then we'll send them to private school when they catch up on English. This way they won't be a drain on the economy.

"Well, Conrad, this is how I see it. When I . . . uh . . . retired from private life to go

on to other . . . things, you took it upon
yourself and laid off all the people at the
plantation. I seem to recall the number
eighty-four somewhere along the way.
Thirty-seven isn't even half of eighty-four,
now, is it? There are vehicles there. Have
someone teach the adults how to drive if
they don't know already. Make sure there
is a tutor for the adults as well as the children so they can learn English, too. Be
sure there's plenty of food for everyone.
Clothing, too. Are you taking notes, Conrad? I bet you don't even know how a weed
whacker works.

"Now, these people are going to need
Social Security numbers, credit cards, and,
eventually, driver's licenses, then pass-
ports. Yes, you can make it happen. Later
on we'll make sure we do it all legally, but
for now it has to be this way. I'm going to
give you a phone number and you will call
this person and then you will report back
to me. Are we clear on this, Conrad?
You're sputtering. How do you expect me
to understand what you're saying? Oh,
your wife's acrylic nails will have to go,
too, along with those two-hundred-dollar
hair salon appointments, as well as that

country club membership. Will you please stop babbling? Oh, one more thing. I know people who can make you disappear, Conrad. Like in *disappear.* Poof. You're gone. Now, does that finish us up, you darling man?"

Kathryn choked on her own laughter as she scurried back to report to the other Sisters. She was just in time to see Joe Espinosa walk into the barn. She wanted to run up to him and throw her arms around him and tell him what Annie had just done for his family, but she just smiled, and asked, "Hey, Espinosa, what's up?"

While Ted pulled aside his colleague to clue him in on the current situation, Kathryn quickly recounted Annie's conversation that she'd listened in on. Her Sisters grinned from ear to ear and high-fived one another. Good old Annie had saved the day for one Joe Espinosa, and he didn't even know it.

No one missed the dreamy-eyed looks Alexis and Joe Espinosa gave each other.

Annie returned to the room, shook hands with Espinosa, and welcomed him to their little group. "Ted, take Joseph down to the old barn so he can see what's going on. It's going to be dark soon."

Annie looked around at the women. "Why are you all looking at me like that? I'm a little worried. I thought being the PW would be a little more fun, but it's a lot of angst. So many things can go wrong. Snowden hasn't called back. We need to have those law officers out of here and on their way to wherever they're being taken before we head for the compound. No loose ends. And still no calls from Myra or Charles. It's almost midnight in London, so I guess we won't hear anything until tomorrow.

"Someone call Lizzie, she should have checked in by now."

Nikki whipped out her cell and hit the speed dial. She spoke for a few minutes, then listened for a good five minutes before closing the phone.

"Before I report on Lizzie, I have a question, Annie. I know we're flying by the seat of our pants on this one, but we all need to know how we're going to get out of that compound once we ... uh ... finish our work there."

Annie looked stupefied for a minute. "Girls! Girls! The same way we arrived here. The crop dusters! But, just as far as Salt Lake City, then it's the Gulfstream the rest of the way. Now, no moaning and groaning." She had no idea if that was feasible or not, but she didn't want the girls to worry about their exit. Maybe she'd have to go to Plan B, or maybe C, or even D. "What's the latest from Lizzie?"

"In thirty minutes, Miss Jennings will have her interview with a reporter from the *Daily Herald*. Supposedly the paper's ace reporter. The plan is she's to call the FBI and lodge her complaint about the pregnant girls. She's going to give her real name and tell them she's being represented by Lizzie. Her friends are going to show up at the Holiday Inn and back up everything she said. I'm sure the headline will read something like, THE ONES WHO GOT AWAY. Bert will be in the Provo field office and take the call. He'll apply for the federal warrant around six tomorrow morning. The way things seem to work around here in regard to the polygamists, it could take as long as six hours before a judge signs off on it. That means we have until dawn or a little after to get in and get out of there."

Isabelle started to giggle. "Tell me again what we're going to do when we get there?"

The Sisters looked at one another and laughed.

# Chapter 12

Lizzie ushered the women into a small conference room she'd booked at the last second. Seven people plus the reporter and the photographer were more than the single room that she'd reserved could hold. Out of the corner of her eye she looked over at Marion Jennings and the other five women she'd invited to participate in the interview. The words "cream of the crop" ricocheted inside Lizzie's mind. The prettiest of the pretty. The chosen ones of the Prophet. His to do whatever he wanted with. She didn't think one of them was past eighteen, except possibly

Marion Jennings. None had a birth certificate, and after hearing Marion's vague
references to what had been going on in
the world the year she was born, Lizzie
wondered whether Jennings was even that
old.

Lizzie felt her stomach start to scrunch
up. She wasn't sure what she could do for
any of them. In the end it would depend on
what they wanted her to do, she decided.

A knock sounded on the door. "Refresh-
ments," she said at the women's startled
looks. "It's just some soft drinks, fruit, and
pizza. I thought you might be hungry.
We're going to be here a while."

Lizzie knew that if she ate anything,
she'd get sick. What was wrong with her?
No case had ever gotten to her like this
one had, and she wasn't even sure what
the case was going to turn out to be. She
signed the bill and took her seat at the
head of the conference table. Where to
start? What to say? More to the point,
how to say it?

"I'm Elizabeth Fox. I know Marion has
told you who I am, but let me tell you
again. I'm a lawyer. I can practice law in
every state of this country except for

South Dakota. I'm willing to work with you to help you in any way I can. I know other people who can help you once we get past the legalities of . . . of whatever you all decide you want me to do. Money for my time is not an issue. Other people are paying me to help you. People who care about all of you. We have a little time before the reporter and photographer get here, so let's make use of it. We'll do it one by one, each one of you telling me your story. The device in the middle of the table will record everything you say. I want you, one by one, to acknowledge that this session is being recorded. I also want you to understand this is all privileged. That means no one else will ever hear it unless you each give your permission. If you understand what I just said, go one by one, say your name, and say you agree to having this interview recorded, then give today's date, and the time and the location."

When the young women were finished, Lizzie, for the benefit of the recording, also introduced herself, gave the date, the time, and the location. She thought Marion seemed the bravest, the one least nervous, so she said, "Marion, you go first."

"My name is Marion. I think my last name is Jennings, but I'm not sure. Our mothers said last names were not important. I was married to the Prophet, Harold Evanrod. By my best calculation, I was thirteen when I was given to him. I was sewing my wedding dress when I was twelve. I remember that because it was the day I got my first period. One of the mothers took me aside and said that was my milestone, and it was time to start my wedding dress. At the time I didn't even know what that meant other than if I did what I was told, I would not be damned to hell and would have eternal salvation.

"We had group mothers. We had our natural mother for our first year or so of life, then we were given over to another mother for a few years and on and on it went until we reached the time when we got our periods. That's when life as we knew it totally changed. We were no longer children. There was no more playtime. That year until the anniversary of that period was spent in teaching us, through the group mothers, how to act and behave once we got married. The indoctrination was so intense I would go to bed at night and cry.

"School stopped. No further friendships were allowed. We were told we had to worship the Prophet, to grovel if that's what he wanted. We were taught to be subservient, never to look the Prophet in the eye, always keep our eyes downcast. We were to do nothing to make ourselves attractive, or to be noticed. Our sole lot in life was to have babies and nothing else. It was intense mind control. I didn't know that then, but I know it now. It was a life of fear and pain. We were to speak in a slow, soft manner and not *ever* to question our husband. We were told there would be other wives, and we were not to be jealous because jealousy was the sin of sins. They never used the word 'sin,' but somehow I knew even back then what it meant.

"They had boxes, cartons, actually, of ovulation test kits. All the *wives* had calendars, and we were to mark the days so our husband could pick one of us. Then when we missed our first period we were to mark it down on the same calendar.

That was so the Prophet, in each woman's case, knew not to bother her again until the baby was born. Ten months after the birth, the calendars started up again. That was my life.

"After the birth of your third child, you were put up for something like an auction, and the Prophet decided who was to take you off his hands. Not your children, just you. Then the same thing started all over again with the calendars. I was to go to someone I think was my stepbrother. He drooled, and his eyes didn't focus clearly. And he had three 'celestial' or 'spiritual' wives at that time. I lied on my calendar, and at that point tried to figure out a way to leave. It was a given that I couldn't take the children, so I had to leave them behind. I naively thought that when I got to the outside, someone would help me and I could get a lawyer. But it didn't work out that way. I had never had any money, so I went to the nearest church and begged them to help me. They did. A very kind, caring family did everything they could for me, then they put me in touch with these other young women, and we all became friends.

"Somehow word leaked out to the HOE that there was a group of women who were going to make trouble, so the pastor of that little church moved us all to the East."

"How did you get away from HOE, Marion?"

"I walked out to the gate and climbed the fence and ran like hell until I couldn't run anymore. I think I walked twenty miles before I found that church. I was so exhausted I couldn't stand up, and I was dehydrated from the sun. But I survived. And so did my friends."

"Aside from the Prophet, how old were your husbands?" Lizzie asked the others.

"They were *old,* they were all old. Here on the outside you would call them grand-father types. No one got a young husband," said a young lady who had the girl-next-door look written all over her. "None of us knew what a movie, television, computer, or telephone was until we climbed those fences and ran away.

"In some ways, the outside people were afraid of us because we were so naive and dumb. We didn't know any better, but I think we all learned real fast," the girl next door said.

"What about the boys?" Lizzie asked.

A fiery redhead reared up. "They were treated like animals and made to work until they dropped. I had a brother who died in there. There were too many boys, so they kicked about two hundred of them out into the world. They have a cemetery where all the babies who died are buried, and there are a lot of them."

"What about doctors and dentists? Who delivered your babies?"

"There's a doctor in Sienna who lives on the outside. If there was a problem, he came to the compound," Marion said. "He was a dentist, too. If it was a natural birth, the mothers could assist—they were all midwives, so they knew what to do. Instead of paying the doctor, he was given a wife and had two rooms in one of the buildings. As time went on he acquired many wives. And it was the same with the sheriff, who is also the judge. The sheriff had his very own house on the compound. He had a *real* wife on the outside and a house there, too. The same thing went for the deputies."

Lizzie's mind raced. "How many children were you expected to have?"

"As many as you could. Or until you're all used up," a dark-eyed, dark-haired young woman said. "When that happened, or if you had too many miscarriages, then you were sent to the long building where the other older women were. There you did laundry, cooked, cleaned, and worked in the gardens. They were tired women, weary, and they hated one another. They pretended to pray; they read old sermons and the books the Prophet said would grant them eternal salvation. Personally, I think they were all just waiting to die. I hated them. I didn't want to be one of them."

Lizzie turned the tape over and pressed the PLAY button. How could something like this go on in the United States of America?

"What's the purpose of those ugly dresses and those awful hairdos?"

The young women all laughed, but the laughter didn't reach their eyes. Lizzie thought she had never seen such haunted eyes in the whole of her life.

"The funny thing is, you don't even own the dresses. You are not allowed to *own* anything," Marion said. "The dresses are pretty ugly and reflect the old times, when life was supposed to be simple and just. The older women wear darker colors and the younger ones wear the softer pastel colors. I always wanted a yellow one, but it wasn't to be. Yellow to me was a warm, golden color, a free color. We are told to let our hair grow because a husband likes a woman with long hair. Supposedly it was a sign of purity. Actually, we were forbidden to cut our hair. That was the first thing I did when I left."

"Let me tell you what this is all about now." Quickly, Lizzie told them all about Pearl's experience, without mentioning names. "Those girls are minors. What was done to them is against the law, but I'm sure you all know that by now. Do any of you have any idea why fourteen young girls, one who might be mentally challenged, were being transported to the HOE compound? Where would they be coming from? Why would so many be moved all at one time?"

"Something must have happened wherever they were living. They would never move them otherwise," Marion said. "I would guess, and it's just a guess on my part, that some outsider figured out what was going on and called in a complaint. Or, it could be as simple as too many welfare filings. That happened once or twice while I was still at the HOE, but I don't recall the details. I just know a lot of activity went on, and the Prophet was livid that he and his people were being questioned. Enormous amounts of money pour into that compound. I wish you could see the Prophet's house and how he lives."

Lizzie nodded. "I'm going to ask a question of all of you. Tell me honestly what you think. How many of the women in that compound would willingly leave if they had the chance?"

The young women all looked at one another. They shrugged as one. Marion went first.

"In my opinion, none of the older ones. They're hard, mean, bitter women. They would be afraid they'd be damned to hell. I think all of the younger ones would leave if given the chance. The most vulnerable are the twelves to sixteens. Remember, they have been brainwashed. They think that all the people outside the compound gates are evil and work for the Devil. They're taught early on that the greatest thing of all is eternal salvation and that only staying within the compound and obeying the Prophet will earn that for them. Then you have to factor in the children. It's the best answer I can give you."

Lizzie addressed another question to all of them. "How do you like life outside the compound?"

The answers ranged from "wonderful" to "scary" to "exciting" to "challenging." When she asked if any of them would willingly go back, they all said no but clarified they would return if they could get their children. But not to stay.

Lizzie nodded to show she understood.

She then started questioning the other women, whose accounts of their life on the compound didn't differ one iota from Marion Jennings's account.

"Did we help you at all, Miss Fox?" Marion asked.

"Yes, you did. I hope you are as forthcoming with the reporter, who should be arriving any minute now. If you hear me object to something, do not, I repeat, do not answer that particular question. I'll lay down the ground rules before we start, and we'll be taping everything you say again so later there will be no doubt about your answers. Your pictures will be taken, just so you know. By the way, is there a hospital or clinic in the compound?"

"There's a birthing station. After all," Marion said bitterly, "that's what it's all about, procreating, isn't it?"

"Unfortunately, yes. I would call it a breeding farm, and the women are nothing but broodmares," Lizzie said. "Ah, I think our reporter is here. Are you all ready for this?"

The women nodded and straightened their shoulders.

Lizzie leaned across the table and lowered her voice. "Someday, somehow, your children will know what you've done to get them back. I promise each and every one of you that I will try my best to make that happen."

Lizzie pushed back her chair and walked over to the door. She opened it to see a young woman in her midthirties, she guessed, followed by a photographer. She introduced herself, then looked at the reporter square in the eye and didn't say a word. The reporter returned her look and gave a slight nod. Lizzie walked back to the table, knowing that the young women sitting around the conference table were in good hands and believing implicitly that the power of the written word had no equal.

# Chapter 13

On the walk back to the old barn, where the sheriff and his two deputies were tied to a rusty snowplow, Jack stopped and motioned for the others to come closer. "You guys know we're winging this whole thing by the seat of our pants, right?"

Harry, Ted, and Espinosa nodded.

"All of us need to understand we're going to be reacting on the fly at whatever comes our way. That's not a good thing. A good thing is a plan, and we don't really have a plan. Right now we're relying on some guy named Avery Snowden, Charles's right hand, or so we're told. I think it's pretty safe to say he doesn't really know our capabilities, and we don't know his. I just know that Murphy's Law is going to rear up and bite us on the ass."

"Once we leave here, are we coming back?" Ted asked.

"I don't think so. When we leave here, the grid goes on. Snowden or his people are supposed to take care of that trio in the barn. I'm not sure how soon that's supposed to happen. At least that's what Maggie said in her last phone call. I'm assuming the removal will be by air or out across the prairie somehow. She said when it happens, she'll confirm. If it doesn't happen the way Maggie set it up, then we are in some real deep shit because those guys are loaded for bear and can identify all of us."

Espinosa crowded closer. "Jack, those three guys are not *official* law enforcement. They're on the Heaven on Earth payroll. It's the same thing as hiring three private dicks, giving them guns, a uniform, and cruisers. That means they answer only to the guy they call the Prophet. So, where's the deep shit you're talking about?"

"Sooner or later someone is going to

notice that the station they work out of is empty. Some sterling citizen is going to call somebody who has some real author- ity. By morning, the *Daily Herald* will be in everyone's hands. The media will descend on that little station, and we all know," Jack said pointedly as he looked at Espinosa and Ted, "how the media will dog it to death."

Espinosa licked at his lips. "Yeah, I get it. So then, what's our next move?"

"We are going into that barn and talk nice to our guests. We need them to tell us how they get into that compound when they go out there. The road leading to the actual compound is approximately two miles long. The buildings and the people can't be seen from the gates. I saw a pic- ture of the gates, and they have some kind of special locks on them. I don't want to have to smash through them since that would then allow the media vipers to follow us in. Maggie said there isn't a single NO TRESPASSING sign. I don't get that part, but if she said there aren't any signs, we have to go with that. It's in our favor because that means we aren't technically trespass- ing if there are no signs. *Capisci?*"

"And these guys here, once they're . . . gone, aren't going to come back to haunt us?" Ted asked.

Jack grinned. "Not in the foreseeable future. At least, that's the way it has always worked when Charles was in charge. People just disappear, never to be seen or heard from again. By that I mean they are simply relocated to a less desirable area of the globe. I have no reason to believe Snowden won't be operating under the same rules and principles," Jack said.

"It's not like we have too many choices at the moment. Let's see what goes down and work from there," Ted said.

"We're going to need pictures," Espinosa said as he flipped out his digital camera. "I have to upload them to Maggie for tomorrow's edition. Even though the paper here is on top of things, the *Post* has to have lead exclusive."

Jack looked over at Harry, who just shrugged. Harry was ready. Harry was always ready for whatever happened. Jack envied his friend's total confidence, his inward serenity, and his belief that he could take on the world and come out on top. Three pedophile polygamists posing as law enforcement officers wouldn't make him break a sweat.

"Then let's do it!" Jack said.

The inside of the old barn was full of rusty junk, an antique wringer washing machine, and wooden boxes full of more junk stacked up against the walls. Rakes, shovels, axes, and picks, just as rusty, were piled in a corner. Two old iron beds, almost rusted through, leaned drunkenly against the washer. The only light in the barn came through a dirty window and the open barn door. The only sound to be heard was the scratching of the rats as they scurried about trying to find a safe hiding place. Then he heard a sound overhead and rather thought it was bats. Bats and rats. A deadly combination no matter how you looked at it.

The foursome advanced into the room and walked over to the rusty snowplow.

To Jack's experienced eye, the sheriff and the two deputies looked defiant. "Gentlemen, this is going to be quick and dirty because we don't have much time."

"And we don't like you," Harry said.

"Yeah, none of us like you child-abusing cruds," Ted said.

Espinosa focused and clicked, again and again. "I don't like you, either. Not one of you is photogenic," he grumbled.

"You have no options," Jack told them, "so let's get that out of the way right now. So, the first one who tells me what I want to know gets to walk out of here. The other two, well, I don't know how to say this, other than to just say it. You'll never see this fine state of Utah again. All those doormat celestial wives you have will just be assigned to some other *schmuck* like you. I want a map of where every little thing is on the compound. I want directions from Point A to Point B, and I want to know how to get through those gates. First one up gets a walk."

"We aren't telling you anything," the sheriff said. "Our people will be out here before you know it, and your ass will rot in jail."

"You mean those Stepford women and men who bow to Harold Evanrod, also known as the Prophet? Our people picked him up a few hours ago when he approached the gates, and right now he's in the same position the three of you are in, at a hidden location," Jack lied, an evil grin on his face. "Ah, I can see you don't believe me. Espinosa, show these guys the pictures you took of that momentous event."

Espinosa's eyes popped wide. What the hell . . . He fiddled with the camera to try to stall for time until Jack could somehow clue him in to what he was supposed to be showing the sheriff.

"Ah, never mind, who cares if they believe us or not? Never mind. Where they're going, it won't matter one bit." Jack walked over to the corner of the barn at the end of the doorway and grabbed a pitchfork that was so old that flakes of rich brown rust dribbled on the floor. He jabbed it into the rotten flooring right in front of the three men.

"Don't think I won't jab this right through your nuts if one of you doesn't start talking real fast, and I don't want to hear one word about my eternal damnation or salvation. I'm going to count to three, and the first one to talk gets a pass. One. Two."

"Okay, okay, I'll tell you what you want to know," the deputy named Clyde said. "Let me loose, and you can ask me whatever you want. I won't lie."

Jack yanked the pitchfork out of the floor. More rusty particles flew in the still air. "It doesn't work that way. First you talk, then we let you loose."

"Then how in the hell am I supposed to draw you a diagram of the compound?"

Jack looked at Harry.

Harry looked at Jack.

"The man has a point," Ted said.

"You right-handed or left-handed?" Jack asked.

"Right," the deputy said.

"Ted, unhook his right hand but hook up his left to the sheriff. Now, draw me a picture," Jack said as he handed him a small notebook he removed from his pocket. "Explain as you draw, so we understand what it is you're doing there. You make even one mistake, and your ass is grass, buddy. But before you do that, how do you guys get into that compound?"

"Remotes on the visors of the cruisers. You just press the red button, and the gates open."

Clyde was like a runaway train as he scribbled and talked. When he finally finished, he mumbled something about having forgotten the pumpkin field.

"What the hell is the pumpkin field?" Jack asked.

"A field where they grow pumpkins. The HOE is the biggest supplier in the state, and they truck them all over. They've been harvesting for the past two days. I was supposed to escort the tractor trailer tomorrow to Provo, and Sam here was scheduled to escort the second load to Salt Lake City. After they unload, they go back for another load. The pumpkins get shipped from Provo and Salt Lake to other parts of the Southwest." He then followed up with a good ten minutes, giving more information on pumpkins than any of the others wanted to know or cared about.

"Hmmm," Jack said. "Who knew the pumpkin business was so lucrative? Who owns the tractor trailers?"

"Clyde, shut up," Ron Finn, the sheriff, said.

"You know what, Ron, I don't want to disappear, and I don't want to rot here, either. The minute you told me to watch out for those pregnant girls coming out to the compound my stomach started acting up. I told you it was trouble, but you and Sam here didn't listen to me. Look at us now." Clyde turned to Jack, and said, "The HOE owns the trucks. They own a lot of things no one knows about. Where do you think all those welfare checks go? That compound is not self-sustaining. They depend on the outside but put up a good front so that people like you will leave them alone. Now can I go?"

It was almost dark, the only light coming from Ted's small Maglite. The barn looked eerie in the limited light. The rats didn't like it, either, and several of them ventured toward the old snowplow. Sheriff Finn kicked out at one of them. It squealed and skittered away.

"No, not yet."

"Come on, man, you promised to let me go if I told you what you wanted to know. I kept my word, and now you need to keep yours," Deputy Clyde whined.

Jack motioned for the others to follow him toward the door so they could talk. "Look, we don't have all that much time. I don't like leaving those guys out here in this damn barn with no light. The place is infested with rats and bats. I need some indication of when they're going to get picked up. Ted, Espinosa, make some calls. Harry, come with me, we need to talk."

When they were outside and away from the barn, the wind kicked up and whispered through the straggly trees to the right and left of the path that had led them to the outbuilding just a short while ago.

Overhead, the stars were brilliant diamond specks in the sky. The moon was a mere half slice in the dark night. Jack wished he was in Rock Creek Park back in Washington, holding Nikki's hand as they went for an evening stroll. Off in the distance, he heard some kind of animal howl. Then a second animal picked up the cry. A pack of wild animals? His stomach started to churn.

"What do you think, Harry? I wasn't prepared for that pumpkin business, I can tell you that. I suppose that just solved one of our problems. I'm thinking we can run with my idea, but I don't have a clue as to how and where. Kathryn used to drive one of those rigs way back when. Cross-country. I believe she knows every trucker on the highways."

"And that means what, *kemo sabe*?"

"I don't know, I'm just tossing stuff out here. We were never in the planning stages on any of the girls' missions. All we had to do was show up and follow orders. I'm nonplussed. Are you non-plussed, Harry?"

"Yeah, Jack, I'm nonplussed," Harry snarled.

"Hey, Jack," Ted said, "I just got the word that there are three guys up at the end of the road. They're heading down here now to pick up those three cruds. They said Snowden sent them. Annie turned off the grid. Look, I see lights."

Jack let out a long, loud sigh as he headed back to the barn to free his three prisoners. He winced when Ted flashed his Maglite and he could see an army of rats skittering off in all directions.

Deputy Clyde was still whining. The sheriff was still telling him to shut up, that he should have known better than to believe a bunch of sinners who were headed for hell and damnation.

Harry took affront to that particular dec-laration. He looked down at the sheriff, who refused to meet his gaze. He bent over, reached for the man's balls, and squeezed. "The pain will let up in July of 2011 or thereabouts. Your balls will stay black long after that. You have anything else you want to say?"

The sheriff doubled over in agony, his balls sending spears of pain all the way to his teeth and up into his brain.

"You guys lied to me, you son of a bitch!" Clyde roared.

His fellow deputy tried his best to look invisible.

"Yeah, I lied. I have a problem with the truth sometimes. You want to do something about it?"

"Goddamn right I do. Unhook me, and we'll see if that lying mouth of yours still works."

Harry looked down at the blustering deputy as though he couldn't believe what he was seeing and hearing. "Man, you don't want to go there. Trust me," he said, his voice taking on a singsong quality to it.

"Shut the hell up, you slant-eyed piece of dog crap."

Harry shook his head from side to side. "Now you've gone and hurt my feelings. He snapped his fingers and tweaked Deputy Clyde's nose.

The deputy fell back against the snow-plow and didn't make another sound.

"You're slipping, Harry. You should have been able to do that in a nanosecond. Took you a full second," Jack chortled.

"Eat shit, Jack. I think our guests' ride is here."

Just then, a set of powerful headlights lit up the inside of the old barn like a baseball field hosting a night game. The rats dived for cover as Deputy Sam cowered. Sheriff Finn was still howling in agony as Deputy Clyde slept peacefully.

With the headlights blinding him, Jack thought from the sound of the engine that the vehicle of choice for his guests was a Humvee. Or another military vehicle. He wasn't sure if the three hulking men standing in camouflage gear were really Utah's National Guard or not, and he didn't care, either. He just wanted to be relieved of his responsibility. "They're all yours. Where are you taking them?"

"That's NTK, buddy."

Harry clucked his tongue. "Yeah, Jack, that's need to know. Even I knew that."

Espinosa was so busy clicking his

camera that he tripped all over his own
feet as he did his best not to get any
frontal shots of the three hulking men carrying out the sheriff and his deputies. He
managed to get two great shots of the
hulks tossing the HOE's law enforcement
into the back of the Humvee. Maggie was
absolutely going to love them. He hoped
she would add a caption that read something like, *"At great peril to himself, Joseph
Espinosa managed to get these pictures
to the* Post *for your viewing pleasure."* He
looked over at Ted, who was text messaging at the speed of light.

When the old barn was locked tight,
and the rats and bats were left in peace,
Jack turned to the others and said, "I don't
think those guys are the type I'd want to
belly up to the bar with on a dark and rainy
night."

"You think those guys were legit? You
know, real National Guard?" Ted asked.

Jack didn't know if they were or not.
"Nah, those outfits came straight out of a
costume shop. They're probably mercenar-
ies on Charles's payroll. Okay, boys, time
to get this show on the road."

The foursome walked on the dark path back to the barn, where the women were waiting for them.

"What took you so long?" Annie grumbled.

"We needed some extra time to get the skinny on the pumpkin venture. We understand it all now. It's a very lucrative business. I now know everything there is to know, and then some, about the business side of pumpkins," Jack said airily.

"Shut the hell up, Jack."

Jack ignored Harry, and said, "Harry only knows the cooking end of pumpkins, whereas I know all about the distribution end. This information is going to prove to be quite valuable. You'll see," he said loftily. "Now, I do believe it's time to head out to the Heaven on Earth compound to see what we can do to . . . help the world move forward."

"Will someone shut him up?" Ted grumbled, his fingers a blur in the dim yellow light spilling out of the Ellis barn as he continued to text Maggie back at the *Post*.

# Chapter 14

Sally Duval, Maggie Spritzer's right hand, looked at her boss and laughed. "We did it again. It's a dynamite front page, Maggie, and, we beat the Utah edition by three hours. I wouldn't be a bit surprised to find out in the coming months that there are going to be a lot of legislators in Utah wringing their hands and finally doing something about those polygamists. About time, too. Hey, want to go get something to eat?"

"I'm too tired and wired to eat, Sally, but thanks for the invitation."

Sally made a face. It was a well-known

fact to everyone at the *Post* that Maggie Spritzer could eat anything at any time of the day or night. Those close to her often called her "BP," for Bottomless Pit.

"I'm going home to take a bubble bath. Then I'm going to sack out for eight full hours. I'll be in late in the morning, so hold the fort. Don't call me unless it's an emergency. And you know what constitutes an emergency—someone bleeding all over my office, the president being abducted by aliens, or the entire food supply in Washington being vaporized by unknown forces."

"I got it, Maggie. Enjoy your bubble bath."

Forty-five minutes later a cab dropped Maggie off in front of her house in Georgetown. She looked back over her shoulder to see the front light glowing on Jack Emery's house a few doors away. She shivered under her lightweight suit jacket. She always felt comforted knowing Jack was in residence three doors away. When he and Ted were away, she felt jittery, antsy, knowing she was on her own. That wasn't to say she couldn't handle herself; she could. She just felt better with backup close at hand.

It was a few minutes before nine and she was about to step into the Jacuzzi when the phone she was never without gave off a soft, keening sound. "Why now?" she groaned as she flipped it open. "Myra!" The bubble bath with the tantalizing lavender-cypress bath salts was forgotten as well as her tiredness. Maggie's reporter instincts kicked in at the sound of Myra's voice. She could almost hear the trouble and anxiety crackling through cyberspace. "Talk to me, Myra."

Three hours after the interview had begun, Lizzie Fox packed up her briefcase, shook hands all around, thanked the *Daily Herald* reporter and her photographer, and prepared to head to her room, where all she wanted was a steaming-hot shower and at least fifteen minutes to talk to the love of her life, Cosmo Cricket. But she knew the young ladies who were now her clients needed to talk a bit more without the reporter and photographer around.

There were three things Lizzie Fox dearly loved about her chosen profession.

The first was the hand-holding: her personal reassurances to her clients that she would work her tail off on their behalf. For some reason, clients never got tired of being reassured. The second thing she liked was the retainer check, which was always big enough to choke an elephant. The third thing was the winning at the end. It was always a given that she would win because she would accept nothing less from herself. The proof of that was that she had never lost a case. Nor would she.

When the conference door closed behind the reporter and photographer, Lizzie said, "I have an idea. Let's all go into that cozy little bar down the hall and have a drink. If you have any questions or are worried about anything, we can talk there. They have a piano bar right alongside so we can all relax. My treat," she said hastily when she saw the look of worry on the women's faces.

She'd learned right off the bat that these women were all working for minimum wage and didn't have ten extra cents to spend. Suddenly she wanted to scoop them all up and carry them off to some safe place where they would never have to worry again. While they were all happy and relieved to be free of the HOE and all the problems associated with living in that commune from hell, they had at least known that if they stayed within the compound they would always be fed and clothed. Outside, on their own, the rules were different, and they had to fend for themselves. The first free moment Lizzie had she was going to talk to Annie about doing something for them.

When their drinks—a margarita for Lizzie and iced tea for the others—and snacks arrived, Lizzie kicked back and smiled. "I thought it all went very well. You are all going to be so famous you won't be able to stand it. Remember now, you don't say a word to anyone unless I'm present. Always wait a second or so to give me time to object."

Lizzie held up her glass, and they all made clinking sounds. "I think we should drink to your freedom to be the persons you all want to be. From here on in, the name of the game is patience. Now, tell me things about yourselves that we didn't talk about back there in the conference room. Tell me about your hopes and your

dreams and what you want for the future."
*Annie, you don't know it yet, but you are
going to be the fairy godmother of all time.*
She wished she could tell these young
women about Annie, Myra, the other Sisters, and Charles just to wipe the haunted
look from their eyes.

"Wait! Wait! I want to make another
toast. But before I do that I want to tell you
there are very few people I admire and
respect 100 percent, but there are some,
and I want to add you to my short list. I
admire you for having the guts to walk
through those gates. I admire you for
having the guts to leave your children
behind, knowing they will be cared for,
because it is the smart person who knows
how and when to fight another day. We're
going to get your children back. I promise.
I never make a promise I can't keep."

There were tears, but Lizzie had
expected them because she had her own,
which she was trying to keep in check.
She needed to text Ted, and she needed
to do it immediately. Now that she had a
list of the children's names along with
physical descriptions, it would help Ted

and make the Sisters' job easier. Since Ted was a master at text messaging, he was the logical one to contact. When she finished, she noticed the young women's eyelids were starting to droop. It had been a long, exhausting day for all of them. They all said their good-byes, with Lizzie promising to be in touch no later than noon of the following day.

There were hugs, kisses on the cheek, then more hugs before Lizzie was left alone at the table. She ordered a second margarita and a hamburger loaded with cheese, onions, lettuce, bacon, and tomato—her all-time favorite late-night "snack." She leaned back and closed her eyes for a few minutes as her mind raced.

Lizzie took a long drink and called Cosmo Cricket. "First things first. I love you, Cricket. With every fiber of my being. Second, I need a favor. I need a large, safe place for a whole lot of people, most of them children. I'm going to need it by midafternoon tomorrow or sooner if you can do it. Someplace secluded, no prying eyes, and it has to have all the comforts of home. I'm breaking the law that you and I both love, Cricket, just so you know. I want you to call Annie. She has an idea, so act on it for all of us. Third, I love you more than I did when I first made this call."

Lizzie waited a moment for the response. She heard the smile in Cosmo's voice and the reassuring words, "Consider it done. And just for the record, I love you *more* more."

Lizzie grinned to herself as she bit down on her burger, which was so big she almost couldn't fit it into her mouth. While she chewed, she text messaged Ted again, then Maggie, who was still up for some reason at midnight.

Her work done, Lizzie finished her burger and her margarita and actually thought about ordering another drink. She convinced herself the first one was never finished so she threw caution to the winds and ordered a third. Just the fact that she could do all this, that she had the freedom to order and pay for what she wanted, made her happy. She took one little sip and pushed away the drink. She paid the bill and made her way to her room. As she walked through the hall, she wondered how people could live with other people making each and every decision of their lives, with no choices at all. How could people lead such a robotic existence? All-consuming brainwashing, masquerading as religious belief, was the only answer she could come up with.

Before she slipped between the covers, Lizzie Fox dropped to her knees and prayed.

The bathwater in the Jacuzzi was cold. The glass of wine sitting in the alcove over the tub had lost its appeal hours ago, along with any desire for sleep. Maggie was gulping at strong black coffee, her fourth cup, her nerves twanging all over the place as she waited for news from Ted and the Sisters. She hoped she didn't come to regret the decision not to call any of them to tell them Myra's news until everyone was safely away from the HOE compound.

Maybe she should change her clothes and go back to the office so she could be ready to make instant decisions in a work atmosphere if needed. Before she could change her mind, she stripped down and pulled on a pair of jeans and a fleece-lined sweatshirt, then slipped into her running shoes. Now she felt like the old Maggie, with grease on her sneakers and ready to set the world on fire. She peeled a banana as she dialed the car service that took her back and forth to work. "I'll be downstairs in ten minutes. Be there!"

Before she left the house, she jammed the last of the bananas into her backpack along with an apple, an orange, several power bars, and a bag of cookies. Then she checked her e-mail on her home computer, which was tied into the *Post*'s e-mail server. Finally, she checked her BlackBerry. She had no messages from anyone. A minute later she was out the door and waiting at the curb. She looked around at the quiet night and was surprised to see two neighbors walking their dogs. They had to be nocturnal people, she thought, something she was not. Several cars went by before her driver pulled to the curb.

"Are you going in early or are you going in late, Miss Spritzer?"

"Both," she said, slumping down in the seat and buckling up. The rest of the trip to the *Post* was made in silence.

When Maggie stepped out of the elevator she ran smack into her assistant, Sally.

"What are you doing here, Sally? I thought you went home when I did. Did something happen? Why didn't you call me? What? What? Tell me."

"Nothing, Maggie. I just decided to stay in case something did happen. I caught a few hours' sleep. I stayed because I knew you'd be back. Now, aren't you glad I did? With me here you won't be alone in this big old place," Sally said cheerfully.

"Nothing came in from Ted or Joe?"

"No. But it's still early out there." Sally looked up at the bank of clocks on the wall. "It's only ten o'clock out there."

"I think we're both nuts. We could be home sleeping in our own beds, but here we are, with nothing to do."

"Are you hoping for another special edition tomorrow?"

Maggie licked her lips. Was she? Of

course she was, a special edition was every editor-in-chief's dream, but that particular dream depended on Ted, Espinosa, and the vigilantes. She nodded.

"What are you expecting to happen in the next few hours? You know you can trust me, Maggie. I'm not seeing it. Anything after the early edition here and the one in Provo will be anticlimactic. Unless you know something you aren't sharing," Sally said as she tried to figure out what else could possibly warrant a second special edition in as many days.

Maggie was too good a newswoman to give away anything no matter how trusted the employee was. "Just my reporter's gut instinct," she responded vaguely as she yanked out a banana from her backpack and started to eat it, wondering as she chomped down if she'd get constipated from having two bananas. She finished it off, then peeled the orange she'd brought along. The orange should level things off, and in case it didn't, she still had the apple. If she factored in her nerves, she rather thought her lower abdomen would be in fine shape. *God, what is wrong with me?*

Maggie looked up at the clocks. Almost eight in the morning in England. Going on eleven o'clock in Utah. Something had to happen soon. It just had to.

The scent of the orange peel wafting over her desk was pleasant. "Sally, what time can we go online to see the morning edition of the *Daily Herald,* do you know?"

"I'll check. Probably the same time you can read ours, around two or three. The papers are on the street by four. Maybe midnight. Be right back."

Maggie scarfed down the orange, juice dribbling down her chin and onto her desk. She swiped at it with the sleeve of her sweatshirt. She debated about eating the apple but decided to let it stay in her backpack. For the moment. She could always chew on her fingernails.

Sally was back within minutes. "Depending on the weather, around 1:30 Utah time. What online has to do with the weather is beyond me."

Maggie looked at the clock and shrugged. The life of a reporter-turned-EIC was to wait for the story. No, that wasn't true. As a reporter, she created the story. It was the EIC who waited for the story. She wished, and not for the first time, that she was out in Utah with the Sisters, watching and helping the story unfold.

"C'mon, c'mon, someone call in—text, fax . . . something," Maggie muttered under her breath as she watched the hands on the clocks across the room.

# Chapter 15

Myra was on her fifth—or was it her sixth?—cup of tea. She couldn't remember. For the most part, the only time she drank tea was when she was in bed with a bad cold or the flu. She longed for a cup of strong black coffee, but it wasn't to be had. In England, you drank tea whether you liked it or not. She got up off the chair she'd been sitting in and walked over to the window to stare out at the gray, dismal day that seemed to be unfolding. She longed for a brisk, sunny autumn day back on the mountain with the girls . . . raking the leaves, with pumpkin pies baking in the oven. She wished for Murphy and Grady begging her to throw a ball or stick so they could fetch it back.

Myra turned her head slightly to see the young woman sitting on the love seat. She wondered how anyone could sit so still for so long, and stare off into space for hours at a time the way that young woman had been doing and was still doing.

Where was Charles? What was going on? Myra looked at the watch on her wrist. It had been hours since Charles came to check on her. He'd said little, his face a mask of pain. She wondered if it was permissible to go outside and walk around. Maybe the young woman named Allison wouldn't rebuff her this time if she asked her to go for a walk, just to stretch the kinks out of their necks and legs. She sighed. She'd never know unless she made the offer.

"Mrs. Barnstable, would you like to join me for a little walk? I think we could both use some fresh air. I'd like to hear about your children if you're up to talking."

Allison Barnstable looked up at Myra and saw nothing other than compassion in the older woman's face. The mention of her children brought tears to her eyes. She blinked them away and got up. She nodded as she followed Myra down one long hallway after another until they reached the front door, where a man eyed them as though they were the enemy.

Myra squared her shoulders and said, "We want to go outside for a little while. We need some fresh air."

The man, or, as Myra thought of him, the guard, hesitated for a full minute before he pressed a button she couldn't even see. The door swished open on some kind of hydraulic mechanism. The two women walked through the opening and down a winding path. There were no people to be seen and no cars or ambulances in any of the parking spaces.

Desperate to say something, anything, to elicit a conversation with the young woman at her side, Myra finally asked, "Do you have many sunny days here?"

"Not really," was the curt response.

At least it was a response, something she could run with, and run she did as she babbled on about the farm in McLean and Big Pine Mountain. She talked about golden sunshine, the rich scent of pine resin on the mountain, of the horses on her farm, and how wonderful it was to ride over the pastures. She talked of her daughter and her passing with a catch in her voice. "So you see, dear, Sir Malcolm has already lost a child. It was a horrible time for us both." She deliberately avoided specific details in order to protect herself, Charles, and her fellow Sisters.

"Tell me about your children. Do you have any snapshots of them with you? Oh, look, here's a bench. We can sit down for a few minutes."

Allison Barnstable was like a robot, easily led, as Myra guided her to a bench that was still wet, but she didn't seem to mind.

"Why are you talking to me? What is it you want from me? Did you see that woman who came here during the night? She comes every night with four men, and they take her to Geoff's room. She stays for thirty minutes, then the men take her away. She was here the first night they brought me here. They wouldn't let me see him, but they let *her* see him. I kicked up a bit of a fuss, and they sedated me. Against my will." Tears rolled down Allison's cheeks.

Oh, dear. "Was it someone you know?" Myra asked. She had her suspicions as to who "that woman" was, but she kept them to herself. "I guess I slept through the visit." She hated lying to this young woman, but she had to protect Charles and *his friend*. Assuming she was guessing correctly.

Allison sniffed. "Of course I don't know her. I think it's Lady Pamela Adamson, but I can't prove that. They always say the wife is the last to know about these things. Well, they're wrong. I do know. I just can't put a face or a name to the woman who was here."

Allison was crying openly as Myra tried to grapple with what she was hearing. Should she say something, or should she just listen? She patted Allison's arm the way only a mother would. Sometimes actions were more powerful than words.

"He's going to die. I know it. I feel it here," Allison said, thumping her chest. "They wouldn't even let me inside that room. I have to look at Geoff through the glass, but they let *that woman* in there.

She holds his hand and talks to him. It should be me sitting there. He's my husband even though he . . . even though we haven't . . . I need to say good-bye, to say I'm sorry I wasn't what he . . . Oh, sweet Jesus, I am so sorry. My mum told me, but I didn't listen. I wanted . . . I did everything I could to make myself into what he wanted, but it wasn't enough. He was so dashing, women always fell all over him. And yet he picked me. Look at me! Take a good look. I look like a milkmaid, and he picked me. I thought I had died and gone to heaven when he chose me to be his wife, the mother of his children. We have three wonderful children, a boy and two girls. I had no help, so I had to do everything myself. Geoff was always away with the training and the flight school and all that it involves. I know now that there were times when he could have come home, but he didn't. He wanted bright lights and parties and women, not a milkmaid wife and children who needed and wanted what he wasn't prepared to give."

Myra patted Allison's arm again, encouraging her to continue as she worked at

processing the information Allison was vol-
unteering.

"A young woman called on the phone
one day. The children were being so ram-
bunctious. I had worked all day and was
tired and trying to cook and do laundry,
and she said she wanted to come and
see me to talk about Geoffrey. I don't know
why I allowed it, but I did. She was so
beautiful. She wore makeup, and her hair
was so chic. She was dressed like a model
and had diamonds in her ears and on her
wrists and fingers. My daughter asked me
when she left if she was a princess.

"I cried all night and couldn't go to work
the next day. I just stayed home with the
children and played with them the entire
time. The princess's name was Pamela
Adamson. Lady Pamela Adamson. She
said Geoffrey wanted a divorce but wasn't
able to face me. She said I could have the
children. Mind you, she said I could have
*my own* children. She said I could
have the house, cottage, actually, as long
as I continued to pay for it. She said Geoffrey would send me a check every month
to help support the children. I told her to
get out of my house and never come

back. I also told her in no uncertain terms what she could tell Geoffrey. That was just a week before Geoffrey had his accident. It's probably all my fault. His mind was on her and me and the children, and not on what he should have been doing."

"Dear God," was all Myra could think of to say.

"All I wanted was to see Geoff, to tell him if he wanted a divorce, it was okay. I don't want a husband who doesn't love me. But I was hoping he would love the children and want to be part of their lives. I wanted that so desperately, but I don't think he cares one whit about them. How do you tell your children their father doesn't love them? That was an issue with Geoff when his mother told him about . . . that man you came here with. I am sorry I was rude to you when we spoke earlier. I just don't know what to do."

She was sobbing, so Myra gathered her into her arms and tried to soothe her the best she could.

"And you still love Geoffrey?"

"Yes. No. Oh, I don't know. I loved the man I married. He was so kind, so nice to me. We had such wonderful times. He was so full of life. So dashing. He loved flying and was decorated many times. When the children were born, he was so proud. At least that's the way it seemed at the time. Then his mother died, and he changed overnight. He wasn't the same man anymore. His mother told him about . . . the man you came with. He couldn't accept or handle it. He started to drink. Then there were the women. Not just one or two but a whole string of them. Mum told me about them, so I'm not sure if it's true or not. She never liked Geoff, but mothers don't lie to their children no matter how old they are, so in the end I accepted it, and Geoff knew I knew. He started giving me less money and I had to get a job and put the children in nursery school. Pilots don't make all that much money, and he needed more and more to support his flamboyant lifestyle.

"Then the health issues started, and he came back home for about a year until he was on the mend. We . . . we got along a little better, and he promised so many things. Then when the doctors told him he could go back to his squadron, it started all over again."

Myra sensed movement out of the corner of her eye. She turned to see Charles standing on the path that led to the front door. Unconsciously, she gripped Allison's arm a little tighter. She knew the news was bad, she could see it in the droop of Charles's shoulders. He shook his head from side to side. It was over.

Allison took that moment to look up and wipe at her eyes. She saw what Myra saw. If Myra's grip on her arm hadn't been as firm as it was, she would have slid to the wet ground.

"You can handle this," Myra said gently but firmly. "I'm right here beside you. I won't let anything happen to you. Now, if you want to see your husband one last time to say good-bye, that man standing there will arrange it."

Her voice shaky, Allison looked up at Myra. "Geoffrey said good-bye to me a long time ago. I just want to go home now to my children. Thank you for . . . for talking to me."

"Look at me, Allison. What you say may well be true, that Geoffrey said good-bye a long time ago. Obviously you didn't respond back then. You need to say your good-bye now. Later, you'll regret it if you don't."

There were no more tears, but Allison's eyes were weary and red-rimmed. "I should never have allowed them to bring me here, but at the time it seemed I had no choice. Well, I have a choice now, and I'm choosing not to go in there to say good-bye. That time has passed for me. The person in there," she said, waving her arm toward the house down the path, "is someone I used to know. And, yes, I'm bitter, but I have every right to be bitter. I'm sorry, I don't even know your name. If you told me, I've forgotten it. Thank you again."

"It's Myra, Allison. Are you sure in your heart this is the way you want it to end?"

Allison straightened her shoulders, buttoned her lightweight coat, settled her shoulder bag more firmly on her shoulder, and turned away, calling over her shoulder, "I'm sure. I don't want anything to do with this place or these people. I'll walk or catch a ride."

Myra was about to run after her when she felt Charles's hand on her arm. "Let her go, Myra. They will see that she gets home to her children."

"But . . ."

Charles's voice turned to steel. "I said, let her go."

Myra whirled around, her own tone matching Charles's but with even more of an edge. "You are not talking to one of *your people,* Charles, and you do not ever, as in *ever,* tell me what to do, when to do it, or how to do it. That's another way of saying 'kiss my ass.'" Without another word she ran after Allison Barnstable.

When she caught up to Allison, she was stunned to hear her say, "We won't get far. They'll come after us and take us back. You do know that, right?"

Myra did know that so she merely nodded. Within minutes two golf carts appeared out of nowhere and both she and Allison were bodily picked up and put into them. Allison's expression clearly said *I told you so.*

Angry beyond words, Myra lashed out one more time at Charles, who was sitting in the second golf cart. "He wasn't who you wanted him to be, Charles. I want to go home, and I want to go home now. And by home I don't mean a hotel room on this side of the *pond.* If you don't arrange it right now, this very minute, I will make a phone call to *MY people,* who will be here to take you and *your people* on. Actually, I already notified them, and they're waiting for me to call back, and if I don't call back, it's—how do you and *your people* say it?—it's a go?" she lied with a straight face.

"Myra, you don't understand. This is not America. They do things differently over here. There are things I am not at liberty to tell you, and I'm sorry about that, but that's just the way it is." He might as well have said, *"Now be a good girl and go sit down until I tell you to get up."*

Myra huffed and puffed. "I'm sorry about that, too, Charles. I want to go home now. Allison wants to go home to her children. What part of that don't you understand? As far as I'm concerned, you can stay here for the rest of your life. But this young lady needs to tend to her children, and I want to get back to mine."

"And that will happen but not right this moment. There are things that need to be taken care of first. You'll be on your way by nightfall."

Allison dug her fingers into Myra's arm.

"And Allison?"

"Mrs. Barnstable will be taken to her home shortly, but before that happens, there are people who need to talk to her."

"What you mean is, people need to try and brainwash her. Say it, Charles. Say it out loud."

"Myra . . ."

Angry beyond words, Myra lashed out again. "Your knight in shining armor was all rusty, Sir Malcolm. It's too late to shine that armor up, but you're going to do the next best thing, aren't you? We both know how that works. As Kathryn would say, 'You backed the wrong horse.'"

Charles's expression was cold and forbidding. "That was a low blow, Myra."

"Ha! You ain't seen nothing yet, Sir Malcolm," Myra said, using another of Kathryn's favorite expressions.

Myra drew her line in the sand. "From here on in, Sir Malcolm, refer to me as 'Mrs. Rutledge.' Now go back to *your people* and tell them I'm not the pushover you thought I was. Remember that call I made. Even you, Sir Malcolm, don't want to go up against my Sisters. They'll chew you up and spit you out before you can count to three."

Myra reached for Allison's arm, who was staring at her like she'd just sprouted a second head. "Who are you, really?" she whispered. "That man is afraid of you, isn't he?"

"I certainly hope so. We'll talk about that another time. For now we have some time to pass. You were going to show me some pictures of your children. Let's talk about them for now.

"Lord, I wish I had some coffee," Myra muttered over and over as she led Allison back into the dreary, dark building.

"Then let's make some. There's coffee in the kitchen. I think I could use some myself," Allison said. "By the way, who is Kathryn?"

"I didn't see any coffee. Show me where it is. Kathryn is . . . a friend back in the States."

"Is she like you, outspoken and with a good heart?"

"Kathryn is one of a kind. Yes, she's outspoken, and she has a wonderful, big heart. She has a dog named Murphy, who is her shadow. She had a terrible experience in her life, then her husband died. It took her many years to come back to the land of the living. She's a wonderful . . . friend. Do you have friends?"

"Not really," Allison said as she watched Myra spoon coffee into a coffeemaker that had been hidden in one of the cupboards. "When Geoff and I were first married we had friends, other pilots and their wives. Life was so exciting back then. But they were moved frequently, then the children came, and a new set of friends came along, other mothers with their husbands, but they were too dull for Geoff. Then, they, too, faded away. I was always too tired to pursue friendships, and when there would be time for me to entertain, Geoff would be gone. I'm chatty with a few of my neighbors, but that's about it."

As the women waited for the coffee to drip into the pot, Myra asked the question that had been bothering her the most. "What will you do now?"

"I'm not sure. What I do know is I can't go back to my mum's house. My father isn't well, and he takes a lot of care, not that Mum minds. The children bother my father, they make too much noise, they run up and down the steps, and that annoys him. I have some savings, and I'm sure Geoff had some insurance. As far as I know, the Royal Air Force takes care of its own. At least I hope that's still the way it is. I'll think about all of that after I get through the funeral."

"Do you have a passport, Allison?"

"Yes, of course, and so do the children. Geoff said it was mandatory. Actually, two years ago, after a particularly randy episode of Geoff's that almost became public, he promised us a trip to the States, but it never came off. Why do you ask?"

"No reason. I was just curious."

Myra poured coffee into delicate bone china cups and held one out to Allison. They carried their coffee over to the corner of the kitchen, where a high bar table sat.

"Tell me about Geoff's father. Tell me everything so I can understand why my husband changed once he found out about him. I need to know. For my own sanity."

So, Myra told her. Everything.

# Chapter 16

Jack looked over at Harry, and said, "Let's go over the plan one more time."

The look Harry shot Jack was so deadly, Jack actually cringed. "Listen, you dipshit, we don't have a plan. We never had a plan. We talked about a plan, but we never developed one. So, what the hell *plan* are you talking about?"

Jack was in awe. Harry never said more than five words at one time, and not even that many if he could condense them to two. That had to mean his buddy was pissed. To the teeth. He debated if he should try to cajole good old Harry, then thought better of the idea.

Jack opted to back off. "What I meant to say was, we need to *make* a plan. If we can't come up with a plan, then we need to at least discuss our entrance into the compound. Even Delta Force has a plan before they invade and take charge of things."

Harry sniffed. "You mean we aren't going to go in like a herd of stampeding bulls? Gee whiz, Jack, you're losing your edge."

Jack sniffed in return. "You talk too damn much, Harry."

Ted took a moment to look up from texting, and said, "You guys need to get a referee, and, no, I do not want the job. Neither does Espinosa." Tongue in cheek, he said, "Maybe you should talk to the girls since this is their deal, and stop worrying about a plan."

Espinosa weighed in. "Yeah. You really should talk to the girls, Jack."

"Fine! Fine!" Jack sniped. "We'll talk to the girls. In the meantime, Ted, check out what's in the box those make-believe National Guard types left us. Maybe they threw in some grenades or something equally devilish for us to play with."

"And if I find some, what should I do with them?" Ted asked curiously.

"Pull the damn pin and sit on it. What's with you, Ted? You just tell me what's inside, okay, and treat the box like it's dynamite with a lit fuse."

"Everyone is so testy this evening," Espinosa said as he snapped a picture of Jack's retreating back and sent it on to Maggie.

"What's our problem?" Nikki asked.

Jack wanted to tell the love of his life there was no problem. He wanted to tell her he would single-handedly take on the whole HOE compound while she and the other Sisters watched him work a miracle. That's what a fool Jack Emery would have said, but that night he was feeling like the emperor of all fools, so he simply said, "We need a plan."

Nikki's lips tightened into a grim line. "I thought you had a plan."

"Yeah, I thought he had a plan, too, but he doesn't," Harry said, looking everywhere but at Jack.

"We can't go anywhere without a plan," Ted said, unhappiness ringing in his voice.

"I keep saying the same thing, but no one listens," Espinosa said.

Jack reared up and exploded. "Okay! Enough with the damn plan poop already! We don't have a plan because Charles is not here. That means we all have to pool our ideas and come up with something that will work. Everyone is going in different directions. It's chaos. Do you hear me, total chaos! Now, before we drive out of this place, I want to hear a damn plan, and I want to know it will work. Otherwise, we sit this one out! Now, who wants to go first?" he demanded.

"It's night vision gear and camo outfits," Ted said.

Jack snapped. "What is?"

"You told me to look in the box, so I looked in the box. No grenades, no rocket launchers. It's all night vision gear. I'm not a member of Delta Force, but I do watch movies, and that's what it looks like to me. And the suits. You know, those . . . speckled brown-and-white things like the guys in the Humvee were wearing. Harry, you're going to have to give up those thong sandals you wear because if you want to be coordinated, the desert boots go with the speckled suits. Same color, actually. Maggie always says you have to coordinate if you want to make a fashion statement."

Harry turned around and flicked his thumb and forefinger at Ted's nose. Ted slid to the ground. Espinosa took a step backward as he peered down at his colleague. He snapped a picture and sent it on to Maggie.

"Harry, you have to stop acting independently and stay with the program. That wasn't nice. Now, where were we?" Jack asked as he looked down at Ted, who appeared to be sleeping peacefully.

"Is the 'program' the same as the plan that you don't have?" Harry growled.

"We were discussing the fact that we do not have a plan," Alexis said as she winked at Espinosa, who immediately got all flustered and forgot to take her picture. "But I see a glimmer of something here. We have uniforms and boots, so that will make us look official. Caps are in there, too, I'm sure. We can all look like a squad, and if we show up in those police cruisers and the two SUVs, we should at least *look* official. I think that's a good jumping-off place, do you all agree?" she asked, deliberately looking at her Sisters as opposed to the guys. She winked again at Espinosa, who got even more flustered. But not so flustered that he forgot to snap her picture in full wink.

Maggie immediately texted him.

**"She's flirting with you, you fool. What happened to Ted? Is he sick?"**

Espinosa ignored the question about Ted and texted,

**"How do you know that?"**

**"I know because I'm a woman. You snooze you lose, Espinosa. Tell Ted I'm going to kick his ass for sleeping on the job—and dock his pay."**

Emboldened with Maggie's assessment, Espinosa moved a little closer to the circle of women and made a kissing motion in Alexis's direction. She grinned and winked again. Espinosa felt faint and almost joined Ted, but he got his wits about him just as the previously inert man struggled to his knees. The night was still young.

"Good thinking, Alexis," Jack said. "Yep, there are some of those soft-billed caps in here," he said, poking around inside the box. Soldiers kind of stuff them in their pockets. "Dress-up time, ladies and gents!"

Ted Robinson was on his feet. He massaged his nose and looked over at Harry. "I forgive you, you son of a bitch, because you know not what you do. Even though you know I don't have a spleen, you knocked me out, not knowing if I would succumb or not, but that's okay because your ass will fry in hell someday for what you just did to me. But, I'm not the type to hold a grudge, so, like I said, I forgive you."

Harry said, "Huh?" just as Ted's hand snaked out.

Ted gave Harry's nose a playful tweak, then stepped back. "I guess I touched you, huh? The untouchable Harry Wong was touched by a reporter he just decked, the same reporter who has no spleen. Not that my nose has anything to do with my spleen. I'm just saying."

"That's enough!" the Mighty Mouse ninety-pound stick of dynamite known as Yoko roared.

Harry didn't exactly cower at his beloved's words, but he moved a little closer to Jack.

"Suit up!" Annie bellowed.

They all scrambled to find suits that would fit. The boots were another problem. In the end Yoko and Harry had to keep their sandals on since the remaining boots were several sizes too large and would have fallen off their feet.

"Now what?" Isabelle asked as she twirled and whirled for everyone's benefit.

"You realize, of course, that we are going to look like aliens when we put on those night vision goggles," Kathryn said.

"Don't you get it?" Annie asked. "That's part of the plan we're coming up with. We're going to scare those people to death. That is the *PLAN,* isn't it, Jack?" Her tone sounded so fretful, Jack wanted to cry.

"I'm thinking that'll work," Jack said. Harry made a hateful sound that stopped Jack in his tracks. "We just have to develop it a little more. The plan, that is."

Nikki looked adoringly at Jack. Then

she shook her head from side to side, as much as to say, *"How stupid is that?"*

It was Jack's turn to cower next to Harry, who tried to push him away. "Get away from me. You're too stupid for me to admit I know you, you can't even wear men's boots."

"What do National Guard troops do?" Ted asked.

"They stand around waiting to get a call to do something, and they get paid while they wait," Espinosa said. "The women are allowed to wear tons of makeup, false eyelashes, and lipstick, and the guys are allowed to be fat with beards, and they can wear earrings. They go away for two weeks every year for some kind of training. Pretend training, because they're all out of shape. I saw that in a movie one time. No one takes them seriously. In the movie, which was a comedy, by the way, no one took them seriously. Would you want those wannabe pretend soldiers trying to put out a fire or pulling you out of a raging river? Jesus, think about it. What if while some female pretend soldier is pulling you out of a raging river her eyelashes fall off? Poof, you're gone while she tries to find her eyelashes. What do you think she's going to try and save? Not your sorry ass, that's for sure."

"When you put it like that, the short answer is no," Ted said. He held up his hand to make a point. "Those people at the HOE compound don't know about the beards, the earrings, and the eyelashes, so they'll just think we're like, you know, the marines, or the cavalry, and they're going to get arrested. Right?"

"Oh, yeah," Alexis drawled as she tilted her head to better see Espinosa, who she thought looked quite cute in his camo gear. She wiggled her eyebrows and winked.

Espinosa got flustered all over again as he jammed his hands into his pockets to steady them. He looked down at his BlackBerry. "Maggie says for the Sisters to line up, caps off. She wants a sweeping bow. For the *before* and *after* pictures. She wants you to look menacing. That's it! Perfect!" A nanosecond later, the pictures were on their way to Maggie.

"I think we should leave now that everyone has aired their grievances," Annie said smartly as she opened the passenger door of Sheriff Finn's cruiser. "Look at

it this way, girls, this is first-class compared to that hearse we took our last ride
in when we were in Las Vegas."

Espinosa took the gentleman's approach
and waited for the women to pile into the
cars. One mighty shove from Ted, and
he almost landed in Alexis's lap. Ted
slammed the door so quickly, Espinosa
had to scramble and, finally, since he was
bigger, maneuvered so that Alexis was
forced to sit on his lap. He grew light-headed
at her scent, which made him think of warm
sunshine and wildflowers. He inhaled so
deeply he coughed, his face turning purple.

Alexis swiveled around and pounded
him on the back, a wicked smile on her
face. "So, Joseph, whatcha been doing
lately besides taking pictures?" Alexis
purred, her face as close to his as it could
be without actually touching.

Espinosa wondered what kind of
comeback Ted or even Jack would make
to a comment like that. Jack would have
some clever remark, while Ted, who was
absolutely no authority on women, would
say something stupid. He was probably
better off on his own. "Just waiting for a
moment like this."

"Aahhh," she said before turning around to face front.

Espinosa rather thought his answer was on the money. "Aahhh" sounded like Alexis liked his response. He felt like beating his chest and yelling, "Me, Tarzan!" Of course that was stupid, and something Ted would do, so he just sat there with his arms around Alexis and waited for his next big moment.

In the lead car, Annie was staring out at the dark night. "Jack, when we get inside the compound, what are you and the boys going to do? I don't know why I say this but I'm thinking the compound is going to be pitch-dark. I know, I know, we have the night vision goggles and a rough map of the place, but what exactly do you see yourself doing?"

"Rounding up all the males while you girls round up the women. I think the men should be separated from the women. I don't really have a clue what we should do about the children, to be honest with you, Annie. As far as I know the sect is not into violence and weapons, that kind of thing. They brainwash, they connive to get money illegally and the leaders live high on the dole. Nikki will be taking on their financials and wreaking a little havoc where all that's concerned. We have the element of surprise on our side. The first thing we have to do is confiscate any and all cell phones, and I suspect there aren't but a few of them. That guy, the one they call the Prophet, Evanrod by name, is tight on control. He'll probably try to call Sheriff Finn or the deputies, but we have their phones. I tossed them on the floor in the back. Before you ask, I turned them off."

In the backseat, Kathryn unbuckled her seat belt and leaned forward. "How are we going to utilize the two eighteen-wheelers that are in the compound?"

"They're full of pumpkins," Jack said. "How many do you think one of those rigs can hold, Kathryn?"

"Thousands," was the immediate response.

"How many people?"

"Adults or children?" she snapped.

"Either/or," Jack shot back.

"Maybe seventy-five kids, and you'd still have room for pumpkins. If you're talking adults, probably the same number plus some pumpkins. Give or take a few.

They won't be comfortable. Is that your plan?"

"It might have to be. Lizzie is supposed to get back to me shortly about a route to Vegas, where Cosmo Cricket is setting up a safe haven. I'm sorry, but I just don't know, Kathryn."

Nikki's voice was cheerful when she said, "Not to worry, Jack, this is in no way your fault. We're pretty good at winging things. I don't see this time being an exception. Actually, this time around we number ten, as opposed to our usual six, and I'm not counting Bert, who will be on the outside by the gates. I think that, all things considered, we're good to go. You know, some scientist once said, 'For every action there is a reaction.' I think maybe it was Einstein. We just have to wait for their action, then we do our thing. Everything is going to depend on how we're greeted and how much opposition we encounter."

Jack wondered why Nikki's little speech didn't make him feel more comfortable.

"Okay, according to this GPS, we're exactly one mile from the gates. So far so good."

"Yeah, so far," Kathryn muttered.

# Chapter 17

Lizzie Fox stared at the text message coming in on her BlackBerry from Cosmo Cricket. She wanted to dance a jig at what she was reading. True to his word, Cosmo had a safe haven waiting for whoever Lizzie was sending his way. Annie's project was a work in progress. He'd asked that she send Nellie and Elias immediately to Las Vegas to be the welcoming committee for whatever guests were coming his way. And gave instructions for Nellie to call Paula Woodley. Not only did Cosmo have a safe haven, he had what he called "getaway vehicles" of all descriptions.

Lizzie laughed out loud as she sent the message on to Jack Emery before she responded.

Lizzie felt warm all over, her face flushed a rosy pink as she typed in cryptic letters that, translated, meant she loved him so much her toenails ached. She hoped she never came to regret the day she'd involved this dear, sweet man in her nefarious doings. Childishly, she crossed her fingers and grinned from ear to ear. Cosmo could handle anything, and if things ever went south, he'd handle that, too. That was a given as far as she was concerned.

Next, she called Maggie at the *Post* for an update. As she waited for Maggie to pick up, she forwarded Cosmo's text message. That would put them all on the same page, she hoped.

When Maggie answered, Lizzie asked, "Anything I should know, Maggie, before I head out to the courthouse to file my lawsuits? I hope to be on my way back to Vegas in case Cosmo needs some help, which I don't think he will, but I want to see him. I should be back in Washington in three or four days. Has anyone heard from Myra? No snafus along the way? By the way, your front pages have been sizzling. We're going to have to buy you a crown because, lady, you are the Journalistic Queen, bar none."

"Thanks, but it ain't over till it's over, and everyone is home safe and sound. Not a word has come through from Myra or Charles to me. Annie said she talked to her, but Myra was just being Myra, which means she didn't give up anything. We're all still pretty much in the dark as far as she and Charles are concerned. I don't know if that's a good thing or not, but if my feet were put to the fire for my honest opinion, I'd say it's not a good thing. This is the part I hate, the waiting," Maggie said.

Lizzie smiled to herself. Murphy's Law— what can go wrong will go wrong. "Yeah, me, too. Gotta go, Maggie, someone is knocking on my door."

Lizzie frowned. She wasn't expecting company. She made her way to the door and looked through the small magnified peephole and was stunned to see Marion Jennings. She unlocked the door and motioned for the young woman to come in. A chill ran up and down her spine at the expression on Marion's face. "What's wrong?"

"Maybe nothing. I . . . I didn't tell you something. I don't know why I didn't. I'm sorry, but . . . the others said I needed to come back and tell you. One of those young pregnant girls is my sister. She just turned thirteen a few months ago. I begged my mother, my real mother, when I left, not to give Sara to those . . . those men. She wouldn't even talk to me when she found out I was leaving. As far as she's concerned, I no longer exist. They are going to try and tell you she's older, but she isn't. What that means is, she was promised to someone before she even became a teen. When I left she was playing with a rag doll. She was just a little girl."

Lizzie wrapped Marion in her arms. "So what you're saying is, you want us to get your sister out of there and not leave her behind for the FBI and the authorities to decide her fate. Is that what you're saying?"

"Yes. She's a baby having a baby. It's not right. I'll be able to take care of her and the baby if you can get her to me. I'll just have to work harder. I'm sorry I didn't tell you. I don't know why I didn't."

Lizzie nodded. "And your mother?"

Marion's expression froze. "I don't much care. She didn't care about me, and she doesn't care about Sara. She didn't care about any of us. I don't want to talk about her anymore. Good-bye, Miss Fox, and thank you again for all your help."

Lizzie locked the door. She walked back to one of the two chairs in the room and sat down. She dropped her head into her hands. How could a mother allow such things to happen to her children? Lizzie sat like that for a long time, tears rolling down her cheeks. It was all so wrong, and no one did anything about it. Well, maybe that would all change in a matter of a few hours.

Lizzie bounced up off her chair. No damn *maybe* about it. It *would* change, she'd make sure or die trying, if it came to that. She wished she knew what was going on out at the HOE compound.

Her satellite phone in hand, Lizzie ripped off a message to Jack, explaining her visit from Marion Jennings. She ended the cryptic message with:

**"The girl's name is Sara. Even if she's kicking and screaming and her mother is threatening you, do not leave that girl behind."**

Less than fifty miles away, Jack Emery read Lizzie's message in the dim light of the sheriff's cruiser just as he was reaching up to the visor to press the remote that would open the HOE compound gates. He turned around and spoke to the girls. "Lizzie said we are *not* to leave a girl named Sara behind. She's Marion Jennings's teen sister, one of the pregnant girls. We're to take her kicking and screaming if we have to. And she says to ignore the mother."

"Which one is she?" Nikki asked.

"Check the pictures Pearl sent on to Maggie. If she didn't give a description, we at least know her name," Annie said. "What are you waiting for, Jack? It's time to kick some ass and take names later. Did I say that right, Kathryn?"

"You did, Annie. What time is it?"

"Almost nine o'clock," Nikki said. "Night vision goggles, everyone."

"Drumroll, please," Jack said in a jittery-sounding voice as he pressed the remote. "Wait just a damn minute here. We didn't decide if we want the sirens and the blue lights or do we just drive in like we belong?"

A ripe discussion followed as Jack pulled ahead so that all vehicles were inside the compound before the gates closed.

"It's the boy in you to want the sirens and the blue lights," Annie said in an indulgent, motherly voice. "We go in like the vigilantes we are. We have the element of surprise so we need to capitalize on that surprise. That's the bottom line."

Jack was disappointed. He'd always wanted to ride in a police car with the flashing lights and siren wailing. He gave in gracefully.

Annie had the map Deputy Clyde had drawn up. "It's a straight two-mile-long road till you come to a long square building. It's the worship center, school, and kitchen. A quarter of a mile to the left is the Prophet's house. There are no buildings around it. There is a flagpole and a huge bell in the center to the right of the worship center. When the Prophet wants to talk to everyone, he rings the bell, and everyone assembles around the flagpole.

"The flag is not really a flag but a huge piece of cloth with the Prophet's picture stitched on it. They lower it at sundown and raise it at sunrise.

"Deputy Clyde said they always park by the flagpole. Behind the worship center is the children's dormitory, ages three to twelve. The baby building is next to it. The women live in a two-story brick building to the left of the baby building. The gardens or the fields where they grow produce is the acreage beyond all the buildings. According to Deputy Clyde, that's where we should find those two eighteen-wheelers. If I understand this correctly, there is a boys' dormitory close to the Prophet's house, and the girls' dormitory is next to the two-story brick building. Both dormitories have house-mothers," Annie said. The men's building is off to the left.

"So what's the plan?" Nikki asked.

"We park the cars in a circle. I get out and ring the bell. I get back in the car, and we wait till everyone assembles. We continue to sit inside the cars so they all start to worry. We keep our cars dark. Nothing like making them sweat a little."

"And then?" Kathryn asked.

"Then we take charge," Annie said, excitement ringing in her voice. "Call Harry and the others to give them the plan. It's not much of a plan, but it's still a plan. Then you ring the bell."

Jack followed Annie's instructions. He looked around in the dark night, expecting someone to accost him, but everything was quiet. There were few stars out because of the dense cloud cover that hid the slice of moon that had been visible on the drive to the compound. He took a second to wonder if it might rain soon. Everything in the world looked green to him.

It took all of Jack's strength to swing the heavy ball that dangled inside the huge iron bell that was every bit as big as the Liberty Bell in Philadelphia. He scurried back to the cruiser after two thundering clangs.

Suddenly the dark compound came to life. Lights blazed in all directions. In the formerly quiet night, they could hear doors opening and slamming shut, followed by the sound of pounding feet.

Annie looked down at her special phone, which was vibrating in her hand. Myra. She took a deep breath. "Not now, Myra," she said. "I'm rather busy right now. No, Myra, there is no one else who can talk to you right now. We're all extremely busy. We just entered the compound, and those . . . people are scurrying around like ants. No, there is nothing you can do unless you can launch a few hellfire missiles in this direction. I know all about satellites in the sky that are watching our every move. Plan? You want to know what our plan is." Annie grappled in her mind for a suitable response. "Our plan is, we have two tractor trailers, the kind Kathryn used to drive, full of pumpkins. Good-bye, Myra!" Annie shoved the phone back into her pocket as she struggled to pay attention to what was being said while wondering about Myra's strange tone of voice.

"If you don't count the kids, I estimate there are about a hundred people standing around that flagpole," Nikki said. "More women than men. That's good for us. Oh, oh, the guys are stepping forward, shielding the women. The Praetorian Guard?" She tittered.

"Could be," Jack said. "They're creeping forward. This reminds me of that movie where aliens made imitation people in pods. This whole place is beyond creepy."

"I saw that movie," Annie said. "There are no pods here unless you count the pumpkins. Now you can turn on the siren and the blue lights. On the count of three, out we go. Jack, Harry, Ted, and Joseph, take the lead. One! Two! Three!"

The man advancing toward them was the Prophet, with his people close behind, and they stopped ten feet from the police cruisers. "You aren't Sheriff Finn!" he said.

"No kidding! What gave it away?" Jack asked. Out of the corner of his eye he could see Ted's busy fingers while Espinosa clicked away.

Jack heard someone say, "Live from the Heaven on Earth compound."

He thought it was Espinosa, but it could have been Ted for all he knew.

"Who are you?" the Prophet demanded.

"Me? I'm just some guy who doesn't

like what you do out here," Jack said, ripping off his night vision goggles. The others followed suit.

"What I or my people do out here is none of your concern. You are trespassing on private property. I'm asking you to leave. You're frightening my people, and I will not tolerate it."

"I didn't see any NO TRESPASSING signs on the ride in. So call somebody if you're worried," Jack said. "Somebody other than the sheriff and his two deputies because they left on vacation. They said they were going to a less stressful environment. They gave us these beautiful vehicles. Wasn't that nice of them? I want you all to turn around. We're going to march nicely, two across, to the house of worship, where we'll decide what to do with you."

The Prophet straightened his shoulders and said, "I will do no such thing. I want you to leave right now. Who is that evil-looking person?" he asked, pointing to Harry.

"Harry! Harry's a terrorist. If you don't do what I say, he will make your brains come out your nose."

The Prophet blinked and backed up a step. "You're the Devil!" He turned to his people and, in the voice he probably used for his sermons, said, "You see, this is the Devil at work! I told you the people on the outside would try to drive us away from our homes and our religion because they don't understand it. They will be forever damned, and there will be no salvation for any of them. I want you to all be strong because we will prevail."

"Cut the bullshit, you creep, and do what this guy tells you, or you'll be picking your brains off your upper lip," Kathryn bellowed.

A hiss of noise from the women could be heard at such blasphemy coming from another woman. The men started to mumble among themselves. Harry stepped forward, his arms outstretched. Ted and Espinosa were working their phones industriously.

The Sisters separated as though they were corralling a herd of sheep. The women strained and struggled to follow the Prophet as they waited for him to tell them what to do.

"Don't look at that asshole," Kathryn

said. "He won't be giving you orders ever again. Right now, you take your orders from us. I'm only going to tell you this once. Move your goddamn feet and head to that female dormitory." If she'd had a whip, she would have cracked it on the ground. The women stood rooted to the ground.

Harry reached the Prophet and grabbed his ear. "Obviously *your* women are attempting to resist taking any orders from *my* women. Tell them to do what we say, or you'll be chewing on your ear."

"Harry, Harry, the charisma you exude just astounds me. Unfortunately, this herd of sheep doesn't appear to appreciate the jewel that you are like the rest of us do," Jack said.

Harry offered up a single-digit salute in Jack's direction. Jack guffawed.

"Do what they say," the Prophet said in a high-pitched tone that stopped just short of being a squeal.

Jack stopped and whistled shrilly between his teeth. Turning to the men he said, "Like the lady said, I'm going to tell you this once. Move to the worship house and make it snappy. When you get in there, you will sit down and not make a sound. Now move!"

The men and the young boys, the youngest around thirteen or so, moved. No one had to be told twice. Jack thought it strange that the women had been prepared to hold out but not the men. *Damn, what the hell kind of place is this?*

"Hey, Jack, this guy over here said we're Satan's disciples," Ted said.

"You have my permission to kick his ass for telling such a bold-faced lie."

Ted did what he was told. The man, who had enough blubber and facial hair to pass for a grizzly bear, stumbled and fell. Ted gave him another kick, and he sprawled forward. None of his people offered to help him.

"Please, God, don't let that man be one of those men the Prophet turns his celestial wives over to when he tires of them," Jack muttered.

Harry stood at the open door watching as the group of men and boys straggled into the worship center. He turned on every light switch he could find. The huge room was suddenly flooded with light. The congregants blinked at the blinding glare. Jack motioned to the rows and rows of metal chairs.

"Sit! Fold your hands. Do not move. Everyone under twenty-one years of age, sit to your left. Those of you who are older, sit to the right. You, Prophet, you sit up here, front and center. Pretend you're preaching to your people. That's good, sit right there under that ugly picture of yourself," Jack ordered.

"Espinosa, you getting all this?"

"You know it! I'd like a couple of the girls in here. I'm thinking Kathryn and maybe Alexis."

"That'll work. We'll hold the fort while you fetch them."

"Ted, I want you to check out the baby building. You can take some shots yourself and send them on. Keep track of the housemother," Jack said.

Then it was just Jack and Harry in the room with the men and boys.

Jack's phone vibrated. It was Nikki. "Tell them all except for the young ones to strip naked. Toss their clothes outside. I'm on my way to the Prophet's house. I'm going to need your help. Can Harry handle things there on his own?"

"Surely you jest. Be there in a few minutes."

Jack whispered to Harry, who grinned. "I'll call you if I need you."

Jack was at the door when he heard Harry say, "Everyone on their feet. That's good. Now strip!"

# Chapter 18

Annie, Nikki, Isabelle, and Yoko led the women into a huge room that was neat and tidy. Blinding overhead lighting suddenly came to life.

"I wonder who pays the electric bill way out here in the middle of nowhere. I didn't see any poles or wires on the way in," Annie said as she looked around at the women who were clustered together.

"Generators," Nikki said. "That has to mean propane. I guess they have it delivered. So much for backward living. I'm thinking these people only pretend to be from the Dark Ages when it suits them.

Look, I have to hit the Prophet's house
and see what I can do over there. Yoko,
you come with me. Annie, you and Isabelle
take over here. Call me if there's a problem. By the way, Annie, call me immediately if you hear from Avery Snowden. His
last call said his people would be here
sometime around ten. I don't know what
the plan is, so run with it if he shows up.
Ted or Espinosa can open the gates."

Within seconds, both Nikki and Yoko
were sprinting across the compound
toward the Prophet's house. Jack caught
up with them just as they bounded up the
two steps that led to a wide front porch.

The lights were already on when Jack
slammed the door behind him. "Wow!"
was all he could think of to say. Nikki and
Yoko echoed his sentiments.

"Guess the Prophet doesn't believe in
prairie living. This says to me the Prophet
indulges himself," Yoko said, looking
around at the costly furnishings.

"Some big bucks went into decorating
this place. I know furniture," Nikki said,
"and that couch and chairs had to set him
back about fifty grand. That's an oriental
carpet. Who knew prairie people even

knew about carpets, much less oriental. And a seventy-six-inch high def TV. There must be a satellite dish outside. Probably brings in over two hundred channels. Wonder if he invites the others to watch sports with him," she added, a distasteful expression on her face.

"Check this out," Jack said, motioning to a shelf that held stacks of CDs. "Five bucks says the Prophet has a porn library. Ah, yes, *Debbie Does Dallas. Peaches and Cream.* I think Debbie is Peaches. Peaches must be her nom de plume."

"Jack! We don't have time for this! Come on, we have to find that guy's study or office. The place where he does all his dirty dealings," Nikki said.

"Here it is!" Yoko shouted as she looked around at an array of electronic equipment that rivaled what Charles had on Big Pine Mountain. "This must be a bigger operation than we thought it was."

Nikki flexed her fingers. "I'll take the computer. It's a given that it is password-protected. I'll try and see if I can crack it. If not, you'll have to squeeze it out of him, Jack. Yoko, start going through the files, the drawers, and the closets. We need a list of every person in this compound. All the information you can gather up to take with us. If I can't crack the password, then we have to take the computer with us. And, this is really important, find the birth and death certificates. That's going to be crucial."

Jack walked back out to the main room. The log-cabin walls were adorned with colorful Chagalls. A fire was blazing brightly in the huge fieldstone fireplace. The mantel held framed photographs of the Prophet with various women in wedding dresses. Jack counted thirty-seven framed photographs. Above the mantel was a huge oil painting of the Prophet himself in a tuxedo, sitting on a throne. The only thing missing was a jeweled crown. A few trees in full foliage stretched almost to the ceiling. Several ferns and other bushy green plants were scattered about the huge room. They looked well tended. All in all, it was a pleasant, cozy room, as opposed to the dreary ambience of the other buildings in the compound.

Jack walked down a short hallway. "Girls! Girls! You have to come and check this out. Wooeee!" Jack said as he held

open the door to the bedroom so Nikki
and Yoko could see what he was seeing.
"Think harem, and this is it!"

Yards and yards of gauze adorned the
huge four-poster. Gossamer hangings decorated the windows. The smell of incense
was so powerful, Nikki sneezed.

Above the bed was another painting of
the Prophet but this time he was naked as
a jaybird, all his attributes, or lack thereof,
showing clearly.

"I'm thinking he was thinking he had a
rocket there. Or maybe a missile." Yoko
burst out laughing as she jumped up on
the bed and reached for the painting. She
had the back off the gilt frame, and within
seconds, the canvas rolled neatly. "I think
we should fly this on the flagpole. At half-
mast. I'm going to call over to the worship
house and have them send someone to
run this up the flagpole."

"Go for it," Nikki said as she headed
back to the computer room.

Even from where they were standing,
both Jack and Yoko could hear the furious sound of the clicking keys of the
computer.

"I was right, Jack," Nikki called, "this is

password-protected. Are you finding any-thing?"

"The guy is one sick bastard!" Jack said as he opened and shut drawers. "We need to set fire to that shrine to himself. I'll call Harry. There's a book here dated 1990. It has a list of names. It looks to me like there are only a handful of first names and just an initial for a last name. There are nineteen women named Julia, twenty-three named Mary, and forty-four named Sara. It goes on like that. There are all kinds of symbols and markings next to the names. It must be some kind of code." He turned away after Harry answered his phone. "Tell his highness we need the password for his computer. Don't take no for an answer, Harry."

While Jack waited for Harry to get back to him, he looked around and saw a pack of cigarettes in what he surmised was the bar area. Next to the cigarettes was a gold lighter engraved with a naked woman holding up her enormous breasts. He looked under the bar itself and saw a large rack holding fifty or so bottles of fine wine that he certainly couldn't afford.

He plucked a cigarette from the pack and lit it with the gold lighter. The flame almost singed his eyebrows. He tapped his foot as he waited for Harry to give him the password, but all he heard were squeals of outrage. He knew Harry was talking, but he couldn't hear what he was saying. Just Harry being extra nice, he assumed.

A sandy-haired young man opened the door and poked his head inside. It was obvious to Jack from the expression on the guy's face that he had never been in the Prophet's home. Jack wasn't sure what he was seeing—awe, revulsion, fright?

Yoko bounded out to the room, the rolled-up painting in her hands. "Take the picture off the flagpole and hang this one," she said sweetly as she unrolled it for the young man to see.

Jack thought the guy was going to faint at the sight of the picture on the canvas.

The guy, who said his name was John, turned away. "I can't do that!"

"Sure you can," Yoko said. "If you don't do as I say, I will personally hang *YOU* from the flagpole. By your dick. What's it going to be?"

John of the sandy hair reached for the painting as though he were reaching for a snake and backed out of the door.

"I sure hope those colors are water-proof," Yoko said as she scampered back to join Nikki.

"Jack, you there?"

Jack tossed his unfinished cigarette into the fireplace. "Talk to me, Harry."

"The password is *salvation.*"

"Is the son of a bitch still in one piece?"

"Depends on what you mean by one piece. He's minus his four front teeth. He's bleeding all over the place."

Jack sighed. "Anyone look like they might revolt?"

Harry laughed. Jack thought it was the most evil sound he'd ever heard.

"Not on my watch, buddy."

"Nik, the password is 'salvation.'"

A minute later he heard her say, "Okay, I'm in. Hey, my phone is vibrating. Will you get it, Jack?"

Nikki's phone glued to his ear, Jack continued to paw through the drawers of the Prophet's massive desk as he listened to the voice on the other end of her phone. He announced himself and waited.

"Avery Snowden, Mr. Emery. I have my demolition people with me along with my caravan. My ETA is ten minutes. Will the gates be open?"

*Demolition people? Caravan? Well, damn.* "They'll be open," Jack said, ending the call.

"That was Avery Snowden, and he said his ETA is ten minutes and he has his demolition people with him. Nik, did you hear what I just said?"

"Hmmm. I guess Annie won't need her hellfire missiles after all." A second later she was engrossed in what she was doing.

Jack called Harry again. "Now we need to know if those gates can be opened from here. Avery Snowden said his ETA is ten minutes. He said he has his demolition people with him. And a caravan."

"Does it mean this is part two of the plan we don't have?"

"Yeah, yeah, Harry, that's what it means. Hurry up, the clock is ticking. Snowden sounded like a mean sucker, so we don't want him and his demolition people to be

kept waiting. Ditto on the caravan, whatever the hell that is."

"Eat shit, Jack. Will it make you happy
if I go after the Prophet's bottom teeth?"

"It will make me positively giddy, old
buddy. How are the others holding up?"

Harry let loose with his evil laugh again.
"Believe it or not, *buddy,* they're waiting
for the women to rescue them."

"You talk too much. I'll hold on while
you . . . uh . . . get me the information I
need."

Jack walked around the main room trying to find a keypad of sorts, something
that would open the compound gates. He
couldn't find a thing. Shit, that had to
mean he was going to have to drive down
to the damn gates and open them himself. He heard a sharp whistle in his ear.
"Yeah?"

"Keypad is in the linen closet, right side,
second shelf."

"How many teeth did that cost the
Prophet?"

"Four more," Harry said lazily. "Just for
the record, I'm getting tired of doing your
dirty work."

"I'm going to make this up to you, Harry.

Yoko said to tell you she loves you," Jack added as he sprinted toward the bathroom. He found the keypad immediately and pressed the red button, not knowing or caring if the ten minutes was up or not.

Jack looked at the contents of the linen closet. Any woman would be proud to call it her own. Stacks of fluffy yellow and pink towels. Scented satin sheets, every color of the rainbow. Jars and jars of bath salts, perfumes, and powders. Another shelf held what looked like Frederick's of Hollywood fashions. Everything was sized extra small or small. Of course, most thirteen-year-olds would require small clothing. One whole shelf was devoted to fragrant candles. "Linen closet my ass," Jack muttered. This was a rape closet, pure and simple. On his walk back to where Nikki was glued to the computer, Jack found himself shaking with rage. He couldn't ever remember being so angry.

Blind with his rage, Jack called Annie and he was like a runaway train as he told her what he had found in the linen closet. "I want you to bring those goddamn women over here and show them this linen closet. I want to know how a mother could send her daughter to this den of iniquity and still sleep at night. Never mind, Annie, I'm just venting. There's no point, they've all been here at one time or another. They have to pay for this, Annie."

"And they will, Jack, they will. What are all those flashing lights outside?"

His anger under control, Jack said, "It must be Avery Snowden and his demolition crew. And his caravan. He called a few minutes ago. Do you know anything about that, Annie?"

"He's part of that plan we didn't have when we first got here. It's better than two trucks full of pumpkins, Jack. Remember, Snowden is Charles's right-hand man, so whatever he wants to do, I say we should just let him do it."

Jack walked out of the Prophet's house to the center of the compound, which was now so blinding white with light he wished for sunglasses. He looked up at the canvas painting of the Prophet snapping in the brisk breeze. "Serves you right, you asshole!" he muttered.

Coming toward him was a tall man dressed the way they all were, in camo outfits. He looked to be in his midfifties and no doubt retired from some secret gung ho Black Ops organization no one knew about. He sported a military haircut and was clean-shaven. His entire toned body shrieked professional something or other. Jack thought he looked bigger than a goddamn oak tree.

The man held out his hand. "Snowden," he said smartly.

Jack felt the urge to salute but jammed his hand in his pocket. "Emery," he said just as smartly.

Snowden turned slightly to indicate the eight men behind him. "These are my men. We can have this place rigged in two hours. Then we'll want another hour to go through each and every building to make sure they're all clear before we implode them. Detonation is three hours from now. That means one o'clock to you. Does that work for you, Emery? What about those pumpkins? I wasn't counting on the pumpkins. The de Silva woman said the pumpkins were part of the plan."

"Yeah, yeah, she did say that. Can we get back to the pumpkins later on? How . . . How much explosives did you bring?"

Snowden's eyes narrowed to slits. "If I

told you that, then I'd have to kill you. If we're finished here, Emery, my men have to get to work. You want those ambulances parked anywhere special?"

"Ah . . . I'm going to have to ask the . . . the de Silva woman." Jack wondered if he looked as stupid as he sounded.

"Three hours," Snowden called over his shoulder.

"I got it, three hours." Jack was glad the guy didn't go with that military time shit. He hated counting backward to figure the time. For some crazy reason, he felt the urge to salute again. Rather than stifle the urge, Jack walked over to the flagpole and snapped off a crisp salute to the naked man and his rocket's red glare swaying in the breeze.

"Who the hell is that?" Snowden asked Jack as he climbed into a military-style vehicle.

"No one you want to know." Jack laughed as he headed back to the Prophet's house.

# Chapter 19

"Jack, can you come here a minute? I have a major problem."

Jack sprinted into the Prophet's work-room and looked questioningly at Nikki. "What can I do?"

Nikki raised her hands. "This is beyond my immediate capabilities with our time frame. Call Maggie and ask her to call her friend Abner Tookus. He's that ace hacker everyone talks about. He's . . . he's helped us before. Give her the password to give to him and have him take everything off every one of these computers. We have

to take them all with us. Then you have to
call Lizzie and tell her not to file any of
those lawsuits. There's enough money
here to set all these people up somewhere for a good long time. I'm talking
food, housing, and intensive therapy, as
well as counseling. Once this place
implodes, there won't be anything here
for any of them except those damn pumpkins. What I'm not sure of is if one of the
other sects, or places, whatever you call
them, would come to rescue them if they
elect to stay behind.

"Tell Harry to call the doctor these
people use. That piece of garbage is not
going to be left behind. He needs to be
punished just like the rest of them. I'm sure
he has a remote that will let him enter the
gates. Have Espinosa or Ted escort him
in. We don't want him turning tail and running or calling someone before we take
this place apart. Then you have to call
Bert, and this is what you tell him . . ."

Jack walked away to make his calls.
He heard Nikki shouting for Yoko. All in a
day's work. He had to admit that when it
got down to the wire like this, his adrena-

line kicked into high gear. He could hear
the conversation between Nikki and Yoko
as he followed orders.

"Yoko, gather up all these cell phones.
How come this guy needs twelve
restricted cell phones? I bet those
women, and probably the men, the ones
who live inside this compound, don't even
know how to work these. For a peaceful
people—if you believe that crap he
spouts—how come he needs two guns
and a shotgun? Poachers? I-don't-think-so!

"As soon as I finish what I'm doing, I'll
disconnect, and we put everything into
the trunk of one of those police cruisers.

"You know what else, Yoko, this land is
free and clear. They paid cash for it ten
years ago. I'm going to print out a quit-
claim deed and the Prophet is going to
sign it over to his people. Lizzie can
finesse the legalities. The last thing we
have to make sure of is that Avery Snowden's people do not in any way harm the
cemetery in back of the buildings. That
must remain intact. I'm not sure about
this, but I think somewhere along the way
the authorities are going to be doing

some exhumations if they don't get the answers they want any other way.

"Okay, I'm done here," Nikki said as she started to unplug the computers lining the room. She shouted for Jack again and pointed at the computers. "We're going over to the women's building now. Meet us there." Her arms full of printouts, she waited for Yoko to gather up the last batch before they ran out of the building toward the cruisers, whose trunks were already open.

Five minutes later, both women rushed through the door of the women's dormitory.

Nikki looked from Annie to Isabelle, who just rolled their eyes and directed their gaze to the women seated in neat rows, their hands folded primly in their laps.

A wicked glint in her eye, Annie said, "They don't want to converse with us even though the Prophet told them to cooperate. They *say* they're worried about the children. They pretend to cry, but there are no tears."

"That's because they're not allowed to cry or show emotion," Yoko said. "They are not permitted to raise their voices, and they speak in almost a singsong tone. Their sole purpose in life is to service the men here sexually and procreate. In between doing that, they cook, clean, do the laundry, and work in the fields. That's it!"

Nikki looked to the left, to where the young pregnant girls were sitting. They all wore serious expressions as they tried to understand that their new home was under siege and what it might mean to them. She pulled the photo of Marion Jennings out of her pocket and looked at it. Then she looked at the girls as she tried to figure out which one was Sara, Marion's sister. "Which one of you is Sara? No, no, don't look at those women. You only look at me. You talk only to me. The Prophet said you are to do exactly what I say." Four girls raised their hands. Nikki blinked. So much for the name Sara. "Okay, girls, who is this?" she asked, holding up the picture of Marion Jennings. Only one girl looked fearful and turned her eyes from the picture.

Yoko took the girl's arm and led her across the room, where she sat her down.

"Where are Marion's children? Do you know?"

One of the women got up from her chair, a furious expression on her face. "Sara, do not speak with these people. They are from the outside. You know what the Prophet teaches us about outsiders."

Quicker than lightning, Annie had the woman by the hair and shoved her back in the chair. "You speak only when I tell you to speak and not one second before."

"Take me to the children, Sara. Marion wants to see her daughters, and you can make that happen. Come along," Yoko said.

"Is Marion outside?" the young girl asked as she got up to follow Yoko. "She promised to come back for me, but she didn't. I miss her."

"We're going to take you to where Marion is. Where's your mother?"

"I have a lot of mothers. Which one do you mean? A man in a truck was supposed to bring us here, but something happened to him, and some lady took us somewhere, then some other men brought us here."

"Where's your ... Where's your ... your ... husband?" Yoko could barely get the hateful words out of her mouth. This whole scene was too reminiscent of her own past.

"Back at that other place. I'm going to get a new husband after I have my baby."

"Like hell you are," Yoko sputtered. She'd heard enough. Right then, that very second, she wanted to kill someone. With her bare hands.

Back in the women's dormitory, Annie was moving up and down the aisles where the women were seated. "We're going to ask you some questions, and you would all be wise to answer them. Then we're going to tell you what's going to happen. After that, we're going to take you over to the worship center, where your men are, those devils who say you all belong to them.

"Nikki, call over to the worship center and tell the girls we can use their help for a little while. Who's watching the clock?"

"I am," Nikki said.

Jack's phone vibrated in his pocket. He flipped it open and waited.

"Snowden here!"

Jack couldn't resist as he again fought the urge to salute. "Emery here."

"Plane is forty-five minutes out. You have just enough time to get those kids into those ambulances. Don't worry if they're a little cramped. Once on the plane, they'll all be fine. My people are standing by the ambulances. Over and out."

Once again Jack couldn't resist. "My people will be ready for your people, Snowden."

Jack blinked and blinked again. "Well, shit!" he muttered as he drew Annie and Nikki aside and repeated Snowden's message. "I think this is part three of that plan we don't have."

Annie whistled sharply to get everyone's attention.

"Are there any mothers here who want to accompany their children? They'll be leaving in roughly thirty minutes. We'll require some proof of parenthood; otherwise, our people will fill in. I should tell you now, and please pay attention, in roughly two and a half hours this entire compound will be leveled to the ground. There will be no place for you to stay or live, and there will be no food. Well, there might be some pumpkins, but I can't be totally sure of that. One other thing, all those welfare checks you ladies have been getting . . . they're gone. No money will be coming in to support your Prophet's lifestyle or your own meager existence."

Annie walked over to the row of pregnant girls and looked at each and every one until she got to the end of the row. "According to the law, you are all underage. So, since those women over there," she said, pointing to the women who were seated in front of them, "seem to have a terminal case of the stupids, I want you all to get up now and go out to the flagpole. Do exactly what the people out there tell you to do, and you'll be fine."

"Do not move," one of the women, decked out in what looked like yards of forest-green sailcloth, said.

Nikki cuffed her upside the head, then ripped off a strip of duct tape from the roll and plastered it across her mouth. "Make one move to take it off, and I'll break your arm."

Alexis and Kathryn blew into the room, Alexis dragging her Red Bag. "We're all yours," she said breathlessly.

"You know what to do," Nikki said.

"I want to know something," Kathryn said, addressing the women. "Is it true that you don't own those ugly-ass dresses you're all wearing? Is it true you have one for the week and one for Sunday, and they belong to that jerk you all call the Prophet? You let that crackpot own your clothes! I guess so, since he owns you all body and soul. What damn fools you are.

"You ready, Alexis? Let's start with that one with the tape on her mouth. Wait! Where are Ted and Espinosa? Espinosa has to take this picture. Maggie is going to need before-and-after pictures."

The words were no sooner out of Kathryn's mouth when both men walked into the room. Espinosa started to click, knowing exactly what the caption would read when Maggie uploaded the pictures: PROFESSIONAL BABY MAKERS. Or, he grinned to himself, BALD PROFESSIONAL BABY MAKERS!

Nikki and Annie walked among the women taking the pins out of their hair. Annie stuck the pins in her pocket, knowing they would come in handy later on, and tied their hair into ponytails—some so long they reached down to the women's knees. Their hair was thick and luxurious, with no sign of chemicals having ever been used. "We'll save all this and donate it to the organization that makes wigs for cancer patients," Annie said. "I know, I know, with the exception of what we're going to need for ourselves."

The women were squirming and clutching at each other as Alexis first cut the hair just above the knot for the ponytails, then buzzed their heads. Annie wasn't sure if it was the loss of their hair or the fact that a black woman was in their midst doing the dirty deed. What she really couldn't understand was why none of them were crying or fighting back. What kind of people were these? Then she remembered seeing the interview Marion Jennings and the other girls had given. The answer was, they simply were not allowed to cry. Crying meant punishment, from the age of one year on. Brutal punishments.

The last woman waiting to be shorn threw her arms up and around her head as Alexis approached. "Remove yourself from my presence. You do not belong here. Do not touch me. You will be damned to hell for what you're doing. You will never see salvation!" she said dramatically.

"If you had put a little gusto in that declaration, I might have paid attention," Alexis said.

"Let me help," Nikki said, as she ripped off a second piece of duct tape from the roll. She slapped it across the woman's mouth and gave her a swat on the side of her head. The woman continued to struggle until Isabelle pressed down on one shoulder while Nikki took the other. The woman went limp as Alexis cut off the ponytail, then buzzed her hair.

"Just to show what an evil person I really am, I'm going to shave your eyebrows." And Alexis did so with a flourish.

"They're all yours, Joseph," Alexis said as she packed up her scissors and shaver and tossed them into her Red Bag.

Isabelle and Nikki started to fill pillowcases with all the shorn hair. When they were done, they had five pillowcases jammed full of hair. Jack picked them up and took them out to the cruiser, where

he plopped them down on top of the computers. He slammed the trunk, then dusted
his hands. He raced back inside to see
what else was going down.

Espinosa was busy sending off his pho-
tos to Maggie while Annie and Nikki were
herding the women toward the door.

"Be sure to march them past the flagpole," Jack told the girls, "and I want to
see them salute their Prophet. Espinosa,
make sure you get a good shot. You
should have enough light out there to set
this place on fire. Is Maggie drooling yet?"

"Oh, yeah! She said she's going to put
a tiny red star over that guy's privates. It
is a family paper, after all."

Jack guffawed as his phone vibrated
again. "Emery," he said smartly.

"Snowden here, Emery. You didn't tell
me those eighteen-wheelers were full of
pumpkins. We need to unload them. My
people are busy right now. What are
your people doing? More to the point,
what are you doing?"

Jack wanted to tell Snowden he was
getting ready to go over to wherever he
was to jam his foot up his ass, but he just

said, "I'm busy. And your point about the pumpkins is . . . ?" Jack looked across the compound to where he saw Ted yanking a guy out of a Mercedes-Benz. It had to be the doctor.

"My point is, the pumpkins have to be unloaded. How else are you going to transport all those young men you have in there? You need to help me out here, Emery. I can't do it all."

"Well, those pumpkins are part of the plan. Why can't those guys sit on top of them or something?"

"Far be it from me to upset your cockamamie plan, but if that's what you want, then herd those guys over here and tell them to saddle up. I want the trucks out of here before the implosion. Someday, Emery, I want you to tell me what part those pumpkins are playing in this little caper of yours. I've never seen such a wacko organization. Over and out!"

"Yeah, over and out, you rascal, you," Jack mumbled as he made his way over to Ted and the doctor.

"This guy's a bastard, Jack. He threatened to call in the National Guard, the governor, and the Prophet to make me sorry for my ways. That's the bad news. The good news is this little vehicle here is a Maybach 62. Sells for around $486,000. That's almost half a million bucks for this yokel. Business here in the HOE must be good. The other good news is, the title is in the glove compartment. We can have him sign it over to us right now. Along with what I bet is a very healthy bank account. He's got a laptop in the backseat. Want me to take it?"

"Oh, yeah, he won't be needing anything where he's going. March him past the flagpole, then take care of business. I have to take the young guys down to the pumpkin patch."

"Damn, did you finally figure out what to do with them?"

"Nah. I think they're just pumpkins. What's Maggie saying?"

Ted laughed. "Do you believe she's speechless?"

"Right now, right this minute, I believe anything anyone tells me. How old is this guy?"

"According to his driver's license he's sixty-four. Back there at the gate, after I beat the shit out of him, he said he had six celestial wives and one for real. And a few hotties here on the compound. You know, just to round out things."

"Son of a bitch!" Jack pulled back his arm and let it fly. The doctor/dentist/pervert crumpled to the ground. "I'd like to send this sorry sack of shit into orbit, but right now I don't have the time."

"Do you see what you just did, Jack? Now I have to drag his fat ass all the way to the worship center."

"Be sure you wake him up when you get to the flagpole."

"Yeah, yeah, yeah!"

# Chapter 20

The vigilantes huddled at the far end
of the room, their gaze never wavering
from the bald-headed women.

"Now what?" Kathryn asked Nikki.

"Now we take their DNA. Alexis has the
swabs. I just don't know what good it's
going to do. If they won't tell us their
names, and if we can't match it up to the
kids, where will that leave us?" Nikki asked.

"Look, let's just do it and let the authorities figure it out," Annie said "We don't
have the time to work them over. This
place is going to be leveled shortly. The
women won't go with us, and I don't see

how we can force them to leave," she added fretfully. "They appear to listen to us, but either they aren't comprehending us, or they are the stubbornest women I've ever come across."

"We have their DNA from their hair," Isabelle said.

"Not really. We just tossed the hair into the pillowcases. We didn't label it, and, like Nikki said, we can't match it up to a name," Alexis pointed out.

"I've never seen such misplaced loyalty," Annie said.

Kathryn snorted. "It's not loyalty you're seeing, it's fear."

"And they believe someone will come for them from one of the other compounds, and we can't shake that belief," Yoko said. "I don't think we should concern ourselves with that aspect since there's nothing we can do about it. The Feds will scoop them up until they can figure out what to do with them."

"Then let's do the swabs and get over to the worship center," Kathryn said.

Nikki dragged a carton over to the rows of metal chairs. She looked at the women, who seemed resigned to whatever was coming next.

It was an assembly line as Nikki swabbed, Kathryn bagged the swab, and Isabelle labeled it with whatever each woman revealed about her own identity. When they were finished, Yoko ran the box out to the police cruiser and dumped it into the trunk. Seconds later she was back with the other Sisters.

"Chop, chop," Annie said as she herded the women toward the door. She turned around and called out to Alexis, "You know what to do."

Alexis nodded as she headed down a long hall toward the sleeping quarters. The women stopped on a dime, bumping into one another as they tried to figure out why Alexis was going where she was going and what she would do when she got there.

Isabelle gave one of the women a hard shove forward. "Move! The Prophet is waiting for you."

It was all the women needed to hear. As one, they picked up their feet and almost ran to the door and outside. They looked like a gaggle of geese as they muttered among themselves.

The women blinked at the blinding light coming from all the vehicle headlights. Annie led the parade to the flagpole.

"Look alive here, ladies! Behold your glorious leader!" she said, pointing to the canvas flag. "Everyone salute!" she said, snapping off a crisp salute.

The other Sisters followed suit.

The Stepford women, their bald heads gleaming in the bright light, tried to huddle against each other, their eyes glued to the canvas snapping in the light breeze. They did their best to look away, but Nikki cracked her invisible whip.

"No! No! Don't look away! This is the man you worship, the man you honor and obey! Take a damn good look because you will never see him again. By the way, just in case you don't know, that picture was hanging over his bed. I bet none of you ever thought you would see it outside that den of iniquity where he hangs his . . . hat. Well, guess what! That picture is going to be on the front page of every newspaper in the country tomorrow morning. By evening it will be global. And

so will your pictures," Nikki said, anger
ringing in her voice.

"Hey, Espinosa, get over here. We
need a picture of these fine ladies paying
homage to this guy's dick," Kathryn said.

Espinosa clicked away with gay aban-
don. The women tried to hide their faces,
but the Sisters jerked them around to face
the camera. Five seconds later the pictures were on their way to Maggie.

"You know what, ladies? When those
pictures flash across the world, none of
your people will want you. They'll be afraid
to come here for you because they won't
want what's happening here to happen to
them. You getting it yet, you dumb clucks?"
Kathryn bellowed.

Annie wasn't sure, but she thought she
saw fear in several of the younger women's
faces. It was a start, but she wasn't hopeful. Her gut told her that when it was time
to leave, the women would elect to stay
behind.

"Time to see your fearless leader!" Nikki
said as she motioned the women to head
into the worship center.

It took a few minutes to seat the women
and for Jack and Harry to organize the

men. The Prophet stared at the bald-headed women with revulsion.

"Behold, your congregants!" Jack shouted gleefully.

The women stared at the Prophet, their hands going to their heads as they tried to cover their baldness. As one they saw the revulsion in their leader's face. Then they turned and presented their backs to him so he wouldn't have to look at their faces.

"This is a come-to-Jesus meeting, ladies and gentlemen," Annie said, stomping her way around the room. "You!" she said, jabbing the Prophet in the arm. "Tell these pitiful women to do what we say. Surely somewhere in that perverted body of yours, there is some small seed of goodness. They'll be left here to starve, and the weather will turn cold in a few weeks. Oh, wait a minute. You don't know what's out there by the flagpole, do you?

"Jack, drag this pile of bones out there and make sure he takes a good look at that flagpole. Joseph, Maggie will want a good picture of him standing next to his personal flag."

In less than five minutes all parties were back inside the house of worship.

The Prophet was a beaten man when Jack tossed him back on his throne. "Those pictures will flash around the world by sundown tomorrow. All your people will see it. No way will any of you be welcome in any of their compounds. Now, do what the nice lady said and tell these women to do what we say."

Yoko walked behind the throne and grabbed a handful of the Prophet's hair and yanked his head backward. "Do what he says."

The Prophet clamped his lips shut as he tried to struggle. Yoko let loose of his hair and clamped her hands on the Prophet's shoulders. She started to hum the lyrics to "Dancing Queen." Harry shivered as he watched his ladylove.

"Ah, he doesn't want to talk. Hold him still, Yoko." Kathryn walked over to Alexis's Red Bag and rummaged inside. Triumphantly, she held up a switchblade and something that looked like an electric cattle prod.

"Normally, we don't offer options, but in this case we're prepared to make an exception because these women's lives depend on your cooperation. Either I cut your dick off, or I shove this electric prod up your ass. You already lost most of your teeth, so to me it's a no-brainer, but then I'm not stupid like you are," Kathryn said as she bent over to plug the prod into the outlet nearest the Prophet's chair.

Harry, Jack, Ted, and Espinosa sucked in their breath. It sounded like a hurricane swooping through the building. Espinosa's hands were less than steady as he tried to focus his camera.

"You people are so cruel and unkind," one of the women bleated. "You will never see salvation, you will be ground to dust and stomped upon for what you're doing to this man. He will never take orders from you."

Kathryn whirled around. "Shut the fuck up, or I'll slice your tits off."

The woman crumpled to the floor. No one moved to revive her or pick her up.

Harry looked at Jack.

Jack looked at Harry and shrugged.

Ted just gawked as he texted Maggie, his fingers blistering the keys he was pounding.

Jack's phone vibrated. Snowden. "Emery," he barked.

"I need an update, Emery."

"Well . . . let's see. Everyone is in the worship house. As far as I know all the other buildings are empty, but you might want one of your people to check just to be sure. Right now we're getting ready to do an either/or."

"What's an 'either/or,' Emery?"

"The girls can't decide if they should cut the Prophet's dick off or shove an electric cattle prod up his ass. Oh, yeah, one of the wives passed out cold. She's lying on the floor. Did I mention the ladies shaved the wives' heads?"

The silence on the other end of the phone drummed in Jack's ear. "What's your update, Snowden?"

"We're done rigging the buildings. We'll be moving the second eighteen-wheeler out to an eighth of a mile from the gates. All the ambulances are gone. We didn't have any problems. The cemetery will remain intact, as promised. Remember, we are not *exploding* the buildings. We are *imploding* them. I can't guarantee the pumpkin patch."

"Why the hell not?" Jack asked, just to have something to say. He thought

Snowden's voice sounded strange. He pressed on. "What's your ETD, and don't give me that military time shit."

"Now, Emery, that depends on you. When will those people be ready to leave the compound? I have a destination but not a time."

"Well, Snowden, I can't give you that right now. It all depends on whether the Prophet wants to keep his dick or give up his ass. I'll call you back. This is Emery, over and out."

Jack looked at the others and shrugged. "What do you want from me? Kathryn?"

"Okay, Mr. Prophet, what's it going to be?" Kathryn asked, jabbing the prod in the Prophet's direction. Blue current sizzled in the air. Then she feinted with the switchblade. "Did I say this is one of those Japanese knives that can cut down a tree? Did I also mention the fate of the free world and these ... uh ... lovely ladies depends on your answer?"

"Do what these people tell you," the Prophet whispered.

"Louder! I can't hear you! These baldies can't hear you!"

One of the women spoke in her

singsong voice. "You're forcing the Prophet to say what he's saying. You are coercing him to say what you want. We know better. He doesn't mean it. Prophet, shake your head if you really mean us to do what you say."

"I'll be damned," Jack said to Harry. "Where are those women's brains?"

Harry clucked his tongue. "You really don't want me to answer that, do you?"

"I was just being foolish, Harry. Please forgive me."

Ted texted furiously.

Espinosa just clicked and clicked. He wondered how much his bonus would be for the job. He hoped it was substantial. His mother's birthday was coming up, and he wanted to get her something wonderful. He planned to ask Maggie for her help in choosing just the right present.

The Prophet, with a prod from Kathryn, bobbed his head up and down.

"Oooh, oooh, the Prophet is saying something," Kathryn cried excitedly. "Louder, so everyone can hear you!"

"Never question anything I say. Leave my sight, you offend me."

The woman who had spoken cowered,

her hands covering her face. She started to shake from head to toe. Her fellow wives ignored her. The woman lying on the floor continued to sleep peacefully. The other women ignored her, too.

Jack's phone vibrated. "Emery. What's up, Snowden?"

"Are the women leaving or staying? Our final check showed no human in any of the buildings with the exception of the one you're in. No animals, either. The truck has been moved. We're ready to implode in nine minutes. Call me the minute you have everyone outside by the flagpole. We are on schedule."

"Whoopee!" Jack said. "We're departing the premises right now. I still don't have an affirmative on the women. The remaining men are good to go. Like now. I don't know if this matters or not, but they're *nekkid!*" Jack drawled.

"Makes me no never mind—naked, clothed, it's all the same to me, Emery."

"That makes me happy, Snowden. Over and out," Jack said dramatically as he watched the nude men parade past the women.

The sleeper was back on her feet,

appalled at what she was seeing. The woman who had dared to question the Prophet was moaning and groaning about the children.

Yoko told her to shut up, then she said, "That bus left an hour ago."

Harry looked so proud of the love of his life, Jack gave him a shove and told him to get with the program.

"And that would be . . . ?"

"Unwrap that guy you duct-taped to the flagpole. Make sure the good doctor here sheds his clothes, and don't be gentle with him."

Outside, the wind was brisk and cool. The moment the Prophet saw his anatomically correct likeness flapping in the breeze for the second time his legs gave out from under him. Harry jerked him upright as Espinosa, grinning from ear to ear, clicked away.

Jack's phone vibrated. Jack took a deep breath as he looked at the vigilantes.

"Five minutes till implosion, Emery."

"Got it." Jack held up his hand, his fingers splayed to indicate they had only five minutes, and so it was time to move toward the road.

The Sisters hustled as they shooed the women the way they would have shooed a group of reluctant five-year-olds, toward the road and far enough away from the compound to keep them safe.

They all watched Snowden's men shove the naked men into two of the parked SUVs. With only seconds to spare, the dark vehicles growled to life and raced down the road and out to the gate, which was standing open.

The moment the two vehicles were through the gates, Jack hit the remote he'd removed from the visor of the police cruiser. Five seconds later and a minute to detonation, Jack's cell phone vibrated.

"My people tell me there is a caravan of satellite trucks and other assorted vehicles heading this way. Keep those damn gates closed and hunker down. Over and out."

Jack had the crazy urge to tell Snowden to stop with the ridiculous "over and out" sign-offs, but he didn't. "Hit the ground, everyone! Ten seconds!"

He followed his own instructions as Espinosa looked confused. Jack reached out to grab his ankle. Espinosa fell forward and landed on top of Ted. "You can take your damn pictures when it's all over. Maggie will kill me if anything happens to you. Cover your ears!"

Twenty-one seconds later it was all over and nothing but piles of rubble remained of the HOE compound. Thick gray smoke hovered overhead, but the brisk wind carried it away, as if by magic. The only thing left standing was the flagpole and the huge iron bell. The Prophet's likeness billowed in and out, inflating, then deflating, his assets. The vehicles that had been moved were intact, as was the remaining eighteen-wheeler full of pumpkins that was in the process of being moved by Kathryn.

Jack got to his feet, his legs wobbly. "Everyone okay?"

"We're all okay," Nikki called out.

Ted and Espinosa were on their feet and running wildly back into the compound. It always came down to the story for their readers.

Jack moved over to Nikki and put his arms around her. "So, are these women going or staying?"

"I hate to say it, Jack, but I think they're

staying. We could make them leave by force, but what will that get us? I wish you could have heard the speech Annie gave them. It made me cry, it really did. But no matter what she said, it didn't register. She told them what real family life was like. She promised them everything under the sun. She talked about life outside these gates and everything that could and would be done for the children. Sometimes, Jack, we forget how lucky we are and how we take everything for granted. Annie didn't miss a thing. I was watching those women, and they simply could not comprehend what she was saying. They have been so beaten down they can't allow themselves to think. Let the authorities take care of them. They might have better luck. We did what we came here to do, and that was get the children safely away. The best we can hope for now is that one day the children will want to seek out their real parents. If that comes to pass, our people will help them. For now, it is what it is. No one will inhabit this place ever again."

Jack listened to the words, but he wasn't satisfied. He thought about the grizzly man and his young girl brides and how obscene it was. "A new Prophet will spring up somewhere else," he said bitterly.

"That's the downside, Jack. But we kicked the door open. Law enforcement has to do something. Will it be enough, will it be what we want? The answer is no. The upside is that now people will be watching these compounds. When Jeffs comes to trial again, the people will rear up. I'm hoping for a domino effect."

"The women might tell the authorities about me, Nikki. Ted and Espinosa are the press, they can defend being here. I can't."

Nikki laughed. "Kathryn already took care of that. "She told them all if they opened their mouths, we would kill the Prophet. That, they understood. We need to make our preparations to leave. Do you want to take a last walk-through to see what happened?"

"I thought you'd never ask. Should we take the women with us?"

"Great idea." Nikki whistled shrilly. "Line up, ladies, we're going for a walk."

Whatever reaction the Sisters were hoping for didn't come to pass. The women were stone-faced as they followed along like docile children. They held hands and chewed on their lips as they looked at the devastation that had once been their home.

"Aha! The pumpkin patch is intact! Look at those luscious pumpkins!" Jack cackled gleefully.

In spite of herself, Nikki laughed.

Avery Snowden, his men behind him, marched single file up to where the group was standing. "They going or staying?"

"Looks like they're staying," Jack said. "The FBI will be here shortly. You guys should get out of here. We'll be right behind you, but we have one or two loose ends to tidy up. We'll meet up with you at the designated spot. Wait for us, Snowden. Here, you're going to need this," Jack said, tossing the remote into the air. Snowden caught it and grinned.

"See ya," Snowden said. He offered up a sloppy salute, which Jack returned.

"Back to the flagpole, ladies!" Annie shouted.

Jack walked over to Ted and Espinosa. "You get it all?"

"Oh, yeah. And then some." Ted snickered. "Maggie said I should kiss you guys, but I'm not doing that."

"Me, either," Espinosa said.

Harry glared at both men as he tried to figure out if they were lying or not. Yoko reached over and took his arm. Harry wilted right in front of them all. Yoko smiled as she whispered sweet nothings in Harry's ears.

"Thanks, Jack," Nikki whispered.

It was Jack's turn to wilt, and wilt he did.

"I think it all went rather well for not having a plan," Annie said happily as she led the parade back to the flagpole.

Off in the distance the group could see lights springing up outside the gates. The compound itself was totally dark, the only light coming from the crescent moon and the twinkling stars overhead.

# Chapter 21

Myra Rutledge sat quietly staring out the window of the small lobby. Thin, watery sunshine was struggling with dense cloud cover. If she had been a gambling woman, she would have bet on rain as opposed to sunshine. She wondered if she'd feel any better if the sun was bright and warm. She doubted it.

She was waiting for someone to take her to the airport. Someone. Not Charles. At the moment she didn't even know where Charles was. She didn't know where Allison, "Call me Allie," Barnstable was, either.

Myra closed her eyes. She was too tired

to think, yet for some reason she didn't feel sleepy. The truth was, she couldn't remember when she'd slept last. She must have dozed from time to time; otherwise, she'd be dropping off right then.

The only thing she knew with any certainty was that Charles was not returning with her. She didn't know how she felt about that. She didn't know how the girls were going to feel about it either, when they saw her returning alone.

Myra looked down at her watch. Her Sisters should be safely away from the HOE compound already. She wanted to call Annie or Nikki but wasn't sure if she could emotionally handle whatever news they would give her. She also didn't want to have to answer questions about Charles and the current situation.

Myra jerked upright when she heard clicking heels coming down the hall to her left. She didn't bother turning around to look to see who was coming her way.

"Madam?"

Myra forced herself to look up. He was tall and incredibly thin with coppery-colored hair. She wondered if he talked into his sleeve or his collar the way special agents did back home. Sunglasses peeked out of his breast pocket. She wondered how often he got to wear them, given the awful weather.

"Yes."

"Come with me, madam. I shall be escorting you to the airport for your return trip."

Myra knew that if she asked questions she wouldn't get any answers, so she didn't bother. She simply got up and followed the tall, thin man down a different corridor. Then she was outside and escorted inside a luxurious-looking car. She wouldn't have cared if it was a scooter as long as it would get her to the airport.

Settled in the car, her seat belt buckled, Myra looked back at the building she'd just left. Was Charles still inside? Was Allison Barnstable back at her home with her children? She continued to stare out the car window, hoping Charles would magically appear and wave good-bye. She knew it wouldn't happen, so she leaned back and closed her eyes.

As hard as she tried, she couldn't imagine her life without Charles in it. Then again, she'd thought she was going to die without Barbara in her life. She'd survived somehow. She fought the tears forming in her eyes, but it was a losing battle.

**"Mom."**

Oh, dear God! "Darling girl," she whispered.

**"Buck up, Mom. I'm here. Don't cry. Your eyes will get all puffy."**

Myra smiled through her tears. "It's just . . . It's just that I've never been totally alone before. I don't like how I'm feeling. I'm worried."

**"Mom, you're never alone. I'm always with you, you know that. All you have to do is call my name. You know that, too, Mom, so why the tears?"**

Myra fingered the pearls at her neck. She did know that. If only she could reach out and touch her daughter, feel a flesh-and-blood person. Her and Charles's daughter. That wasn't going to happen, either, and she knew it.

**"It will be all right, Mom. This is a bump in the road. A rather big bump from where you're sitting, but it's a mountain for Charles. He feels worse than you do, Mummie."**

Myra felt herself literally swoon at her

spirit daughter's endearing title. When Barbara was little, she'd always called her 'Mummie.' Then when Nikki came along, Barbara had started calling her 'Mom.' Myra had loved that title, too.

"Darling girl, Charles told me I did a despicable thing when you . . . when you passed over. He said I told Nikki, or rather asked her, why it hadn't been her instead of you. I know Charles would never lie to me about something like that. I'm sick in my heart over that. And yet, Nikki never once said a word. How I must have hurt her."

**"Mummie, Nik understood. Nik loves you, has always loved you. Trust me, I know. Please don't ever go there. That was a long time ago."**

"Are the girls all right? I should call, but I can't bring myself to do it."

**"It was a bit tricky back there for a little while, but everyone is fine. I should go. Your plane is waiting. Fly with the angels, Mummie."**

Myra felt something brush her cheek just as the car came to a stop. She looked through the dark glass to see the coppery-haired man getting ready to open the door for her. Her hand went to her cheek. It felt warm and soft. A kiss? A touch from her spirit daughter? It pleased her to think it was so. She smiled through her tears as she stepped out of the car.

There was a spring to Myra's step as she followed the man, who was leading her to a special aircraft sitting all alone on a private runway. She could hear the sound of the jet engine as she climbed the steps. She didn't know how she knew, but she knew she would be the only passenger on this particular flight.

Myra turned, hoping against hope that she would see Charles somewhere in the gloom. In the movies the man was always waiting in the wings, his eyes sad as he watched the love of his life fly away. There was nothing to be seen except the huge black car racing back across the tarmac.

Myra settled herself. The interior was beyond luxurious. The leather seats were soft and buttery. Seating arrangements. A shower and a bedroom were somewhere down the aisle. She wasn't sure, but she rather thought this was the equivalent to one of the planes used as Air Force One back home. Suddenly she felt important.

A young woman with blond hair and a fashionable uniform asked if she would like anything until breakfast was served. Myra shook her head, but she did have a question. "Tell me when I can make a phone call."

The young woman nodded as she made her way to her own seat to prepare for takeoff.

As the special plane rose in the sky, Myra leaned back and closed her eyes. Within seconds she was sound asleep, both her hands clasped around the treasured pearls at her neck.

When the pilot announced their cruising altitude, the flight attendant poured coffee and carried it forward to the lone passenger. She noticed the smile on the woman's face and wondered if the mysterious passenger was dreaming of angels. She carried the coffee back to her own seat and drank it herself. Obviously breakfast was something her passenger could do without. She started to think about preparing her passenger's lunch as she attacked the scrumptious breakfast so that it wouldn't go to waste.

*   *   *

While Myra snoozed on the luxurious British plane, her fellow Sisters were running against the clock in Utah as the media started to broadcast from outside the gates of the HOE compound.

The Sisters clustered near the vehicles, far enough away from the HOE women, who had elected to stay behind, so that their conversation couldn't be overheard.

"What's the plan as of this moment?" Alexis queried as she rummaged in her Red Bag. Piles of clothing were heaped willy-nilly on the ground at her feet as she searched for the last items they would need to make a safe getaway.

"Has anyone heard from Bert?" Jack asked.

They all looked at Kathryn, who shook her head. "The last I heard was what you told me, Jack. He's supposed to get here before it gets light out with some of the men from the local bureaus. He'll be waiting for the federal warrant so he can enter the grounds. That's it in a nutshell. There's no way he can be tied to all of this, Jack."

"He won't be. It's those crazy-ass media people out there we have to worry about.

By now they have to know they can't reach or locate the sheriff and his deputies, so they're going to go to the state police. They'll be here like fleas on a dog in—my best guess—about thirty minutes. So, let's get out of here while the going is good," Jack said.

"But what's the plan?" Harry demanded.

Jack tried to see what the women were doing, but all he could see was a lot of movement. Suddenly he heard a lot of grumbling, then laughter and giggles. What the hell?

"What do you think?" Nikki demanded as she whirled and twirled for the boys to see. In spite of himself, Jack doubled over laughing.

"Well, damn!" was Ted's contribution.

Espinosa was laughing so hard he had a hard time focusing his camera. At the very least, all this should get him a long paid weekend at some posh resort.

Harry clutched at Jack's arm, his eyes frantic. "This can't work!"

"Harry, these bonding sessions have to stop. Next thing you'll be wanting to hold my hand. I can't allow that. It will work. The girls never do anything that doesn't work."

# 342 Fern Michaels

Jack turned to Espinosa. "Hey, Joe, play your cards right, and I bet you can get a gig on *Jerry Springer* with what you've got going on there."

"I hate these dresses," Isabelle said as she looked down at the old-fashioned outfit she was wearing. "Who knew they wore petticoats under these god-awful things. The material in the dress alone must weigh ten pounds!"

"What color is this?" someone asked.

Someone else shouted, "Puce!"

"What? What? You want muddy green, puke green, or *maroon?* It wasn't like I had a rainbow of colors to choose from," Alexis said. "Now, hold still so I can give you a pompadour with all this damn hair we shaved off those women," she demanded between fits of giggles.

"What's the damn plan, Jack?" Harry asked menacingly.

"The plan is . . . The plan is . . ."

"Shut up, Jack, and let me glue this goatee on you. Here's your Smokey Bear hat and the deputy's shirt. Put it on," Kathryn said. "You, too, Harry," she said, slapping a beard onto Harry's chin. Then, to his chagrin, she settled a Smokey Bear hat on Harry's head as well.

Jack laughed like a lunatic. "You look like Fu Manchu, Harry, only shorter!" He danced away before Harry could take a shot at him.

Jack sobered almost immediately when he saw Harry raise his arm for silence. "I hear a siren somewhere. Five miles out, maybe seven."

No one ever disputed Harry's hearing.

Jack moved forward. "Okay, Ted, you drive one cruiser. Girls, pile in. Espinosa, you drive the other. Once you get through those gates, you drive like hell, for two, maybe three miles down the road. Harry and I will meet up with you there. Harry, you drive the SUV and park just outside the gates. Now, here's the plan. Listen up. I'm going to drive the eighteen-wheeler full of pumpkins and block the road on this side of the gates. That means no one gets in here. The only way they'll be able to move it is to blow it up. That's the *PLAN!* Now move, people! Sirens, blue lights! The whole ball of wax."

The people moved.

"What are you waiting for, Harry? You wanted a plan! I just gave you a plan! A sterling plan! A magnificent plan! Now, move your ass."

"Sometimes you are so damn smart I can't stand you. By God, I think it might work," Harry said grudgingly. "See ya!"

Jack watched as the three vehicles—the cruisers, sirens blasting, blue lights flashing, Harry hot on their trail in the SUV—raced toward the gates.

Jack climbed into the cab of the eighteen-wheeler and took off, downshifting as he felt the power under the hood. Pumpkins. Who the hell knew from pumpkins? From that moment on, pumpkins were his favorite . . . fruit? Vegetable? Food.

It took a lot of fancy maneuvering on Jack's part to bring the behemoth to a stop, then back it up, then turn it parallel to the gates; but somehow he did it. He hopped out and made it through the gates and into the SUV Harry was driving with an inch of space to spare. Pedal to the metal, Jack collapsed into the backseat, the door hanging open as Harry sped down the road. "Did the gates close?" Jack gasped.

"Yeah, before anyone knew what the hell happened. I hear sirens, Jack."

"Ignore them and keep going," Jack said as he untangled himself and bounded over to the front seat so he could better see what was happening. "Annie told me this is HOE property all the way to within two hundred feet of the main road. She down-loaded a plat plan from the Provo building office or someplace like that. Technically, all those media people are trespassing. Bet they don't know that, either. Wonder if Bert knows. I think I'll give him a call right now and tell him to get his ass out here right now. No sense waiting till dawn, with sirens coming this way. Do ya think the state police know this is private property?"

"How the hell would I know that, Jack? Shit! Here come some of the media. What do you want me to do?"

"What do you mean, what do I want you to do? I want you to speed up and get us to the girls before the media overtake us is what I want you to do. You're screwing up the plan, Harry. I'm not going to forget this, either," Jack said as Bert picked up.

"Bert! We're out on the road. You need to get here right now. Where are you?"

"I was kissing Kathryn until you called me. I'm right in front of you, you *schmuck*. I'm one of those rare people who actually makes a plan and works off that plan. I've been sitting here for three hours waiting for all of you, and yeah, I know this is private property. How'd those implosions go, buddy?"

"Like clockwork. Did you get everything out of the cruiser trunk? Oops, here comes the media," Jack said, as Harry ground to a stop.

"Got it all. The girls are ready. Stay in your truck, Jack. Whatever the hell you do, don't say a word."

"Got it!"

Jack and Harry watched in awe as the Sisters climbed out of the two police cruisers, followed by Ted Robinson and Joe Espinosa, who had their hands high in the air.

"Up against the cruiser, spread 'em, hands on the hood!" Annie bellowed as she waved a gun around. "That goes for you, too, Mr. FBI Director! You, the one with the camera, you can turn around and take a picture when I give the word. But you have to wait a minute while we take off your distributor caps. And shoot out your tires."

Alexis walked over to the men and hooked them together with FlexiCuffs. "Joe will cut you loose when it's time," she whispered.

A breathless gaggle of media ground to a halt, then backed up when Annie shot off the gun, the bullet going skyward.

"Stay back!" she bellowed a second time.

"Hey, you with the camera!"

"Yeah, yeah, that's me," Espinosa said, his voice quivering with excitement.

The Sisters lined up in the headlights from the cruisers and the SUV.

A gasp went up from the horde of media. "It's those women who live out here! You can tell by the hair and the dresses," someone shouted.

"You have it all wrong," Kathryn shouted. She lowered her voice, and said, "Okay, on the count of three, peel and dive into that SUV. One! Two! Three!"

The pompadours and the prairie dresses with the Velcro bindings that Alexis had attached earlier were suddenly flung skyward.

"It's the vigilantes!"

Espinosa, knowing what to expect, clicked, and a nanosecond later the pictures were on their way to MSNBC, compliments of Maggie Spritzer of the *Post* in a special deal she'd arranged with the powers that be at the network. As the SUV raced out to the highway, the vigilantes were once more making news in real time.

"Where to, ladies?" Jack asked the giggling women in the back of the SUV.

Deadly quiet descended.

"Okay, okay, I was just having some fun. We're going back to the Ellis farm, where the crop dusters should be waiting. They'll take you as far as Salt Lake City, where you will board Annie's Gulfstream."

"Good plan, Jack," Nikki said, leaning over the seat to plant a kiss on his cheek.

"Yeah, it was pretty good, wasn't it? What do you think will happen to all those pumpkins?" he asked fretfully.

"Who cares?" Nikki asked, kissing his other cheek.

"Certainly not me," Jack said, reveling in his moment of glory. "For sure not me," he reiterated.

# Epilogue

It was a magnificent late-fall day on Big Pine Mountain. Beautiful russet and gold leaves swirled in the late-afternoon wind that whispered among the stately pines as birds chittered in their nests high in the trees. No one other than the dogs seemed to appreciate the wonderful day as they raced after the falling leaves that were like an orange and gold carpet on the ground. None of the women had the urge to go out and play in the leaves the way they'd done the autumn before when Charles had issued his mandate to rake leaves or go without dinner.

Annie decided she didn't like what she was seeing: glum faces and inertia. They'd been back not quite twenty-four hours—time for all of them to shower, change clothes, and take a nap. As yet they hadn't had what Charles always called "the debriefing" after a mission was completed.

"I've had all I'm going to take from the lot of you!" Annie said, her voice stopping just short of being angry. "We need to focus here. We need to think about dinner. We need to debrief and fill out our reports, since . . . since there is no one else here to do it. And, that's exactly what we're going to do. We also need to take stock of our current situation, and by taking stock I mean we have to think about the coming months.

"We are virtually cut off from the world up here, as we all know. We all took for granted that the generators would always give us electricity, but none of us know where the gas is or how we get it. It's just there because Charles took care of that. Our larder is not overflowing. What that means, ladies, is unless we replenish it, we will starve up here in the winter months. I do not relish having to hunt for my food with a bow and arrow. Do any of you know how that was done? No, you do not. Nor do I.

"So, what I suggest is that you all get off your asses and come inside so we can take care of business. Scratch that. 'Suggest' is too mild a word. I'm ordering you inside so we can take care of business."

Murphy and Grady stopped their wild dash around the compound to sit on their hindquarters and stare at the women. Neither dog had ever heard such a tone of voice from Annie, who was usually all sweetness and light when it came to them. They waited to see what the outcome would be, sitting still as statues.

"I'll meet you all in Charles's lair as soon as I find something to put in the oven for dinner. No more glum faces. I mean it. Move it, ladies!"

It was an order they couldn't quibble with, so the Sisters rose from where they were sitting on the steps and headed toward the main building.

The only word Murphy and Grady related to was "dinner." They followed Annie, who was always good for a belly scratch and a treat or two.

When Annie joined her fellow Sisters, she announced, "Meat loaf for dinner, baked potatoes, and a salad. Charles already had a meat loaf made up in the freezer. He always prepared ahead, so we need to write that down on our list."

Nikki pulled a yellow pad closer and wrote, "Prepare food ahead of time."

By the time Annie took them through the domestic issues, Nikki's pad was full of things that needed to be taken care of. They argued among themselves as to who was going to do what and finally came to an agreement about it all.

"What about Myra?" Isabelle asked. "Something must have happened. When she called the last time, she said she would be here by noon. It's late afternoon and she isn't here and she hasn't called."

Annie was worried, too, but she tried not to show it. "Just assign her some duties, and she and I can swap if she doesn't like hers. I'm sure there was some kind of delay at the airport. She is a fugitive, so *those people* have to be careful not to blow her cover and get her here safely. Myra can take care of herself. Let's move on now. Briskly, girls."

Nikki took the floor. "The FBI has taken a big hit. Bert is playing it all just right by saying he couldn't invade the compound until he had the federal warrant in his hands. Which, by the way, didn't arrive until we were all in the air in those damn crop dusters. The women have been taken to a federal facility in Salt Lake City, and there is absolutely no press coverage on that other than what the FBI wants to give out. What that means to us is, the women are not talking. Period. He did say that the other compounds, or sects, whatever you want to call them, are screaming about religious persecution. But the general public is in an uproar, so the FBI is kind of playing that down."

Kathryn said Maggie told her earlier that the *Post* is up for some one-of-a-kind award for her print coverage, and they are commending her as EIC for sharing and getting the on-the-spot news to MSNBC, since she couldn't get out a special edition on time. Win-win for Maggie and the *Post.* She said she's going nuts with all the papers in Utah calling her and promising big things, yet thanking her for being so—as she put it—'in everyone's faces.'

"Maggie also said she gave Ted and Espinosa a week's paid vacation. Espinosa went to see his family because his mother's birthday is soon, and he asked Maggie to ask Annie if she wants him to name his firstborn after her. She said he cried. Maggie and Ted are going to Bermuda, or one of those islands, for five days and said, no matter what, we are not to call her. Oh, she also said Abner Tookus, her hacker/guru, wiped the HOE's accounts clean, then burned everything to a cinder. All of Avery Snowden's people have been paid to date as well as Snowden himself."

Isabelle started to laugh as she got ready to offer her contribution. "Maggie made sure we made the half over the fold. According to the article, the vigilantes single-handedly blew up the entire HOE compound, leaving behind a gaggle of bald-headed women who were taken into federal custody and have refused to talk. Great detail was given to the picture/flag, whatever you want to call it, that was flying at half-mast when the FBI arrived. Bert confiscated it, saying it was evidence, but he was extremely fair to the media by first allowing them to take all the pictures they wanted."

Kathryn simply glowed at Bert's accomplishments.

Yoko took the floor, and said, "No one can figure out how we got in and out of the compound. They're still trying to figure out the truck with the pumpkins. Some wiseass in the media said the only way they are going to catch us is to send in Delta Force, and even they are no match for us."

Alexis was next. "Pearl, Nellie, and Elias are still in Nevada. Lizzie, too, but for how long I don't know. They're helping Cosmo, and, yes, Paula Woodley showed up and has things in hand. Marion Jennings has been reunited with her sister and her own children, as have the other young women that Lizzie met with. Annie, your friend Mr. Fish helped out a lot and asked Cosmo when he could expect to see you. Cosmo said he sounded excited at the prospect." she said.

Annie's face turned pink. She was so flustered she forgot to talk.

"And to think we did all of this without a plan," Nikki said. "You know what I mean—without a diagram, a road map, a list, the kind of thing Charles always sent us away with."

At the mention of Charles, the group grew solemn again.

Annie finally found her tongue. "We should have heard something by now. But since we haven't, we have to make some decisions. I want to take a vote now. Winter is coming, so we have to decide if we plan on staying here on the mountain or if we should ask Avery Snowden to relocate us. It would appear that Charles will not be returning. Should we continue as if we know what we're doing and at some point hope we attain Charles's exalted position? Or should we pack it in?"

The other Sisters looked at one another. Without a moment's hesitation every hand shot in the air including Annie's.

"I'm voting for Myra in absentia," she said.

"Seven to zip," Nikki said gleefully. "Come on, girls, Charles is just a guy. We're *women!* There's nothing we can't do if we work together. We have a hell of a team here. Even the FBI says so. So does the *Post.* And let's not forget the TV news."

Murphy and Grady growled deep in their throats, the fur on the back of their necks standing on end as they raced to the door, the Sisters right behind them.

Off in the distance they could hear the sound of an engine and see a speck in the sky.

"Maybe it's Myra!" Annie cried, as she and the others raced over to the helicopter pad.

Holding hands, the women waited. They could barely hear the dogs' barks with the earsplitting sound of the helicopter as it prepared to land. A man jumped out, then reached up to pick up Myra and settle her on the ground. There was no sign of Charles, but they already knew he wouldn't be with Myra.

Bending her head to clear the wings, Myra ran as fast as she could to the waiting women, who were all laughing and crying at the same time. The two dogs vied for attention. Myra bent over, then sat down in a pile of colorful leaves as she tickled and crooned to both animals.

Once her Sisters realized she wanted to stay where she was for the moment, they all sat down, everyone talking at once.

"Is Charles all right?"

"Is Charles coming back?"

"Do you know anything about the generator?"

"Why didn't you stay for the funeral?"

Myra stopped tickling the dogs long enough to hold up her hands. "One at a time, girls. Charles is . . . I guess 'okay' is the right word. It would seem at first blush—no, that's not true. According to Geoffrey's wife, Charles's son was a cad, and I believe Charles is having a hard time accepting that fact. And Geoffrey wanted nothing to do with Charles when he found out who his father was, and from what I was able to gather, Geoffrey has known for a long time about Charles. Charles's people do . . . What they do . . . is . . . Let's just say they make our people look incompetent. They wouldn't even let his wife into her husband's room. Then they whisked her away. More than likely to shut her up so she didn't talk to the press about the hero that wasn't such a hero after all. There were other women involved. It's rather sordid, so let's not talk about that anymore.

"I don't know if Charles will be returning or not. I would hope that he will try to make some overtures to his daughter-in-law if she allows it, which I don't think she will. She has three children and is worried about how to take care of them. I want to believe Charles will step up to the plate.

"As to why I didn't stay for the funeral. Charles and his people did not want me there. As I said, they do things differently. And before you can ask, I'm fine. I couldn't wait to get here. What's for dinner?"

The dogs bounded up and raced for the house at the sound of their favorite word.

"Meat loaf," they chorused as one.

"Well, meat loaf is better than scones and that . . . that pissy tea I had to drink over there. Now, it's your turn, tell me everything that happened, and tell me everything I missed out on. Don't leave a thing out."

"Myra, we'll tell you over dinner. Right now, you can't handle hearing what we went through."

Myra huffed and puffed, and said, "Wherever did you get the idea I am some kind of delicate flower, Annie? If you handled it, I could have handled it."

"If you say so, Myra. We lost half our hair and most of the skin off our faces when we flew in those crop dusters. We had to puke in bags. Going and coming, Myra."

Myra fingered her pearls. "Well, I would have given it a fair shot, Annie. I don't want to think I would have embarrassed myself or the rest of you."

Annie threw her arms around Myra. "Welcome home, Myra."

"When it comes right down to it, Annie, it's the only place to be. And, believe it or not, I do know about the generators."

"Myra, I cast your vote to continue without Charles at the helm. I hope that was all right and the way you would have voted."

"Charles who?" Myra asked as she and Annie walked together toward the main building. "We'll all be fine, Annie. I know it. I feel it in here," she said, thumping her breast. "Barbara talked to me on the ride to the airport," she whispered. "She said it's going to be okay."

Annie smiled as she hugged Myra again. The other Sisters had run ahead and were lined up on the porch shouting and hollering that it was time to celebrate their recent victory.

"We're coming, you darling girls, we're coming!" Annie and Myra shouted in unison.

If you enjoyed *Under the Radar*,
don't miss the next exciting novel in
Fern Michaels's Sisterhood series!

Turn the page for a special preview of
RAZOR SHARP

# Chapter 1

Cosmo Cricket looked at the Mickey Mouse clock on his desk, a gift from a grateful client. Because, as the client put it, what do you give to a man who has everything except maybe a part of his childhood to remember? For some reason, this particular clock meant the world to him and not because Mickey Mouse was part of his childhood—because he hadn't really had a childhood, at least not a normal one. Someday, when he had nothing else to do, he'd figure it all out. He wished he could remember the client, but he couldn't. Mickey told him it was the end of the workday. But the city that he lived and worked in, one that never slept, was about to come alive just as he was about to head home.

This was always the time of day when he sat back with a diet drink and reflected. On his life. On his work. On his past. And, on his future. He never reflected on the present because he knew who he was and what was going on, right down to the minute, thanks to Mickey. He'd known who he was from the day he was born. There were those who would take issue with that statement, but those people didn't know his mother and father. There wasn't an hour of his life that he didn't know about because his parents insisted he know everything. He always smiled when he got to this point in his reverie.

He knew he weighed fourteen whopping pounds when he was born and looked like he was four months old at birth. He knew that his parents fought over who got to hold him. And was told that he was rocked in a chair from day one until he was three years old, at which point he'd announced he was no longer a baby and needed to be a big boy, and he wanted his *own* chair, which appeared within hours, thanks to his doting father. There had been a succession of rocking chairs as he grew. He was sitting, right now, this very second, in the last one.

The rocking chair was battered and worn, and was on its tenth, maybe even its twentieth, set of cushions, he couldn't remember. The chair was at odds with the rest of his plush office and a far cry from the kind of furnishings that were in the house he'd grown up in. Everything in this penthouse suite of rooms was elegant, as top-of-line as the decorator could make it. Ankle-deep carpeting, an array of built-ins, pricey paintings on the walls, soft, buttery furniture, and a view of Las Vegas that had no equal. The palatial suite had its own bathroom, where everything was oversize to accommodate him. He was almost ashamed to admit he never used anything but the towels. He did like the bidet, though. The suite was one massive perk arranged by the Nevada Gaming Commission to get him to sign on as their legal counsel. He'd argued over the Gaming Commission's contract, saying he wanted to be able to practice law with a few select clients and do some pro bono work, and he wouldn't budge. He'd actually walked away when they wouldn't cave in, but they caught up with him at the elevator and agreed to his demands, then threw in what they thought was the clunker, but to Cosmo it was the icing on the proverbial cake. He was to be on call to all the casino owners, who would pay him his six-hundred-dollar-an-hour fee for whatever work he did for them plus a year-end bonus. The only stipulation was that his private clients and the casino owners not interfere with the commission's work. It was a solid-gold deal that worked for everyone.

Twenty-three years later he had so much money, he didn't know what to do with it, so he let other people manage it, people who made even more money for him.

In the beginning, when the money started flowing in, he moved his parents to a mansion, got them live-in help, and bought them fancy cars all without asking them first. That lasted one whole week before they moved out in the middle of the night and went back to their little house in the desert, where they had lived out their lives. He still owned that house, and it was where he himself lived. He'd updated it and was snug as a bug in a rug.

Cosmo chuckled when he thought of the other perk he'd negotiated, the entire floor below his suite of offices. He'd been disappointed that he hadn't had to go to the mat on that one. The "powers that be" gave in meekly, and he rented it out for outrageous sums of money, which he, in turn, donated to his favorite charities.

Cosmo looked at Mickey again and saw that it was almost six o'clock, which meant it was almost nine o'clock back East. He looked forward to calling Elizabeth and talking for an hour or so. God, how he loved that woman.

Mickey told him he had fifteen more minutes to reflect before he headed home. Thinking about Elizabeth Fox made him smile. Never in his wildest dreams had he ever thought a woman like Elizabeth would fall in love with him. Or that he could love her as much as he'd loved his parents. It just boggled his mind.

Cosmo's smile widened when he remembered his parents sitting him down when he turned six and was about to go off to school. They told him how he was different and how the other children were going to react to him. He'd listened, but he hadn't understood the cruelty of children; he learned quickly. It hadn't gotten any better as he aged, but by the time he went off to college, he didn't give a shit what anyone said about him. He accepted that he was big and that his feet were like canoes and that he was ugly, with outrigger ears and a flat slab for a face and that he had to have specially made clothes and shoes and a bed that would accommodate his body. He was comfortable in his own skin and made a life for himself.

And then along came Elizabeth Fox, or as she was known in legal circles, the Silver Fox. At first he couldn't believe she loved him, or as she put it, *I don't just love you, Cosmo, I love every inch of you.* And she meant it. He was so light-headed with that declaration, he'd almost passed out. She'd laughed, a glorious, tinkling sound that made him shiver all the way to his toes. Then she'd sat him down and told him everything she was involved in.

"You can walk away from me right now, Cosmo, and I will understand. If we stay together, you will know I'm breaking the law, and so will you. I'm giving you a choice."

Like there was a choice to be made. He'd signed on and never looked back. He was now a male member of that elite little group called the Vigilantes.

Cosmo looked over at Mickey and saw that it was time to fight the Vegas traffic and head for home. He looked around to see where his jacket was. Ah, just where he'd thrown it when he came back from lunch, half on one of the chairs and half-dangling on the floor. He was heaving himself out of his rocking chair when he heard the door to his secretary's office open and close. Mona Stevens, his secretary, always left at five o'clock on the dot because she had to pick her son up from day care. Mona had been one of his pro bono cases. A friend of a friend had asked him to help her out because her husband had taken off and left her and her son to fend for themselves. He'd hired her once he'd straightened out her problem and gotten her child support, and he paid her three times what other secretaries earned on the Strip. She was so grateful and loyal she would have brushed his teeth for him if he'd allowed it.

Cosmo opened the door to see a woman sitting primly on one of the chairs. She looked worried as well as uncomfortable. When the door opened she looked up, a deer caught in the headlights. "Can I help you?"

She was maybe in her midforties—he was never good at women's ages—well dressed, with a large leather bag at her feet. Her hair looked nice to his eye, and she wasn't slathered in makeup. All in all a pleasant-looking woman whose husband had probably gambled away their life savings and the house as well. He liked to think he was a good judge of character and always, no matter what, he waited to see a client's reaction to meeting him for the first time. This lady, whoever she was, didn't flinch, didn't blink, didn't do anything other than ask, "Are you Mr. Cricket?"

"I am. I was just leaving. Do you have an appointment I forgot about?"

"No. I did call three different times but . . . no, I don't have an appointment. Should I make one and come back? If I do that, I might not . . ."

"I have time. Come on in," Cosmo said, stepping aside so the woman could enter. He knew little about women's fashion and wondered what she carried in the bag that was heavy enough to drag her shoulder downward. He wasn't even sure whether the bag should be called a handbag, a backpack, or a travel case. His mother always referred to her bag as her pocketbook. It was where she kept a fresh hanky with lace on it, a small change purse, a comb, and a tube of lipstick. This woman's bag looked like it contained a twenty-pound rock and maybe the hammer she'd used to dig it out. He felt pleased with his assessment when the bag landed next to the chair with a loud thump.

Cosmo made a second assessment.

The woman didn't want to be here. But she was, and she'd called three times, and had hung up probably because she lost her nerve. For some reason women did that when their problems involved errant husbands. He reached into a drawer and pulled out a clean yellow legal pad and a pencil. He never used pens, just in case he had to erase something. His first rule was: never commit something to paper you don't want anyone else to see.

Pencil poised, Cosmo spoke, his tone gentle for such a big man. "We've established that I'm Cosmo Cricket, attorney at law. Who might you be?"

"Right now I'm Lily Flowers. Last week I was Crystal Clark. Before that Ann Marie Anders. And before that I was Caroline Summers. I don't care to tell you at this time what my real birth name is. I have"—she bent down to poke in the bag at her feet, her voice muffled as she fumbled around for what she wanted, finally finding a small envelope and spreading the contents out on Cosmo's pristine desk—"a passport in each name, a driver's license in the same name, along with a credit card that matches the picture ID on the driver's license. Each one of these identities has a bank account with minimal activity, rent receipts, and utility receipts. In different parts of the country. And a birth certificate," she said breathlessly.

Cosmo made no move to inspect the documents on his desk. "I assume you got these," he said, pointing to the lineup on his desk, "illegally."

"It depends on your definition of the word 'illegal.' That's me in every photo. Just a different hairdo, a little spirit gum here or there to alter the facial features, a little shoulder padding, but it is me."

"At the outset I say to all my clients, 'Tell me the truth, or I can't help you.' I'm sure you are aware of the confidentiality agreement between client and lawyer. If you aren't, what that means is I can never divulge anything you tell me to a third party. So whatever you say to me today, here in this room, I cannot tell another soul. Whatever your secrets are, they are safe with me. Having said that, I now need to ask you why you feel you need four identities other than your real one? What kind of trouble are you in?"

The woman of many names drew in a deep breath and let it out slowly. "Right now I am not in any trouble, but I will be very shortly. I'm here because . . . because . . . I want to know if there is any way I can head it off. What my options are, assuming I have any."

"Okay. But you have to tell me what type of trouble you think is headed your way."

Lily Flowers took another deep breath. "You don't know who I am, do you?"

Cosmo shook his head. "No, I don't recognize you. Should I? Have we met somewhere? Right now you appear to me to be a potential client in distress. Like I said, you have to tell me your problem; otherwise, I can't help you."

"I operate the Happy Day Camp for Boys and Girls in Pahrump. Until a month ago, our revenues exceeded those of Sheri's and the Chicken Ranch. Uh, that's according to my accountant."

*Shit! Good judge of character, my ass.* "Prostitution is legal in Pahrump, which is over sixty miles from Vegas. What's the problem? Did your girls fall short of the medical requirements?"

"No, nothing like that. I operate the cleanest, safest brothel in the state. My girls are the highest paid in the state. My problem is that some of my powerful, wealthy clients asked me to branch out for special occasions. They arranged all the details, a rustic atmosphere, right down to the summer camp theme I operate here. There was nothing in my name. I made sure of that. My girls are independent contractors and pay their taxes and everything that goes with it. As you know, there is no state income tax here in Nevada. I can give you an operations lesson later on. Right now word has filtered down to me that I'm likely to be arrested for my activities. Not here in Nevada but back East."

Cosmo felt his stomach muscles tie themselves into a knot. "Where back East?"

"The nation's capital. That's where all the action went down for Happy Day Camp. The clients, or johns, if you prefer, were all politicians. After the election a few months ago, when our first female president was sworn in, things went south with the opposition and quite a few of the current members of the new administration. They've been trying to keep the lid on it all, but word leaked out. It always does.

"It wasn't all that long ago that the woman they called the D.C. Madam supposedly killed herself. And just for the record, I don't believe that for one minute, and neither does anyone else who is in this business."

By then Cosmo felt like he had an army of ants squirming around in his stomach. "Why did you do it? You could operate safely here. Why go to a location like D.C. of all places?"

"Believe it or not, I didn't want to. I called a meeting of my girls, laid it all out, and—like a fool—allowed them to make the decision. I can understand how none of them wanted to say no, the money they were offering was outrageous. A few of the girls planned to retire when they got back. We only did it twice. Once before the election and once again afterward. 'Celebrations,' for want of a better word.

"The minute word came down to me, I closed Happy Day Camp and sent the girls off to a safe place to await instructions from me. I traded in Crystal Clark and went back to being Lily Flowers five days ago. I put a sign up that said Happy Day Camp was closed for heavy-duty plumbing repairs. This is the fifth day, and my phone has been ringing constantly. People are looking for me. That's why I'm Lily Flowers at the moment. I want to know if I should join my girls or stay and fight it out."

Cosmo twirled the pencil in his hand. He licked at his dry lips and bit down on his bottom lip. "What do *you* want to do?"

"Anything but go to jail. The johns get off scot-free, and the women go to jail. Tell me where the justice is in that? Will they extradite me back to D.C.?"

"Yes. And I am not licensed to practice law in the District of Columbia."

"I thought that's what you were going to say. Okay, that means I have to take off and hope for the best. But I want to leave something with you for safekeeping. I'll pay your retainer if you agree."

Cosmo watched as Crystal again

started digging around in the oversized bag. She finally came up with book after book, and plopped them on the desk, one on top of the other. "My check registers, my little black books. My business cell phones, all my records. And here," she said, counting out bills from a stack of money in a brown envelope, "is your retainer. Do not let those books fall into the wrong hands. Will it be all right if I call you from time to time to see . . . you know . . . how things are going?"

"Look, Ms. Clark, I know quite a few very good attorneys in Washington, D.C. One in particular who is excellent. Any one of them can help you. You really should think about this before you make a rash decision."

"I did think about it on the way here. No way am I going to let them come after me. Let them go after the johns. Why should they get off with no penalties? Do you really want to pick up the paper some morning and read that I killed myself? That's what will happen if I go there and lawyer up. You didn't answer my question, Mr. Cricket. Will it be all right for me to call you from time to time, and will you keep all these records safe until such time as I want them back?"

Every bone, every nerve in Cosmo's body wanted to shout *no, no, no*. "Yes," was his response. "Will you be okay?"

The woman of many names laughed. At least Cosmo thought it was a laugh. "I'll be just fine. I knew this day might come, and I've prepared for it."

Cosmo watched as she gathered up all her identity papers and shoved them into the bag, which now sagged together on the sides, then plopped it on top of Cosmo's desk. "What about money?"

"It's offshore. I'm not stupid, Mr. Cricket. Like I said, I prepared for this day a long time ago. And those records," she said, pointing to the pile of black books and check registers teetering precariously on his desk, "are the originals. The phones are real, and I have no others. The duplicate books and records are in safe hands and being delivered to the intended recipients, that's as in plural, as we speak."

The woman of many names stood up.

Cosmo thought she looked taller without the weight of the heavy bag on her shoulder. "Don't you think you should tell me who has the copies? Just in case." *Christ, how lame did that sound?*

The woman laughed. This time it was a delightful, wicked laugh. She winked at him and laughed again. She held up her index and middle finger in the sign of a *V* before she sashayed out of the office.

*Was that a* V? Damn straight it was a *V*. The only *V* he could relate to was the *V* in the word "Vigilante." It couldn't stand for "victory," given her circumstances.

It was Cosmo's turn to laugh, and laugh he did. He couldn't wait to get home to call Elizabeth. He opened the huge safe behind the minibar by pressing a button. He started to secure the woman's records when he noticed a piece of paper sticking out of the uppermost black book. Curious, he pulled it out and read a signed statement giving him permission to use the records as he saw fit to help bring the johns to justice. After he returned the paper to its place in the top book, he closed the safe and moved the minibar back into position.

Waving to Mickey, Cosmo turned off the lights, locked the door, and departed. He was still laughing when he climbed into his Porsche for the long ride out to the desert. He hummed an old Fleetwood Mac ditty as he tooled along, marveling at what a small world it was.

# Chapter 2

It wasn't your ordinary retirement party, with laughter and balloons and bubbly gushing out of a fountain. Judges for some reason thought their parties should be bland, boring, and sedate. Perhaps it had something to do with this judge's age, which was seventy-seven. Maybe Big Foot, as Judge Paul Leland was affectionately called in the cloakrooms, didn't know how to have fun. Although, given his current wife, who was thirty years his junior, one wouldn't have thought so. On the other hand, maybe the poor old dear was just worn-out, thanks to his social-climbing young consort.

Lizzie hated these command performances. Soggy canapés, less than satisfactory wine, not even champagne, and no music to speak of. She refused to acknowledge the violin player who circled the room doing his best to annoy people. She glanced down at her watch and wondered if it was late enough to make her excuses and head for home. Three hours of torture was her limit. It was coming up to ten o'clock, time for this party to end, for her at least. She looked around to see if anyone else was getting ready to leave. Maybe she could start a trend. She really wanted to get home so she could talk to Cosmo. All day she had looked forward to her glass of wine and the phone call. After talking to him, she'd fall into bed with a smile on her face. God, how she loved the man with the funny name.

All eyes were on Lizzie as she made her way through the crowd to reach the judge, who was surrounded by a sea of white hair and bald heads, men and women as old as he. A little while ago she'd seen the young wife guzzling wine with a tall, buff lawyer who was married but cheated like crazy. All the younger lawyers clustered together at the far end of the room, the not-so-old judges at the other end of the room waiting to be excused or for a bomb to drop so they could leave. She was surprised no one had pulled the fire alarm to clear the room.

The sea of white moved in tandem as the geriatric crowd parted for Lizzie to move closer to Judge Leland. Every eye was on the black sheath she wore like a second skin, on the stiletto heels that allowed her to tower over the man she was congratulating. No one missed the outrageous five-carat diamond Cosmo had slipped on her finger three months ago and which sparkled on her left hand; nor did they miss the three-carat diamonds winking and glimmering in each ear under the bright fluorescent lights, another present from Cosmo. The untamed mane of silvery hair tumbling down her back and around her shoulders looked like spun silver.

And then she was in front of the judge, every ear tuned to the conversation. "I'm so sorry, Judge Leland, but I have to leave this enchanting party because I need to double- check a motion I want to file in the morning. I hope you have a wonderful retirement and don't miss all of us too much."

The judge's voice was raspy and yet frail-sounding when he said, "Ah, Miss Fox, I will sorely miss listening to your outstanding oratory in the courtroom. My wife always quizzed me on your fashionable attire when I got home. Thank you so much for coming this evening to help me celebrate my retirement. I'll look forward to reading about your courtroom dramas in the days to come, as opposed to witnessing them firsthand."

Lizzie laughed, that tinkling sound she was famous for. She bent down and, to the amazement of just about everyone in the room, kissed the judge soundly on the cheek. She smiled, and the room grew brighter as she waited for the sea of white heads to part once again. Two minutes later she was out of the room and headed for the checkroom to retrieve her cashmere coat. But maybe she needed to visit the restroom first.

Inside the elegant restroom, she met three colleagues she knew quite well. They were whispering among themselves. "Okay, ladies, it's safe to leave. I paved the way for all of us to call it a night," Lizzie said.

"There is a God," one of the lawyers said dramatically. "Lizzie, have you heard?"

"Heard what?" Lizzie asked curiously as she headed to the far stall.

The three women as one moved down the length of the vanity and all of them started talking at once.

Lizzie exited the stall and started to wash her hands. She had trouble keeping up with what she was hearing.

"Biggest scandal since . . . God, I don't know when." "Practically the whole damn cabinet . . . even some of the Secret Service . . . try the vice prez . . . jeez, what's this all going to do to Martine Connor's new administration?" "Congress and the Senate . . . more than you can shake a stick at."

Lizzie was about to weigh in with a dozen questions when the door opened and a gaggle of women entered the room. All conversation among the lawyers screeched to a halt. Lizzie rolled her eyes as she held the door for the others.

Lizzie retrieved her long white cashmere coat, slipped into it, and almost ran to the exit. She handed the valet her ticket and waited for her brand-new Porsche to be brought to where she was standing. Her head buzzed with what she'd heard and what she hadn't heard. Imagination was a powerful thing.

Her car roared to a stop. For some reason, Porches driven by anyone other than their owners always seemed to roar. Lizzie slipped a ten-dollar bill into the valet's hand and slid behind the wheel. The powerful car purred and growled to life as she raced down the circular road that would lead her to the main highway. Another scandal in Washington. What else was new? She didn't want to think about scandals, she wanted to think about Cosmo Cricket and the coming weekend when she would fly out to see him.

Five hours later, Lizzie rolled over on her lavender-scented sheets as she struggled to figure out what had woken her. The phone, of course. She squinted at the clock on the nightstand. The large red numerals said it was 2:59. No one called her at this hour unless it was a dire emergency. Her first thought was Cosmo, but she discarded that thought immediately. He'd said he was going straight to bed when they hung up from their call, and she had done the same thing. One of the Sisters? Surely nothing was happening on the mountain that couldn't wait till morning. The caller I.D. said PRIVATE CALLER. Did she even want to take the call? No. She rolled back over, sniffed her pillowcase, and settled down to go back to sleep when the phone rang again. *Damn*. She rolled back over and picked up the phone. "This better be really, really good because it's three o'clock in the morning, and I was sound asleep." Lizzie didn't care who was listening to her tirade.

"Lizzie, it's Martine Connor. I am sorry to wake you, truly I am, but I do not have a minute to myself these days. This is the only time I can call you. I need to talk to you, Lizzie."

"Madam President," Lizzie said, bolting

upright and swinging her legs over the side of the bed at the same time. "Is this how we're going to chat from time to time? Is something wrong?"

"First things first, cut out that 'Madam President' stuff. You only have to call me Madam President if the press is around. No, we are not going to chat in the middle of the night. No, I take that back, yes, that's about the only time we can talk. I can't sleep in this job. I haven't had a good night's sleep since I moved into this damn place. I used to sleep like a baby and, yes, something is wrong. I'm surprised you haven't gotten wind of it all, even though they're trying to put a lid on it. You know whenever they do that, an explosion always follows."

Lizzie's mind raced as she made her way out to the kitchen to make coffee. She knew there would be no more sleep for her that night. She thought about the conversation in the lavatory with her colleagues at the Hay-Adams a little while ago.

"I think you need to be a little more precise, Martine. I did hear something tonight at Judge Leland's retirement party, but it was in the restroom. Lawyers talk, you know that. Nothing seemed out of the ordinary in the party room. I think I would have picked up on it. Every damn judge and lawyer in this town was there. Also, there were quite a few congressmen and senators present. Give it to me straight up. Martine, does anyone know you're calling me? Aren't there invisible eyes and ears on you?"

"I'm on that crazy phone you gave me. I carry it on me at all times. Yes, my dear, in my bra if I'm wearing clothes without pockets. I have it set on vibration mode. I'm also in bed. Alone. There are no eyes and ears here that I know of. There damn well better not be."

Lizzie poured her coffee, added cream, then rummaged in the fridge for something to munch on. She reached for some chicken legs her day lady had left on a platter of southern-fried chicken along with a side bowl of potato salad. She poked at the other bowls and saw a salad and some fruit. With the phone cradled between her ear and her shoulder, she carried everything to the round wooden table. "Talk to me," she mumbled.

"It's that old devil sex. It's reared its ugly head in my administration. This is worse than the scandal that erupted before I took office. You remember the D.C. Madam, don't you?" Not bothering to wait for a reply, President Connor raced on. "This time around, half my staff attended that damn party. I'm told there were Secret Service there. I lost count of the federal judges and congressmen who attended that damn camp weekend. Not just once, but twice," Connor screeched. "They had such a good time, they did an encore after I was sworn in. And don't tell me 'boys will be boys.' I don't want to hear it. I think every politician in this damn town was involved in one way or another. Do you know how this makes me look?" Again she didn't bother to wait for a reply. "I have an administration of perverts. Say something, Lizzie."

Lizzie for some reason enjoyed hearing Martine venting. *Welcome to Washington* was what she wanted to say. Instead, Lizzie said, "I heard there were quite a few senators who . . . uh, went to camp, and I also heard several of your fancy-dancy ambassadors and a few of their friends were also in attendance." Lizzie licked at her fingers and reached for a second chicken leg. "I hope you aren't calling me to ask me to represent any of those perverts because the answer is *no,* Madam President. I have long believed that the johns should be the ones who are arrested and punished, not the working girls and madams. The men went to the summer, or winter, camp, whatever it was, of their own free will, and they were willing to pony up outrageous sums of money for the pleasure. No one twisted their arms. Then they walk off scot-free, and the women take the fall. What's wrong with this picture? No, Madam President, I can't help you."

"Lizzie, you have to help me. Not directly, I realize that. I want you to get in touch with the Vigilantes and ask for their help. I can't think of anything else. I guess you can see I'm desperate, or I wouldn't be calling you."

"Martine, *no!* They won't help you! You're already running a tab with the Vigilantes. You owe them a pardon that has not been forthcoming. I'm sure they're on the same page I am when it comes to the johns. If you weren't sitting in the office you won, you'd be on our page, too. You know that, Martine."

"Lizzie, I could go down the tubes with what's going on. I'll be the laughingstock of the free world. The first female president, and I have an administration whose members can't keep their pants zipped. This is going to be a circus. I have to try to do *something*."

"Chop them all off at the knees right now. By them, I mean every man within spitting distance of what went on, those that attended that . . . uh, camp. Go back to all your short lists and work from there. Make everyone involved who is a part of your administration resign. Then move on. There's no way you can contain this. You have to know that, Martine. We both know the media will be on this like fleas on a dog. You have to be aggressive. Whatever you do, don't go giving speeches, or just slapping any of the 'boys' on the wrist, and don't try to hide anything. That's the best advice I can give you right at this precise moment." Lizzie attacked the potato salad, eating right out of the bowl. She couldn't believe this conversation. And she couldn't believe she was eating cold fried chicken and potato salad at three o'clock in the morning. She refilled her coffee cup.

"So, what you're saying is you won't help me, is that how I'm to read your response, Lizzie?"

Lizzie sighed. She'd been friends with the president for more years than she cared to remember. As women, they'd been through a lot during that time. Together they had been in the box, out of the box, and over the top of the box, always coming out the victors. "What kind of help are you asking for, Martine? If you're asking me to defend any of those Happy Campers, the answer is *no*. I'll tell you something else, I'd represent the madam *for free*. I think the Vigilantes will be of the same mind. Having said that, I must be dense because I don't know what it is you think either the Vigilantes or I can do."

"I know, I know, Lizzie. I'm out of my

mind. To be honest, I didn't know who else to call. I guess I thought you would have a magic bullet of some kind. It just isn't time for the pardon yet. I'll keep my word, but I can't do it yet. Damn it, I just took office. I've never, ever broken my word, Lizzie, and you damn well know it. Christ, I'll probably be impeached within my first 180 days in office. Can you imagine what the guys on the other side of the aisle are going to do with this?"

Until then Martine Connor had sounded like an agitated old friend with a terrible problem, calling for help and advice. Suddenly, she was back to being the first female president of the United States.

"I'm sorry, Lizzie, for waking you and bombarding you with my problem. I understand where you are coming from. I'll deal with it some way, somehow. Go back to sleep, Lizzie. Good night."

Like she was really going to be able to go back to sleep. Lizzie wondered if she'd ever be able to sleep again. Right now all she wanted to do was call Cosmo. She looked at the clock. It was a little after midnight in Vegas, and Cosmo slept soundly.

Morning would be time enough, as he was an early riser. Cosmo would talk her through her angst then—when he was bright and alert. Simply put, she didn't want to be responsible for Cosmo losing any sleep.

Lizzie wrapped the platter and bowls of food and put them back into the refrigerator. She couldn't believe she'd consumed the whole pot of coffee. She consoled herself with the fact that it was a small pot, with only four cups, and somehow the fourth cup always seemed to evaporate.

The kitchen clock over the doorway said it was 3:45. If she took a shower and dressed for the day, she could make a second pot of coffee and not feel guilty. She knew she would need the adrenaline rush coffee gave her when she called Big Pine Mountain. Lizzie looked around to make sure she was leaving her kitchen nice and tidy before she went back upstairs.

Maybe she should call Maggie Spritzer before she called Big Pine Mountain. Or better yet, maybe she should make two phone calls before she called Big Pine Mountain. Calling Jack Emery and Maggie Spritzer was the way to go, she thought. Both lived within a mile of her house, and maybe she could get a better fix on things if she agreed to meet them at one of their houses. She'd offer to bring the donuts and coffee. Now, that was a plan. She'd think it through while she showered. For some reason she did some of her best thinking while standing under a stream of hot water. A good long shower always left her with a clear head, and she usually came up with a solution before she got out to towel off.

She knew for a fact that Jack got up at five o'clock and was usually at Harry Wong's *dojo* to work out by six. Maggie liked to be in the office by six o'clock, six thirty at the latest.

Lizzie's mind raced as she ran through what she had scheduled for the day. She thought about what she could postpone, reschedule, or blow off totally. When she was satisfied in her own mind, she picked up the phone and called her secretary, knowing full well she wouldn't reach her. Lizzie left a voice mail and knew Sandy would take care of things the way Sandy always took care of her schedule the moment she opened the office.

Cosmo would have to wait.

# Chapter 3

Lizzie couldn't believe her good luck when she found a parking space right in front of Jack Emery's house in Georgetown. And from the looks of things, Jack was up and moving around inside because the house was lit up from top to bottom. She looked to her left, three houses down, and could see that Maggie Spritzer was up and about, too, her house lit up just the way Jack's was.

Lizzie was out of her car a moment later, an enormous paper sackful of cinnamon buns and three huge cups of coffee in hand. She set down her purchases on the stoop, called Maggie, and said, "Jack's house. Now!" Then she rang Jack's doorbell.

Jack opened the door, took in the sack of sweets and the coffee. He looked at Lizzie, and said, "Oh, shit! What now? It's only quarter to six!"

"Leave the door open, Maggie is on the way," Lizzie said, heading toward Jack's kitchen, where she rummaged for a plate on which to set the buns. "Come on, Jack. You need to smile when you greet your guests. It's the only way to start the day. And, I brought breakfast! That alone should put a smile on your face." She was turning around to reach for a stack of napkins when Maggie breezed into the kitchen, her freckled face alight with questions. High heels in hand, she was in her stocking feet.

Maggie reached for a bun, rolled her eyes, and sat down. "Oooh, these are soooo good, and I need this right now. What's up?" she asked as she happily munched away.

"Honey, if you thought that little gig in Utah was Pulitzer material, wait till you hear what I have to tell you. Right now, right this minute, I can probably give you enough fodder for your paper for the entire year! Banner headlines for a solid month. You are absolutely going to love what I am about to tell you," Lizzie said, reaching for a bun she knew she didn't need. But she wanted it, and she never denied herself anything if she could help it. That was what life was all about in her opinion.

"What about me, Lizzie, am I going to love this?" Jack grumbled as he eyed the cinnamon buns and tried to exercise willpower. Finally, unable to resist the sugary treat, he snatched one and shoved it into his mouth. "I hate Starbucks coffee!"

"Oh, boo-hoo," Maggie said as she swigged at the strong coffee. "Tell us, Lizzie, all the little 'ifs,' 'ands,' and 'buts.' Don't leave anything out!"

"Guess who called me at three o'clock this morning?"

"Cosmo? He asked you to marry him!" Maggie said.

Lizzie shook her head. Maggie looked crestfallen, as did Lizzie.

"Charles? He's on his way back, and the girls are planning to flog him?" Jack suggested.

Lizzie shook her head again. "You'll never guess, so I'm going to tell you." She paused dramatically. "Martine Connor. *President* Martine Connor."

Jack's face lit up like a Christmas tree. "She's going to pardon the girls! She's coming through on her promise!"

"No! Not yet. She said she can't do it yet, but she will. I told her what the consequences would be if she reneged. No, she called asking for help. I turned her down on behalf of the Vigilantes because she's already running a tab with the Sisters. No freebies, ladies and gentlemen. I hope I wasn't out of line. I haven't even called the girls yet. I have to tell you, she made me a little angry."

"I don't think they'll fault you, I would have done the same thing," Maggie said as she bit into her third cinnamon bun. "The president made you *a little angry*. So what's the deal?"

"A scandal of mega proportions involving her brand-new administration. Actually, last night at Judge Leland's retirement party, I heard some lavatory gossip but wasn't able to follow through on it at the time. Then when I got home, Cosmo called, and, as luck would have it, he has a client who is tied to the scandal. He suggested that she consult one of the "very good attorneys" he knows in D.C."

"Cosmo's in Vegas. How does that tie in to the president calling you in the middle of the night?" Jack asked as he contemplated a second cinnamon bun.

"What? What?" Maggie snarled.

Lizzie grinned. "It seems that our new president has an administration of perverts. It would also seem that a good many of them, like fifty or so, enrolled in the Happy Day Camp for some . . . unorthodox . . . uh . . . activities. It would appear that when Martine won the election, they, the perverts of the current administration, got carried away and had a little camp outing. Then they had another camp outing after Martine took the oath of office." She waited for a reaction, and when she saw only blank expressions, she said, "A brothel. Happy Day Camp is a brothel in Las Vegas. Actually, it's a little more than sixty miles from Vegas. As you know, prostitution is legal in Nevada in counties with fewer than 400,000 residents. However, when the madam was contacted to bring her dog-and-pony show to the nation's capital, she balked, but they, the perverts, convinced her and her girls that there would be no blowback. It appears they were wrong."

"Oh, shit!" Jack said.

"Wow! You were right, this is big stuff. Do you have names?" Maggie asked as she picked frosting from the remaining cinnamon bun. Jack slapped her hand away from it.

"I don't, but Cosmo does. The madam is on the run and she gave him her books, financial records, and cell phones for safekeeping. The administration is trying to contain the situation, but the other side of the aisle must have gotten downwind of it somehow, and they're going to blow it wide-open. I don't know when, but I have to assume very soon. She's going to end up being known as not only the first female president but, she'll also be the laughingstock of the free world. Actually, the whole world."

Maggie snorted. "They'll go after the madam, string her up, and the johns will lose face, their jobs, and go on with their lives. Half of them will probably end up as lobbyists or CEOs. That's how it usually works. Wait a damn minute here. Are you saying the president wants the Vigilantes to . . . cover for all those guys so they can keep their jobs and not embarrass her administration, meanwhile letting the madam get slammed into jail?"

"Yeah," Lizzie said.

"Well, damn, I think the girls will take this one on for free. No way are they going to do what she wants, pardon or not. By 'books' do you mean Cosmo has the madam's little black books?" Maggie asked.

"Yes, and some of those clowns actually used their credit cards. The woman was no dummy, she made sure she got fingerprints of the whole bunch, and she's matched them up to the payments. The reason she's on the run is she was tipped off that this was going to go down. She didn't waste a minute. She sent her girls off to the far corners of the globe, and she's taken on a new identity. She also told him that copies of all the materials she gave Cosmo were on their way to the 'intended recipients'—and then she winked at him and gave him the *V* sign! So Cosmo thinks she might mean the Vigilantes! How she would know where to find the girls, I have no clue. However, there is every possibility she knows Rena Gold. You remember Rena, who helped us with that little caper at the World Bank and then again in Vegas when things went sour there last year? After all, it is Vegas. Anything goes in Vegas, we all know that."

"What is the objective?" Jack asked in a jittery-sounding voice.

"What, Jack, are you so dense you can't figure it out?" Maggie asked as she drained the last of her coffee. "The madam wants the johns to be punished. It's as obvious as the nose on your face. She's the one who, in the end, will hang by her toenails. She'll be rotting in jail, and the politicians will be dining at the Jockey Club. Eventually they will all weasel their way back into some political arena. Think back to the D.C. Madam. She ended up dead, and you know there were some who said she did not take her own life. Did even one thing happen to her clients? I think not. Every single one of them is going on with his life, and she's dead. *D-E-A-D*, Jack."

"Cosmo said his client made mention of that, and those on her side of the fence said they do not believe she took her own life. But right now the D.C. Madam is not our problem. So, Jack, to answer your question, Cosmo's client wants the johns to be brought up on charges, and she wants jail time for them. Or, she wants them . . . *taken care of*. She has no intention of going to jail herself. She provided a service, the johns paid. That's her bottom line."

"And as women you agree?" Jack asked tightly.

"Well, yeah," Maggie drawled. "Guys who think they're above the law need to get brought down a peg or two. If justice was doled out equally, I'm sure the madam, whoever she is, would take her punishment like any woman would. Favoritism will not work in a case like this."

"And you don't think losing a job, maybe his family, and his reputation is enough punishment for the john?"

Maggie got up, reached for the last cinnamon bun, and smashed it in Jack's face. "Does that answer your question?" she snarled.

"You're vicious," Jack snarled in return as he licked at the frosting smeared across his lips. He then dunked his head under the kitchen faucet and dried off with a length of paper towels. "All I did was ask a question."

"Yeah, well, it was the wrong question," Maggie snarled a second time.

Maggie turned to Lizzie, and said, "I'm on it. When can you get me the names in the black books?"

"Hold on here, ladies. Isn't that violating the attorney-client privilege?"

Lizzie smiled. Jack cringed. "She gave it up, Jack. We have permission to run with this. Cosmo said she's one tough lady, and she 'is not going to roll over and play dead for a bunch of dick-dead men.' Those are her words, *in writing*. She okayed, *in writing,* for Cosmo to do whatever he had to do."

"Okay, okay," Jack mumbled. "What's the plan? Just so you know, if the girls jump on this, I'm not budging without a plan. I know I'm speaking for Harry when I say we need a plan."

Lizzie and Maggie both nodded. "I think a meeting is called for," Lizzie said. "I have plans to fly to Vegas this weekend. If you all want to arrange a meeting on the mountain, I can attend via webcam. If there's any way I can arrange for a meeting with our new client, I want to jump on it. The only problem with that is that we have no way to contact her. Cosmo said she's gone to ground and will call in from time to time. I'm thinking she's already out of the country since Cosmo said her money is offshore. That's where she'll head. Always follow the money. You know that's the first rule. Maggie?"

"Hey, I'm on it. The minute you get me those names, we'll start raising some hell. This city will tremble. I can see the headlines now!"

"Guess my work here is done, then," Lizzie said. "You'll bring Harry up-to-date, Jack?" Not bothering to wait for a response, she moved on to Maggie. "Stay in touch, and I'll call the mountain and clue everyone in. Still no word on Charles, I guess?"

Both Maggie and Jack shook their heads.

All three left Jack's house, and waited while Jack locked his door. Maggie headed toward her house, where her car was parked. Jack said his was parked on the next block and started to jog toward it before Lizzie could offer him a ride.

It was raining, a steady, heavy rain that would flood the roads in Georgetown within a few hours.

Lizzie slid into her Porsche and was at the end of the street before Jack reached his car. She gave a light tap on the horn. She could see Jack raise his hand to show he heard her good-bye.

Thirty minutes later, Jack breezed into Harry Wong's *dojo* just as his early-morning class was disbanding. He screwed up his face so Harry would know something was up before he decked him for being late. Harry Wong was a pain in his ass.

The love-hate relationship between Harry and Jack boiled up, as it always did.

"I hope you're going to tell me you have

a raging case of shingles and a huge boil on your ass, and that's why you're late."

"Sorry, my little buttered muffin, but the only thing I can complain about this morning is a hangnail. Listen, something has come up. Let's have some of that shitty green tea you think has miraculous powers, and I'll tell you all about it." Sensing a smart-ass comeback, Jack said, "Yoko said to tell you she loves you." Any time Jack wanted to bring Harry to his knees, he would throw Yoko into the mix. Yoko was the only person who could put the fear of God into one Harry Wong. Jack delighted in seeing his best friend in the whole world crumble at his feet.

"Eat shit, Jack. And I'm not afraid of Yoko. I love her," Harry blustered weakly.

"Tsk-tsk," Jack said, clucking his tongue. "Listen up, and don't say a damn word until I'm finished. Your reward at the end will be me telling you we're going to head for the mountain tomorrow afternoon. You ready, you miserable excuse for a human being?"

When Jack finished regaling the martial arts expert, Harry looked at him like he was crazy. "Tell me you're jerking my chain! Please, Jack."

"Nah, it's for real. I tried protesting, but the two of them," he said, referring to Lizzie and Maggie, "damn near castrated me right there in the kitchen. The knife block was close to Maggie. My blood ran cold, I can tell you that," Jack said dramatically.

Harry was so into blood and guts and dismemberment, especially when he thought it could be Jack's, that he actually looked mellow at the moment.

"You know the girls are going to be on this like white on rice."

"Yeah, I know," Harry mumbled. He slurped from his tiny cup of green tea as he waited for whatever else was going to tumble from Jack's lips.

"There's no plan. As yet," Jack added hastily.

"No plan!" Harry screeched.

"Easy, Harry. I'm not even sure the girls know about it yet. Lizzie is calling them. We're going up tomorrow so that means we'll be there to uh . . . uh . . . help with the plan. Read my lips, Harry. *We-will-have-a-plan!*"

"That's what you said the last time, Jack," Harry said ominously. "Your cocka-mamie plan was a truckload of pumpkins."

"It worked, didn't it?"

"Just shut the hell up, Jack. I need to think about this. I hate guys who can only get it by paying for it," Harry muttered as he paced. That is, Harry thought he was pacing, but he was actually stomping around in his bare feet, powerful feet that could kill a man with one little kick, one big toe placed in the wrong place. Harry was a killer. Jack was glad his "archen-emy" was one of the good guys.

"You done thinking yet?" Jack demanded a minute later. In the blink of an eye he was on the floor, looking up at his wiry friend.

"Yeah. Serves you right. You know bet-ter than to talk to me when I'm thinking." Harry reached down for Jack's hand to pull him to his feet. And then Harry was on the floor, with Jack straddling his chest. "Say it!"

"Up yours! You're a wuss, Emery!"

They went at it for a good fifteen min-utes until both men collapsed, with no real winner. Huffing and puffing, both of them got to their feet, their eyes wary until Jack roared, "Enough! That was my workout for the day."

Harry extended his hand. "Pretty good, Emery. In ten years, you might be almost as good as I am."

"My ass. It was a draw. You want to drive tomorrow or should I?"

"We'll make better time on my cycle. Your call."

"Whatever gets us there the quickest," Jack said.

"Then it's the Ducati," Harry said, all smiles and sunshine.

"You are a piece of work, Harry Wong."

"You know, Jack, you are absolutely right. I am. And you are one damn lucky son of a bitch to have me as a friend."

Jack knew there was no way he could ever win an argument with Harry, so he let it drop. "Listen, I have to get to court. How about calling Bert and filling him in? Ask him if he wants to go to the mountain with us. I'm not sure about Maggie or Ted. I'm thinking they're going to be rather busy in the next few days. You know how Maggie loves a good headline."

"OK, I'll call Bert. You want some tea to go?"

"What? You gonna slip something in it so I fall asleep in court?" Jack asked in pretended outrage.

"Never happen."

"Yeah, yeah, yeah."